HOW MUCH DO YOU *Love* ME?

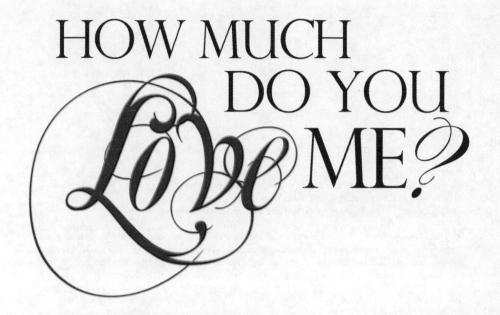

HOW MUCH DO YOU Love ME?

PAUL MARK TAG

SWEETWATER
BOOKS
AN IMPRINT OF CEDAR FORT, INC.
SPRINGVILLE, UTAH

This is a work of fiction. The characters, names, incidents, places, and dialogue are products of the author's imagination and are not to be construed as real. The opinions and views expressed herein belong solely to the author and do not necessarily represent the opinions or views of Cedar Fort, Inc. Permission for the use of sources, graphics, and photos is also solely the responsibility of the author.

ISBN 13: 978-1-4621-1447-4

Published by Sweetwater Books, an imprint of Cedar Fort, Inc., 2373 W. 700 S., Springville, UT 84663
Distributed by Cedar Fort, Inc., www.cedarfort.com

LIBRARY OF CONGRESS CATALOGING-IN-PUBLICATION DATA

Tag, Paul M. (Paul Mark), author.
How much do you love me? / Paul Mark Tag.
    pages cm
Summary: James and Keiko marry quickly before James goes to World War II and Keiko to an internment camp. Sixty years later their daughter Kazuko, born in the camps, uncovers a secret that could overwhelm the family.
ISBN 978-1-4621-1447-4 (perfect : alk. paper)
1.   Japanese Americans--Evacuation and relocation, 1942-1945--Fiction. 2.   World War, 1939-1945--Concentration camps--California--Tulelake--Fiction. 3.   Tule Lake Relocation Center, setting. 4.   Intermarriage--Fiction. I. Title.
PS3620.A335H69 2014
813'.6--dc23
                                   2014013390

Cover design by Kristen Reeves
Cover design © 2014 by Lyle Mortimer
Edited and typeset by Melissa J. Caldwell

Printed in the United States of America

10 9 8 7 6 5 4 3 2 1

Printed on acid-free paper

To the 120,000 Japanese Americans
held in US internment camps during World War II

CONTENTS

CONTENTS

PREFACE

The internment of 120,000 Japanese Americans during World War II is a stain on the historical consciousness of the United States. My intent in writing this book has been two-fold. First, I wanted to write an interesting mystery/love story. Beyond this objective, my goal was to remind us all, particularly the younger generations in the United States, of a noteworthy episode from our country's history. Most of the time our country has acted honorably, and we can be proud of our accomplishments, both in peacetime and war. However, there are instances when we have acted neither nobly nor fairly and for which we need reminding so as not to repeat our mistakes. The unjustified internment of Japanese Americans following the bombing of Pearl Harbor on December 7, 1941, was one of those times.

This book is a work of fiction. That said, I have attempted to create an interesting story set within the confines of accurate historical events. To assist the reader during his or her reading, please note two sections that I have added to the end of this book: Cast of Major Characters and Glossary.

ACKNOWLEDGMENTS

There are many who helped me research, read, and proofread this novel. Foremost among them is my wife, Becky, who besides her patient readings, provided love and encouragement. I always looked forward to her afternoon visits while I was writing, fortifying me with coffee and a snack.

Beyond Becky, my overwhelming thanks go to Robin Brody. Robin helped me develop the plot and faithfully reviewed every chapter immediately after I wrote it. Our weekly luncheon reviews kept me focused and provided stimulating conversation that invariably led to ideas for upcoming chapters.

Several first readers provided important contributions once the book was completed, discovering errors and making valuable suggestions for improvement. In alphabetical order, they were: Franette Bell, Leonard Dickstein, Peggy Dold, Mary Godfrey, Michael Guy, Glenn Handlers, Fran Morris, Daura Palmer, Ann Schrader, Debi Williamson, and Mihoko Yamane. Pam Harbor evaluated and corrected my medical references. Megan Carlisle and Heather Trescases of the Eastside Heritage Center of Bellevue, Washington, provided and suggested references regarding the city of Bellevue in the 1930s.

Two other individuals require special recognition. They are my superb editor, Alissa Voss, and the cover design artist, Kristen Reeves. The following books supplied important reference material:

- *Bellevue: Its First 100 Years* by Lucille McDonald (Bellevue, Washington: The Bellevue Historical Society, 2000).

- *Bellevue Timeline: The Story of Washington's Leading Edge City From Homesteads to High Rises 1863–2003* by Alan J. Stein and The HistoryLink Staff (Baltimore, MD: University of Washington Press, 2004).

- *Farewell to Manzanar* by Jeanne Wakatsuki Houston and James D. Houston (NY: Houghton Mifflin Company, 1973).

- *Looking Like the Enemy: My Story of Imprisonment in Japanese-American Internment Camps* by Mary Matsuda Gruenewald (Troutdale, OR: NewSage Press, 2005).

- *Only What We Could Carry* by Lawson Fusao Inada, editor, with the preface by Patricia Wakida and afterword by William Hohri (Berkeley, CA: Heyday Books, 2000).

- *Strawberry Days* by David A. Neiwert (NY: Palgrave Macmillan, 2005).

Beyond the above, I enthusiastically credit the Densho Digital Archive. Without this web-based database with its searchable interviews and reproductions of internment camp newspapers, my book would not have the historical richness that I intended. From their website, I quote: "Densho: The Japanese American Legacy Project is a digital archive of videotaped interviews, photographs, documents, and other materials relating to the Japanese American experience. Additional information on the project is available at www.densho.org."

I save for last my thanks to my uncle August Kern of Somerset, Pennsylvania. He was one of those people from "The Greatest Generation," as Tom Brokaw's book of the same name referenced. Uncle August served on USS *Santa Fe*, the "Lucky Lady," the same ship that my book character James Armstrong served on in the Pacific. Many of the details that I relate from James's experiences on that ship come from interviews with my uncle.

Finally, if there are mistakes remaining in the manuscript, you can blame me alone. I obviously did not do a good enough job reading the references or listening to the excellent comments and suggestions of everyone mentioned above.

PROLOGUE
INTERNMENT

Japanese Internment Camp at Tule Lake, California
Saturday, July 25, 1942

Her name that summer was Keiko Armstrong, but it hadn't been for long. Some five months earlier, back in Bellevue, Washington, her name had been Keiko Tanaka. Keiko figured that she was probably the only Nikkei at the Tule Lake War Location Center with an Anglo surname.

Keiko's family had arrived at Tule Lake in northern California one week earlier. They missed their home in Bellevue, where paranoia and mistrust had taken hold following the bombing of Pearl Harbor the previous December. Anyone who looked Japanese was suspected of being an enemy agent of the Japanese emperor, Hirohito. Executive Order 9066, signed by President Roosevelt, had devastated their lives. On February 19, 1942, this legislation dictated that all Japanese who lived along the coast in the western states, 120,000 strong, be shipped away from the Pacific where everyone feared the Japanese military would invade. Even Nisei, those second-generation Japanese Americans born in the United States—and thus legal citizens—could not escape the Juggernaut.

Keiko and her Japanese family had traveled to Tule Lake by way of Pinedale to the south, near Fresno, California, because the camp at Tule Lake was not yet finished when they departed Bellevue on May 20. For the most part, Japanese families from Bellevue had traveled

1

together. They had arrived first at what were called Assembly Centers. Pinedale was one of fifteen such temporary locations.

The journeys to Pinedale and then Tule Lake had been especially unpleasant. They had traveled by train and only at night. Other trains had priority during daytime, and the hot days found their cars motionless on sidetracks. To make matters worse, the trains were old and smoky, dropping soot everywhere. The first part of their journey—925 miles from Bellevue to Pinedale—had taken four long days and nights.

Keiko and her family arrived at Tule Lake to discover a huge facility designed to house internees in row after row of barracks. Cheaply built, each barrack consisted of four apartments. Keiko, her parents, two sisters, and brother had to make do with only one of these, a space measuring sixteen by twenty feet. A single bare bulb provided light, and a coal stove represented their source of heat.

Keiko hated the place, particularly the dark nights. Wind and dust made its way through cracks in the walls and floors. When she awoke that first morning after their two-month journey from Bellevue, she found her bedding black with dust. Their family, and everyone else in the compound, spent days scrounging for anything to stuff cracks in the floors and walls.

Because no one knew how long the war would last or what the government had planned for them in the interim, everyone was scared. Keiko missed her old life and especially her husband, who had gone off to war. Worst of all, she worried for her baby, who would arrive by January.

1

COMA

Community Hospital of the Monterey Peninsula
Monterey, California
Wednesday afternoon, October 25, 2000

o you think she can hear us?" This was the voice of Kazuko Armstrong, Keiko's daughter. Since a stroke three days earlier, Keiko had been in a coma.

Keiko's son, Patrick Armstrong, responded. "I asked the doctor, and he said no. He says she senses nothing." Keiko heard her son sigh. "It doesn't look good. The doctor says that the longer she stays like this, the worse her chances of recovery."

Keiko couldn't open her eyes, move her body, or respond in any way. Still, her mind functioned, and she heard and understood what her two children were saying. It didn't bother her that she couldn't communicate or that her hours were numbered. Keiko had come to terms with what had happened and was ready to join her ancestors.

Keiko's life had been a full one. A good husband, two fine children, and enough creature comforts along the way to make life enjoyable. It was only in the beginning that fate had hit her hard. She had hidden that portion of her life from her children. Even in her own mind, she had compartmentalized much of what had happened. After the war, few Japanese wanted to discuss the internment—partially due to their culture but also because of their shame at what the government had done to them.

For those reasons alone, Keiko had chosen to forget and move on. Her parents, Isamu and Akemi Tanaka, had proved less resilient. The disgrace of the internment experience overshadowed the rest of their lives.

But for Keiko, there was another reason why she chose to forget that terrible period. And that was a secret she vowed to carry to the grave.

"Did you ever think it would end this way, Patrick?" Kazuko's voice broke the silence. "Mom and Daddy both out of it at the same time. Mom with her stroke, and Daddy with his Alzheimer's. I wouldn't be surprised if they're somehow communicating with each other and have decided to go out together."

Patrick continued Kazuko's thought. "Have you ever known anyone more in love than these two?"

If she could have, Keiko would have nodded her head in acknowledgment. For as long as she could, she had borne the load herself, caring for a man stricken by that terrible disease at the age of seventy-two. As the situation became more difficult, her children began insisting that the burden had become too much, concerned that the stress and exertion would kill her. She had agreed, reluctantly, to put him in the nursing home. She'd done her best afterward, spending as many hours as possible each day with him. But, ultimately, the lonely nights had taken a far greater toll on her well-being than the strenuous days beforehand ever had.

The stroke had come three days earlier, on a Sunday. Keiko considered herself fortunate that her children had not been around to witness it. It was her sister, Shizuka, who happened by and called 911. Skilled paramedics attended to her quickly and sped her to the hospital. There, a skilled neurosurgeon performed brain surgery. All of this prevented immediate death, but it did nothing to change the fact that, except for the respirator tube coming out of her mouth, a casual visitor might think she was dead.

Patrick continued the conversation. "How do you want to handle Dad? Mom hasn't visited him for four days now. He must suspect something's up. Do you think we should tell him?"

No, don't do that! Are you out of your mind?

"I don't think that's a good idea."

Kazuko to the rescue!

"What if Dad asks us?"

"Has he said anything? You saw him yesterday, and that had been three days. Did he ask about Mom not coming by?"

"No. But you know as well as I that he has his moments of clarity."

Keiko heard the exasperation in Kazuko's voice. "Think about it, Patrick! If Daddy never asks, it won't be an issue. If he does have one of his moments of clarity—as you say—do you really want him to know Mom had a stroke and may die? No!"

Thank goodness! Kazuko understands these things.

"And if Mom dies? We still don't say anything?"

Oh, Patrick. Give it up!

"I don't know. At the rate his mind is failing, hopefully he'll never notice that she isn't coming by anymore. It's sad to say, but that's what I pray for right now."

"You're probably right, Sukie."

Keiko had always smiled when she heard Patrick call his sister that name. They had been close as siblings since they were toddlers.

Well, at least that's settled, thought Keiko. Now the important thing was to get on with the process of dying. She'd heard Patrick say that it didn't look good; so hopefully it wouldn't be much longer. But with her remaining time, she wanted to relive her life as she remembered it. She would recall it slowly and savor the memories, beginning back in Bellevue before the war. That would give her great pleasure.

If they were here to listen to her story, others in the family—at least those who had been there during the internment—would say that Keiko had bent the truth a little. No matter. This was her story, and she'd relive it the way she wanted.

5

2
HISTORY IN THE MAKING

Bellevue, Washington
Sunday afternoon, December 7, 1941

The cliché was appropriate, Keiko recalled. *I'll remember this moment until the day I die.*

The day had been sunny and cold. The Tanaka family was returning home from church when the announcement came on the car radio: the Japs had bombed Pearl Harbor.

"Where's Pearl Harbor?" Masao was the first to respond.

In the backseat of their black 1938 Ford, Keiko sat sandwiched between her two sisters: her twin, Misaki, and her younger sister, Shizuka. Their parents, Isamu and Akemi Tanaka, straddled her brother, Masao, in the front seat. Keiko and Misaki had just turned nineteen, having graduated from high school the previous spring. Shizuka was three years younger. Masao, the oldest, had turned twenty-one earlier in the year and was considered to be the most sensitive of the children. Once, when he was younger, Masao had become hysterical when he discovered his mother squashing a spider inside the house. From that day forward, Masao became the go-to person for insect and rodent removal, peacefully moving the creatures from their home to the world outside. The story had become family legend.

Respectfully, the children waited for their parents to explain. The answer didn't come immediately. They knew that something was wrong as their father pulled off the road, turned off the engine, and stared into the distance, hands frozen to the steering wheel.

More silence. *What's going on!* thought Keiko.

Motionless, Isamu replied. "Pearl Harbor is a naval base in Hawaii."

"Why would they do that to us?" asked Masao.

Isamu and Akemi, although first generation Japanese, had learned to read and write English, and their children were fluent in both English and Japanese. The whole family, children included, knew that Great Britain was at war with Hitler's Germany in Europe. France had already surrendered. Compared to many of their Caucasian friends, Keiko knew much more about current events. Isamu insisted that whenever they had a newspaper in the house, everyone read it and pass it around. After dinner, Isamu would randomly call upon one of his children to give a summary to the rest of the family. When this happened to either Keiko or Misaki, they often embellished it with editorial comments that led to further discussion. Isamu knew that his twins were smart and especially good at debating and making their points.

It took only a moment before Keiko, thus knowledgeable about current events, realized the importance of what they had heard on the radio and why her father had pulled off the road. Everyone sitting in this car had Japanese blood flowing through their veins, and it was the Japs who had bombed Pearl Harbor.

Isamu restarted the engine, and they continued home. Nothing more was said. A chill passed through Keiko's spine as she realized the implications. Most Japanese living in Bellevue wanted to believe that their ancestry had nothing to do with the international troubles to the east in Europe or to the west in Southeast Asia.

But from her careful reading of the newspapers, Keiko knew that there had been trouble in the wind for years before Pearl Harbor, culminating in the Tripartite Pact of September 1940 when Germany, Italy, and Japan formed an alliance. Not long afterward, the FBI took note, watching the Japanese and looking for anything that might suggest that their loyalties lay beyond American shores.

Keiko and her siblings had never been to Japan. Most Nisei, second generation Japanese who had been born in the United States, never had. Keiko's parents had been born there, but they had never returned and had no intention to. Two full generations had elapsed since Isamu had made his way to Hawaii in 1905.

* * *

Keiko knew that her father had sailed to Hawaii that year for the same reason other Japanese men had: searching for work. Hawaii needed labor to raise and process its sugar cane. Searching for further opportunities, Isamu boarded a ship a year later to the mainland state of Washington.

Isamu had told his children that his timing couldn't have been better. From her history books, Keiko was aware that the Gentlemen's Agreement between the United States and Japan ended Japanese immigration in 1907. This accord followed years of anti-Japanese sentiment that crested not long after the great San Francisco earthquake of 1906. In October of that year, the San Francisco Board of Education decided that Japanese-American children should attend Chinese-American schools. When word of this decision reached Japan, it caused a furor. The Agreement was the result. In exchange for the Board of Education backing off its decision, Japan agreed to halt immigration.

Isamu tried a variety of jobs before settling on farming. From his experience in Japan, he knew how to grow fruits and vegetables on small tracts of land—called truck farming—work his white neighbors found demeaning and not worth the trouble.

Keiko remembered hearing about the nonromantic nature of her parents' marriage. In 1919 when Isamu turned thirty-three, he decided that it was time to find a wife. Pickings were meager in the States. So like many other Japanese males, he ordered from Japan what became known as a Picture Bride. Fortunately, immigration of women was still legal under the Gentlemen's Agreement.

Akemi had explained to her children how it had gone down in Japan. Isamu's family had arranged the union with Akemi's family. In fact, the marriage was legally binding long before bride and groom ever laid eyes on each other. The luxury of marrying for love would have to wait another generation or so.

Akemi arrived in San Francisco in the summer of 1919 to a waiting husband who had traveled by train from Bellevue to Angel Island in San Francisco Bay. To the relief of both, they hit it off, and the union was a success. Such was not the case for some of Isamu's friends, Akemi told her children.

* * *

As Keiko pondered the implications of the Pearl Harbor bombing, the family arrived at their home in Bellevue, solemnity overshadowing further discussion. When they got there, Isamu seemed on a mission. He went inside and dug out his possessions that had originated in Japan: an old Japanese flag, family heirlooms and mementos, Japanese documents of various kinds—anything that might be considered an indication of his loyalty to Japan. All of these made their way to the barrel behind the house where they burned trash. Because of a short news bulletin on the radio, these items had abruptly transformed from priceless keepsakes to symbols of potential trouble. Although Keiko and Misaki understood the reasoning, Masao and Shizuka appeared dazed as they tried to comprehend what was going on.

About seven that night, the family knew that something was up when Shizuka's collie, Princess, started barking outside. It was already dark. Isamu opened the door to two men in suits.

"We're sorry to bother you, but in light of what's happened in Pearl Harbor, the government needs to take precautions concerning the resident Japanese population. You don't mind if we look around, do you?"

Isamu stepped aside as the men didn't wait for a reply. "I can assure you, we have nothing to hide."

Frightened, Keiko sat in the corner of the room.

The visitors walked from room to room, examining everything visible, and then going so far as to open closets and drawers.

Isamu tried to help. "Please sir, if you'll tell us what you're looking for, we'll help you find it."

The man who seemed to be the leader emphasized that everything they were doing was routine. "It's important that we locate any Japanese saboteurs that might be hiding in our midst."

"I can assure you, my family and I are completely loyal to the United States. And I can tell you that except for a few remaining relatives, we have had no contact with anyone from Japan."

Suddenly, Akemi came to life. She hadn't said a word since the earlier radio announcement in the car. Keiko knew her mother's temperament well: she had a long fuse, but once spent, everyone in the family knew to stand back. At five foot one, she didn't present much of a physical presence. But what she lacked in stature she made up for in intensity. She walked right up to the men and made her point with unambiguity. "My four children have all been born here, and they are American citizens. As citizens, they have rights, and you should not be going through their things." The veins in her neck pulsed, and her face flushed.

Keiko watched her father as he stood and watched, obviously impressed with his wife's bravery. To the family's chagrin, the men ignored her.

After less time than it seemed, the two men exited the front door with the family's AM radio, their ancient Kodak Brownie camera, and a rifle that Isamu and Masao used to hunt rabbits.

Perhaps thinking that he needed to say something, the leader offered an explanation. "We're taking the radio because we don't want anyone communicating with Japanese ships off the coast."

Masao asked his father how such a thing was even possible with an AM radio. Isamu turned his hands face-up and made a face. "I have no idea."

The FBI men weren't finished. "What do you keep in those storage sheds out back?"

"That's where we keep our tools and baskets, all the things we need to grow and pick our fruits and vegetables."

There the two men from the FBI discovered the dynamite that Isamu used to blow up tree stumps when clearing land, and they took that too.

Before long, they were gone. Truth be told, they hadn't been rude or outwardly threatening. From her point of view, Keiko was sad to see the radio go—that modern miracle had been a welcome addition to their home a year earlier. She would miss Fibber McGee and Molly and especially the new program, Hopalong Cassidy, a western.

Following that unnerving incident, Isamu decided that a family meeting was in order. Somberly, they gathered around the kitchen table.

While the rest of her family waited, Akemi boiled water for tea.

"This is not going to be good," Isamu began. "If what we've heard about Pearl Harbor is as bad as it sounds, the United States will have no choice but to declare war on Japan. And if that happens, we'll probably get involved in Europe too. What we experienced this evening is just the start, I'm afraid."

Masao, who had been quiet since his initial question in the car, joined the conversation. "But why would the FBI suspect us? You and Mama have been here for decades. This isn't fair!"

Isamu reached for Masao's hands. "You can't blame them, Masao. They're scared. From what we've heard on the radio, it's reasonable to assume that a lot of people died in Hawaii. Everyone's afraid that the West Coast will be next. And because we're Japanese, they're scared of us too."

Isamu paused, obviously giving thought to what he wanted to say next. "But there's one thing that is very important, and I want you children to remember. As your mother so bravely said, you are citizens, and you have the same rights as everyone else. No matter what happens, because of this country's constitution, you are the equals of our Caucasian neighbors, just as they are the equals of us Japanese."

* * *

Keiko's father's ability to see both sides of an argument had always impressed Keiko. She recalled a story her mother had told about an incident that epitomized his character. It occurred during the early 1930s, following the stock market crash of 1929, when times became tough for everyone. Isamu and Akemi were established with their truck-farming business and were getting by, but with little cash to spare.

One evening following dinner, Isamu heard noises in one of their packing sheds. He went to investigate and discovered a Caucasian boy somewhere in his late teens. The boy startled, his arms full of vegetable produce left behind from the day's pickings. He dropped everything and ran toward the back door of the shed. Isamu yelled at him to stop. The boy turned around, shaking so hard that he cowered as Isamu approached, obviously expecting a beating at the least.

Instead, Isamu asked the boy's name. "Anthony Parker," he replied. Isamu extended his hand in a sign of friendship. "I'm Mr. Tanaka."

Knowing full well why the boy was stealing food, Isamu put his hands on the boy's shoulders and told him not to be scared, that he had no intention of punishing him. Instead, he reached for an empty seed bag and filled it with the vegetables the boy had dropped. He also told him that he if he'd care to come by to help on the weekends, that he could then take as much produce home as he could carry.

* * *

Masao continued. "You were there, Papa, in Hawaii. Do you remember Pearl Harbor?"

"That was a long time ago, Masao, thirty-five years. I did live on that island, Oahu. That was where Pearl Harbor was, but I don't remember much. I remember the water and seeing ships, but that's all. I'm sure that it's built up a lot since then." Isamu collected his thoughts. "What all of this means is that we Japanese must show ourselves as loyal Americans. Which we are! Our neighbors and friends know that. Once the government realizes that we pose no threat, I'm sure we'll be treated the same as everyone else."

Keiko and Misaki looked at each other across the table, realizing the irony in their father's comment. Their parents may have been loyal Americans, but they were not citizens and couldn't vote. The 1790 Immigration Act made sure of that, stating that naturalization applied only to "free white persons." Congress updated the law in 1870, but only to include Africans. The children were different. Two years before the Immigration Act update, in 1868, the Fourteenth Amendment to the Constitution made it official that anyone born in the United States was automatically a citizen.

Conversation at the table continued for a while until there was another knock at the door. Knowing that Princess would have barked had it been a stranger, no one was worried this time.

Akemi answered the door. It was James Armstrong, the son of the owner of the three acres of land that their family leased. He and his family lived a couple of miles down the road. He and the twins were the same age and had gone to school together, and he was well liked by the whole Tanaka family.

Out of breath, James briefly caught Keiko's eye, but then addressed her father. "Mr. Tanaka, have you heard what's happened? Pearl Harbor? Dad says it's going to lead to war. He also said that he heard that the FBI was going around and questioning the Japanese. He told me to come over and check on you. Have they been here?"

As Isamu explained what had happened, Keiko crossed her arms. From her point of view, the timing of the news that day couldn't have been worse. She and James might have to rethink their strategy—their way to reveal their secret.

Of the family, only Misaki knew that James had proposed to Keiko a month earlier.

3

MIXED MARRIAGE

Bellevue, Washington
Sunday evening, December 7, 1941

Isamu told James that the FBI had already visited and had searched their house and sheds. Keiko felt it important to elaborate. "They took our AM radio, James. They said they wanted to make sure we didn't communicate with Japanese ships. What do they think we know that would be so important to a Japanese ship? I suppose we could give them directions to all the Japanese restaurants in Seattle."

Misaki, Shizuka, and Masao giggled at Keiko's joke, but her parents failed to see the humor. Isamu looked sternly in her direction.

James didn't laugh either. "It's all so ridiculous," he said.

James then said he needed to head home and update his father. Keiko offered an excuse about seeing James out and followed. They walked toward the road out of earshot. Keiko could sense her father's scrutiny from the window.

James spoke first. "This is bad, Keiko. Dad says he's heard grumblings among people in the town. Idiots, all of them."

"What are they saying?"

"Nasty things, about how no one should trust the Japanese."

Keiko nodded. "Papa says that what's happening is understandable. The bombings in Pearl Harbor were terrible, and he says that people are scared."

14

"I know, Keiko, but that's no reason to turn against your neighbors. They're so—" James stopped in mid-sentence.

"What is it, James?"

"Gosh, Keiko, you are so beautiful. I am so lucky to have you."

Keiko blushed and got caught up in the moment. "I wish I could touch you." After a moment she refocused her thoughts. "James, we've got to keep our heads. What do you think we should do now?"

James stuffed his hands in his pockets. "Maybe we should call things off and wait and see what happens."

This wasn't what Keiko wanted to hear. "Why? As far as I'm concerned, this hasn't changed anything. The only problem that we have to face is our families. Beyond that—"

James cut her off. "No, Keiko, it's more than that. We'll soon be at war with Japan. And Dad says that if that happens, we'll be dragged into the fight in Europe too. If I don't enlist, it won't be long before my name comes up in the lottery."

Keiko had considered this possibility but had rationalized her way around it. Until this morning, there had been no war, and James had been planning to start college the following fall. She had been counting on some kind of abnormality that would make him ineligible for service. But Keiko hadn't even considered that he might enlist. "James! Promise me that you won't actually volunteer."

"It's what will be expected of me, Keiko. And I'm not a coward. That's what guys my age talk about. Enlisting and defending our country."

Keiko couldn't control herself. She walked smartly toward the mailbox and then made a hard left turn for the seclusion offered by one of their sheds. Once there, she motioned for James to follow. Now out of her father's sight, she threw herself into his arms. She then grabbed him by the shoulders and held him at arm's length. "If there's even a chance of that happening, we need to tell our parents now. We've got to get married sooner rather than later."

"Do you really think that's the right thing to do, Keiko? What if . . ."

Keiko wanted to hear this. "What if what?"

"You know what I mean. I love you, but . . ." James had trouble finding the words. "We have to face the fact that if I go off to war, I might not come back."

"You listen to me, James Armstrong." Still holding him by the shoulders, she stared him in the eye. "Repeat after me: nothing is going to happen to me. Say it!"

In almost a whisper, James did as Keiko asked.

With that settled, Keiko released her hold and asked the obvious question. "How do you think we should do this? Should we tell our parents separately?"

James shook his head. "I'm not so sure that's a good idea. I worry about my parents, but I'm sure that you're going to have a worse time of it than me."

Keiko well knew that James was right. "That's why there's safety in numbers. My parents wouldn't dare murder one of their twins in front of both you and your parents. Multiple witnesses. Think about it." Keiko giggled.

James smiled weakly. "I don't know. This is going to be a shock to everybody. Do you know of any other mixed marriages around here? I don't."

Keiko couldn't help but tease James. "What mixed? We're both from Christian families." Her parents had converted to Christianity before their first child was born. As part of a devout Methodist family, Keiko couldn't remember missing a Sunday service in years. Of course, James and his family were heathen Unitarians, as she had heard other Methodist parishioners proclaim. None of their ilk would make it anywhere near the gates of heaven, they said.

"You keep making jokes, Keiko. This is serious."

Keiko chose to set the record straight. "Pearl Harbor's serious! Our going to war is serious! You and I getting married is serious too, but in a very different way."

"Okay, Keiko. You win. But we need a plan."

"Keiko! Are you coming into the house? It's late." Isamu's voice pierced the silence before Keiko could think it through. If her father called, she had to go.

"Let's think about it. We'll decide tomorrow." Keiko gave him a quick peck on the cheek, turned, and ran back to the house.

* * *

As she approached the house, Keiko's pace slowed. Thoughts of their yearlong romance flooded her mind. All of their carefully thought through plans now lay in ruins, forced to the surface because of some ridiculous far-off war—now wars—oceans away from their quiet little town of Bellevue.

Keiko smiled as she reminisced about how this impossible romance had come about. A year prior, neither James nor Keiko had been actively seeking a girlfriend or boyfriend. It had just sort of happened. Casual conversations at school moved toward more intense discussions, followed by some serious eye gazing that led to an initial attraction between the two. It didn't take long before they realized that what each saw was a duplicate soul, so in sync were their values, their views of the future, and even their reactions to daily events.

Of course, both understood that what they were contemplating was nothing short of taboo within their society. Interracial marriage was not something done in those days. Keiko knew that, however James's family reacted to their association, her own parents' response would be worse. For that reason, both had been secretive to the point of absurdity to prevent anyone from suspecting their longer-term plans. And they had succeeded! Except for her identical twin, the world outside their intimate cocoon suspected nothing.

But all of their carefully laid plans would now have to change—and fast.

4

OF ONE BLOOD

Lingering on the porch for a few seconds, Keiko steeled herself. She opened the door and slinked past the severe look of her father. She avoided eye contact and headed straight to the bedroom she shared with Misaki. Masao and Shizuka each had a smaller bedroom.

Misaki glanced up as Keiko entered the room. She was sitting at her desk. Keiko noticed that she was poring over one of the volumes from their family's World Book Encyclopedia. The complete set had been an expensive addition to the Tanaka household, a purchase their father had made two years earlier. "Start reading at A and don't stop until you've hit Z" was the order to his children. Keiko figured that her sister was rereading the section on Japan. Under the circumstances, that was what Keiko would have done.

Keiko pointed to the bed where they could sit next to each other. In a house where the walls sometimes had ears, whispers were the occasional mode of communication. What was to be discussed was hush-hush indeed.

Misaki couldn't wait. "So what are you going to do now? The world is coming apart, and you and James are caught in the middle. There's going to be trouble for us. I'll bet you that what happened in our house this evening is just the beginning. You see how worried Papa is."

"I don't know. But I suggested to James that we get married right away."

Misaki's eyes got big. Although she was aware that James had proposed, Keiko had told her sister that she and James planned for a long engagement, culminating in their marriage sometime after James had begun college the following fall. They figured that would give both families time to get used to the idea.

Keiko waited for Misaki's reaction. It came quickly. "What does James think of the idea?"

"I think he was shocked, but I made a convincing argument. He's like you. He's worried about the future after what happened in Pearl Harbor."

"You made a convincing argument. And that was?"

"I said there was no reason to wait. That with all the uncertainty about what's going to happen, that's the very reason we shouldn't wait."

"And what did he say?"

"He said our parents were our biggest obstacle. He predicted that his family would put up less resistance than mine."

"That's for sure. Papa will have a fit."

Keiko raised her finger. "But then he said something completely unexpected, which made me realize even more that this is the right thing to do. I assumed that James wouldn't have to go into the Army. I was hoping that the fact that he wears glasses would make him ineligible."

Misaki nodded. "He's practically blind without them."

"Exactly!" noted Keiko. "That's what I have been counting on all along. But then he goes and throws a monkey wrench into the whole thing. He says that if our country goes to war, he will have no choice but to enlist, that it would be unpatriotic for him to stay home. I couldn't believe it."

"And what else did he say?"

Keiko hadn't intended to reveal the rest of the conversation, but Misaki had asked. "James was worried about me. He thought that we shouldn't get married because there was the possibility that he wouldn't come home." Keiko's lips began to quiver. "I was strong, Misaki. I told him that was ridiculous, and that I knew he'd be okay. In my own mind, though, I thought that was all the more reason why we shouldn't wait."

In contrast to her behavior in front of James, Keiko's emotions surfaced. With tears flowing freely, Keiko hugged her sister. She held tight and waited for Misaki's reaction, hoping for some words of encouragement.

Keiko backed away, wiped her face, and regained her composure. "Misaki, I need to know if I'll have your support when the time comes. And it'll be soon. You know how Papa is. I need to know that you'll be there for me."

Misaki wiped a tear below Keiko's right eye. "What do you want to do? Elope?"

Keiko shook her head. "I couldn't do that to our family, not to Papa. No, I've got to do this right, no matter how hard it's going to be. I've told James that we should make the announcement together, in front of both families at the same time."

"I don't know if that's the right thing to do or not." Misaki grabbed Keiko by the upper arms. "But you do know that you didn't have to ask. You can always count on me."

Misaki got up, walked to her desk, opened the drawer, and removed the razor blade. Their ritual wasn't new; they had adapted it from a movie they had once seen. Usually done for some silly reason, this time it was different, and both knew it. Misaki sliced the meaty pad of her left index finger and then handed the blade to Keiko who did the same. Each girl held her finger horizontally as the blood began to pool.

Misaki reached for Keiko's finger and pressed it together with hers. "We are sisters and of one blood, Keiko. I will always be there for you. Whatever you say, I will do."

5

UNEXPECTED VISITOR

Monterey, California
Late Wednesday afternoon, October 25, 2000

Kazuko glanced about the living room of her mother's home in Monterey. It felt strange, standing alone in a house whose owner was unconscious and might die. She had filled the watering can a third time, having watered plants in the kitchen, sun porch, and two bedrooms. As her mother had taught, Kazuko stuck her finger into the dirt to check for moisture.

Except for nighttime, Kazuko and her brother had remained by their mother's bedside since her stroke Sunday afternoon. In light of the situation, both Kazuko and Patrick had informed their employers that they would be out until further notice.

Their Aunt Shizuka, Keiko's sister, a night owl, insisted that she be the one to stand vigil after dark. Like Kazuko, she could survive on just a handful of hours sleep a night. At four thirty in the afternoon, when the shift nurse assured them that she would phone immediately if there were any changes, brother and sister chose to call it a day and agreed on a time to meet in the morning.

Kazuko took a break and sat down on the sofa. The last few days had been such a blur that she checked her watch to confirm the day: Wednesday. Their mother had suffered her stroke on Sunday. How long could this last? She'd heard stories of people living for years in such a state. Kazuko knew that her mother would not want this. In fact, Keiko had made a point of telling her children about her living will, a document that put down on paper her request that no heroic measures be taken to keep her alive.

That document revealed itself on Monday, the first day after the stroke. Keiko's family doctor, Samuel Zloh, reminded them that Keiko had left him a copy. When Patrick asked how they should interpret her request, he said that was often not an easy decision. An intravenous drip would maintain her mother's fluids for the time being, he said. If the coma continued, however, at some point they would have to decide whether to insert a feeding tube. He emphasized that they were days away from such a decision. No doubt coming from his earlier life as a Navy physician, Zloh's advice seemed appropriate: "For now, steady as she goes."

Kazuko returned the watering can to the kitchen closet. Next was the outside watering. The lawn had automatic sprinklers, but the bedded plants required individual attention. As Kazuko walked around the corner of the house to retrieve the hose, she noticed a car pull up on the street adjacent to her mother's white picket fence. Figuring that it was someone visiting a neighbor, she continued to the side faucet. As she returned, uncoiling the hose as she went, she saw a man approach the gate and wave.

Kazuko dropped the hose and walked toward him, taking in the presence of an older Japanese gentleman in white slacks and a multicolored short-sleeved plaid shirt. He was carrying a basket of fruit. "Hello. Can I help you?" Knowing that few visitors realized how cool the Monterey Peninsula could be, even during the summer, Kazuko concluded that he did not live here.

"You must be Kazuko," the man said, a pleasant smile softening his wrinkled face.

He knows me? I've never met this man in my life. "I'm sorry. You are . . . ?"

The man bowed slightly, the smile fading. "Forgive me, please. My name is Takeo Sato. I am an old friend of Keiko's. She hasn't mentioned me? I've been corresponding with her for nearly a year, and a couple of weeks ago we decided to get together. I flew in this morning from Seattle and have been calling all day, but she hasn't answered. Is she here? She's expecting me."

Kazuko had to think fast. Her mother had never mentioned anyone by that name. A hoax? Unlikely. The kind, expressive face certainly seemed sincere. "Mr. Sato, would you care to come inside?"

Kazuko led the way, opened the door, and waited as he caught up. He smiled again as he crossed the threshold and handed her the basket. "Keiko always liked fruit."

Kazuko accepted the basket, thanked him, and gestured toward the sofa. "Please, sit down. Can I offer you something to drink?"

"If you don't mind, I would like a glass of water. Thank you."

"I'll just be a moment." Kazuko walked slowly toward the kitchen, trying to decide the best way to tell him. He was in for a shock.

As Kazuko placed the fruit on the countertop, she saw Sato walk around the room, taking in the multitude of hanging pictures, all of them blown-up, framed photographs taken by Kazuko's father, James, an amateur photographer. The finished display, however, was a joint effort. Keiko had taken to framing and had become quite adept at choosing appropriate matting and framing materials. More than once, friends had suggested that she do it professionally.

Kazuko returned with water from the refrigerator and found Mr. Sato staring at one picture in particular. "This is a picture of Tule Lake where we were interned," he said.

"Yes. Daddy took that sometime in the early fifties, I think. I was around eight or nine at the time and didn't appreciate the significance of what I was seeing. Our family had gone on a road trip because Mom wanted to have one last look." Kazuko pointed to the wall. "That picture is the only physical item I've ever seen associated with our family's war experience there. I think that Mom purposely got rid of anything that reminded her of that time in her life."

Kazuko handed Sato the water and motioned toward the couch. Sato took a long drink.

He looked at Kazuko expectantly. "Do you know where your mother is? She had planned to meet me at the airport. I must say I was a little concerned when I couldn't reach her on the phone. So, I rented a car, checked into my hotel, and here I am."

This isn't going to be easy. "Mr. Sato-san." On purpose, Kazuko added the suffix to Sato's name as a way of showing respect to a fellow

Japanese. "I can't believe what has happened myself, but I'm sure it will be even more of a shock to you. Mom had a stroke Sunday and has been in a coma ever since."

The lively sparkle in Sato's eyes that Kazuko found so mesmerizing vanished instantly. His face crumpled, and his mouth fell open. He looked to the floor, his hands unconsciously opening face-up in front of him. His left hand rose to his forehead. "I am so sorry. I received an email from your mother just last Friday. This is unbelievable."

Kazuko decided to give the man some time. This sudden sad information had obviously caught him off guard.

Sato looked up. "You say that she's in a coma. Do the doctors hold out any hope?"

"We don't know. It happened Sunday afternoon. We were lucky, though. Aunt Shizuka found Mom here at the house not too long after it happened."

A spark of life returned to Sato's eyes. "Shizuka? I remember her well. Your mother told me that she lives in Monterey too."

Kazuko decided that it was her turn to ask some questions. "Mr. Sato-san. How was it that you knew Mom and Aunt Shizuka?"

"You don't know?" Sato seemed surprised. "No, I guess there's no reason that you would if your mom never mentioned me. We were all in the same internment camp. My family—my parents and one sister—and the Tanaka family all came from the Bellevue area of Washington. I knew of your family back in Bellevue, but I got to know them well at Tule Lake."

Tule Lake. Kazuko was ashamed to admit that she knew little about the place. As she grew up, talk about the internment had been scarce. She knew that her mother's family had not escaped the Japanese roundup, but, when pressed, Keiko had brushed the subject aside, saying she'd rather not talk about it. Kazuko would then ask her father who would send her straight back to her mother. He'd gone off to war in the Pacific and couldn't offer much on what had happened back home, he had said.

Surprisingly, Kazuko had gotten an identical response from her Aunt Shizuka, Kazuko's talkative favorite aunt, the fun one in the family. No one wanted to say anything, it seemed. Kazuko always suspected what the reason was: Keiko's twin sister, Misaki, had died there of influenza during the spring of 1943. Kazuko figured that this subject was too painful to discuss.

Kazuko shook her head. "Mom didn't talk very much about that period in her life. Aunt Shizuka either."

Sato nodded. "I'm not surprised. What you experienced is typical. We were all so humiliated by what happened that we never wanted to discuss it again. I'm sure you understand."

Being the curious child, Kazuko had had to make do. "Since I couldn't rely on the personal experiences of my family, I read books that filled in the details. I do understand what you're saying." Kazuko's eyes bored into Sato's. "In my mind, though, I always suspected that my family blamed the government for Aunt Misaki's death."

"That wouldn't be hard to do. The winters there were cold and the buildings drafty. We all got sick at one time or another." Sato's lips pressed together firmly. "But, you know, we Japanese have a way of plodding through the worst of times. I know that losing Misaki took me a long time to get over."

"Why? What do you mean?"

Sato's eyebrows rose. "Oh!" He seemed disappointed. "Your parents obviously didn't tell you anything. Misaki was my fiancée. After I got back from the war, we were going to get married."

6

UNANTICIPATED REACTION

Monterey, California
Late Wednesday afternoon, October 25, 2000

Kazuko couldn't hide her astonishment. "You were engaged to Aunt Misaki? I never knew Aunt Misaki had a fiancé."

Sato took another sip from his glass, set it down on the coffee table, and leaned back into the soft cushions of the sofa, a sobering look darkening his wrinkled features yet again. "I'm surprised that you didn't know. I have no idea why Keiko or Shizuka would hide such a thing." Sato's disappointment transitioned into a shy smile. "It's not like I was a delinquent or a criminal."

Kazuko was feeling sorry for the old man. She leaned forward, hands folded between her legs. "Mr. Sato-san, I wouldn't take it personally. Mom didn't tell us anything about those times. Like I said, what I know about the internment camps I learned from books. They did talk about growing up in Washington before the war."

Sato nodded. "Thank you for that. You're very kind."

Caught up in the strangeness of the moment, Kazuko realized that an opportunity had dropped into her lap, and she needed to take advantage of it. Sato might be the last person in the world who had known her family in the camp and who might talk about their experiences. "Mr. Sato-san, could you tell me what you know about Aunt Misaki? When exactly did you meet her? What kind of person was she? Since she was Mom's twin, was she like Mom?"

Sato nodded. "Both of our families had come from the Bellevue area of Washington. Your family had a successful truck farm business."

"That I know. I remember Aunt Shizuka complaining about how much work there was to do during the summer."

"That's how I got to know your family. Many of the Japanese had truck farms. As a teenager during the summer, I made extra money working for different farmers, helping them sell their produce in Seattle. That's how I came to stop by your parents' farm, looking for work. I remember yours especially because of Keiko and Misaki. I had never seen female twins before, and I was infatuated."

Sato's eyes softened as his mind retreated into the past. "They looked so much alike, with their bright eyes, delicate features, and jet-black hair. They styled it the same, you know, making it impossible to tell them apart." Sato's eyes refocused, and he looked up. "You know, don't you, that they were special, those two, and not just because they were so smart? I can say for a fact, because I was there, that they were the most beautiful girls in the camps. They'd turn heads. And they had to know that. But to their credit, they never let on.

"You can imagine the effect they had on a boy like me. I was just one year older. With time, I got to where I could tell them apart. But it wasn't from their looks." Sato shook his head. "Misaki was the one who interested me more. It was her personality. She was more reserved, and I liked that. Like me, quiet, you know."

Kazuko was mesmerized. In front of her sat an eyewitness to the camp where her mother, uncle, aunts, and grandparents had lived. Sure, her mother and aunt had described many of their memories of life before World War II. But here, right now, she might get some insight into that mystery called the internment. "This is fascinating, Mr. Sato-san. Mom is definitely different from the way you describe Aunt Misaki. She's outgoing and doesn't hold back when it comes to giving you her opinion. So Aunt Misaki was the quiet one."

Kazuko thought about her next question. She had so many and didn't know where to start. "Please tell me how you two got together."

"We arrived at Tule Lake by the end of July." The pace of his delivery increased; Sato seemed to relish telling his story. "That was in 1942, only seven months after Pearl Harbor. We had gotten there by way of Pinedale, California . . . not far from Fresno. We were there for more than a month in this temporary facility, what they called an Assembly Center. It was so stinking hot, I was really glad to leave. All of us from Bellevue were used to the mild Washington climate. When we arrived at Tule Lake, at least the temperatures were a little better. Tule Lake's about four thousand feet above sea level. Of course, that changed in the winter when it was much cold—"

"You know that I was born there, in that camp, don't you?" Kazuko interrupted. "In January 1943. Patrick, my brother, wasn't born until after the war."

Sato smiled. "Of course, I know that. I was there the day you were born, and it was only three months or so before your Uncle Masao-san and I headed off to basic training in Mississippi. I remember Misaki telling me how proud she felt to be an aunt." He paused. "You asked how Misaki and I met. It wasn't long after we arrived at Tule Lake that I got to know your family well—because of my interest in Misaki, I have to admit. She and I started to spend time together."

Kazuko felt like a child, her mind soaking up these fascinating details.

"Of course, everyone from the Bellevue area either knew your family or had heard of Keiko."

"Why was that? My family wasn't famous for anything, were they?"

Sato chuckled and shook his head. "Forgive me for laughing. Times have changed so much that we don't even think about it today. Your parents' marriage—back in March 1942, as I recall—was quite the sensation, even with the war starting up and the threat of internment hanging over us. Your parents represented the first mixed-race marriage any of the Japanese there had ever heard of. Rumors were flying at the time. Mostly about the war in your family. Your grandfather nearly disowned his daughter, but it all eventually worked out."

Kazuko had suspected that her parents' marriage must have been groundbreaking at the time. Still, she couldn't remember anyone in the family ever talking about it.

Sato changed the subject. "By the way, I know about your father, James—about the Alzheimer's. Your mother's written me. I'm so sorry. I met him once when he came to the camp, but I didn't really know him. Back in Bellevue, he had enlisted and shipped out not that long after he and your mother married."

"You said he visited Tule Lake?"

"Yes. He had finished whatever training the Navy had sent him to but hadn't left the States yet. He requested leave to see his new baby."

Kazuko blushed, and she felt warm inside. "When was that, Mr. Sato-san?"

Sato squeezed his mouth with his hand. "Let's see. You were born in January—"

"January nineteenth."

"Well then, it had to have been sometime before I left for Mississippi at the end of April. I do remember him hiring a photographer to document the occasion. I assume that you've seen those pictures."

Pictures? "No, I can't say that I have."

"Well, if you ever find them, please let me know. I'd love to have copies because your Dad insisted that Misaki and I get our pictures taken too. Everybody in your family got their pictures taken." Sato took another sip of water, but then something seemed to catch in his throat. "I'd like that because I don't have any pictures of Misaki, let alone one of us together."

"You can count on it."

Sato stared at Kazuko, his face taking on a reflective look. "When I look at you, I can see both your mother and your father."

Kazuko felt embarrassed at Sato's comment, without knowing quite why. She had never once been ashamed of being the product of a mixed-race family. Even while she had been growing up back in Washington, during her teenage years and then again at college, few people had ever made an issue of it.

Kazuko wanted to get back to the interesting parts. "So you say that you and Misaki started to date not long after you arrived at Tule Lake?"

"I guess you'd call it dating. In August, we started to hang out together and got to seeing each other more and more. Eventually I proposed, and she said yes." Sato beamed. "Up until then it was the happiest day of my life, I'd have to say. Here was this beautiful young girl that I had fancied back in Washington. Ironically, at the time I didn't view the disaster of the internment camp as a negative. That camp was the reason my life had suddenly turned for the better.

Being young and in love made the stress and monotony of our lives there seem irrelevant."

Kazuko had read about the harsh life in the camps, and it made her feel ashamed of the easy times she and her brother had had growing up. "So what happened then?"

Sato shook his head. "Around that time was when things started to get complicated. What you also probably don't know is that I had become friends with your Uncle Masao-san. Like Misaki and me, we had similar temperaments." He looked up and swallowed. "Your uncle was the most sympathetic and thoughtful person I've ever known in my life."

Sato composed himself and continued. "But unlike our parents, we were Nisei and thus American citizens. That was part of the reason that from the time we arrived at the camp, we wanted to join the service and go defend our country."

Kazuko knew this part of the story because her Uncle Masao had died fighting with the famous 442nd Regimental Combat team, a Japanese-American unit that garnered great fame because of their heroism and the numbers of combat medals they received. She also knew about the citizenship part and the fact that the Issei, Japanese aliens like her mother's parents who had not been born here, had to wait until 1952 before they could become citizens.

"Back in Bellevue, the government had turned us down and said we couldn't enlist. The selective service classified us as IV-C, Enemy Aliens."

Kazuko knew about this as well. "That's so unreal! You and Uncle Masao were American citizens. How could they justify that?"

Sato ignored the question and continued. "Things really came to a head in February 1943. That was when we males were asked to fill out Selective Service Form DDS 304A." He looked up. "Isn't it something that I still remember the number?"

In her books, Kazuko had read about that too. There had been a separate form for females. She had an idea where this conversation was going. The forms had been very divisive.

"There were two questions which ended up dividing camps and even families. First, they asked us Japanese men if we would serve in combat if ordered; but then they also asked us to swear unqualified allegiance to the United States. I think you can see the problem. Here Masao-san and I, both US citizens, were confined in what seemed like a concentration camp, sitting behind barbed wire, being asked to fight and swear allegiance when our rights had been taken from us.

"As bad as that was, it was worse for our parents, who weren't citizens and had no way of becoming citizens. If they answered yes to both questions, they'd literally become people without a country. This was a terrible situation. Your grandparents voted yes/yes, but mine voted no/no. Masao-san and I knew that if there was any hope for us to serve our country, we had to vote yes/yes. We figured that joining the army was one way for us to gain respect for our people."

"What did Aunt Misaki think about your going off to war?"

"She didn't want me to go, of course, but she understood. I was just finishing basic training when I got the news about her." Sato took a handkerchief from his pocket and wiped his eyes. "Even all this time later, I still wonder if it might have been different if I hadn't left the camp. I think it's human nature to think like that."

Kazuko could feel her heart breaking for this man. Now she wished she knew more about him. Surely he had found someone else after the war? But this wasn't the time to ask.

Kazuko wanted to touch on another sad memory. "Please tell me what you remember about Uncle Masao."

"Like I said, Masao-san and I were buddies. We enlisted together and left Tule Lake at the same time. In Mississippi, we trained together and later sailed to Europe together. We were in different units when he was killed. I remember talking to some of his comrades, and they told me how brave he had been."

Kazuko knew that her uncle had received a medal. "Please tell me other stories you remember about my family in the camp."

The conversation continued for another forty-five minutes. Kazuko was fascinated by anecdotes that provided new insights into her family. During that time, Sato opened up a little about his life after the war. Abruptly, the sound of an opening door broke her concentration.

"Why is the hose uncoiled outside?" her aunt asked before noticing that Kazuko had company.

Kazuko and Sato stood as they heard Shizuka's voice.

31

"Aunt Shizuka," Kazuko turned and smiled. "We have a special visitor who you might remember from way back when." She gestured. "This is Mr. Takeo Sato-san. He's been telling me all about Tule Lake, all kinds of stories about our family back there."

Kazuko waited a beat before asking. "And why have you been holding out on me? You never told me that Aunt Misaki was engaged to be married."

Of the range of emotions that she might have expected, what Kazuko saw revealed on her aunt's face in the next few seconds was not one of them.

7

ANNOUNCEMENT

Bellevue, Washington
Christmas Day, Thursday, December 25, 1941

In the weeks following that fateful morning of December 7, the Tanaka family's hoped-for improvement to the Japanese situation never came. Things got worse. Several Japanese men who held positions of prominence in the Bellevue community found themselves arrested and removed from the community. Did the FBI think they were spies?

Several Caucasian neighbors with whom the Tanaka family had previously had cordial relations turned cold and avoided contact. Not all, but some. James Armstrong's family, who owned the land from which the Tanakas made their living, stood solidly behind them and made the situation tolerable.

It wasn't long before Shizuka reported something that Keiko found disturbing: Caucasian schoolmates who in the classroom remained friendly but, after school, pretended not to know her. Keiko and Misaki, who both had part-time jobs in Bellevue, soon sensed stares and mumblings behind their backs. Just as bad, hateful signs started going up in the windows of some stores. Japs not wanted here. Japs go home. It was getting harder for the Tanaka children to believe that what their father had said was true: that everyone was just reacting to fear caused by the bombing of Pearl Harbor.

The building animosity and controversy concerning the Japanese played itself out in newspaper columns and editorials. Every Japanese American, even those who previously could not have cared less about current events, read every word in the newspaper or had it read to them. Their futures seemed to hang between what the government thought was best for the country and current popular opinion.

Unfortunately, both sides seemed to be converging toward a similar solution. Talk was building about removing the Japanese from areas crucial to the defense of the United States, specifically the western coastal waters. Newspapers were quick to point out that because many Japanese lived close to Navy bases, they were positioned perfectly to sabotage operations in advance of a Japanese invasion. Keiko and her family wondered where all of these Japanese saboteur spies were hiding.

James maintained his resolve to volunteer if the United States pressed forward into war, which happened within days of Pearl Harbor. Following December 7, the United States immediately declared war on Japan, together with Britain, Australia, and other Allies. Hitler's Germany returned the favor, forcing the United States to respond to that challenge as well on December 11. It seemed to Keiko that her country was going to war with the entire world.

James's decision to enlist as soon as he could had not gone over well with his parents, who had been looking forward to their firstborn going off to college. Having graduated from high school the previous spring, he had already decided to delay college by one year, arguing that he could save money by working in his father's law office. Since he had already lost one year, they urged him to wait to see how the draft lottery played out—that his name might never come up. When they realized that he wouldn't budge, they brought in the family Bible, suggested strongly that he place his hand on it, and got him to promise to start college when he returned from the service.

With the mind-numbing speed of world events, Keiko and James agreed that the problems they would face with their families would be no different whether they sprang their news now or later. They decided that Christmas would be the ideal date, a day of general happiness and joy that would surely overshadow any concerns over a marriage.

The Christmas Day idea was, in fact, James's. In light of the community's increasingly ill will toward the Japanese, he suggested to his parents that inviting the Tanaka family to their house for a Christmas dinner would be an appropriate gesture. James's parents, Harrison and Barbara, agreed; so the stage was set.

The Tanaka family arrived at the Armstrong residence around two in the afternoon. Barbara had informed Akemi that she intended to have a traditional American dinner but suggested that, if she wanted, Akemi could bring some Japanese favorites.

Besides James, the Armstrongs had two other children, also boys. James was the oldest at nineteen, with Benjamin and Wally each two years younger than his next older sibling. Keiko admired the thoughtful planning that had gone into the age distribution. Of the family, James said that his mother was always the fun one to be around. She constantly made jokes and pulled pranks. James's father was the opposite, reserved with a quiet manner.

The Armstrong house was one of the grander ones in the neighborhood, fitting for a respected local attorney who had obviously done well for his family. It included a dining room and table suitable for such a large gathering. Keiko had always admired the house from the street, but had only once been inside, on a rare occasion when the rest of James's family was away. As James had shown her around, she marveled at its size and luxury, an opulence that Keiko had never experienced. As her family entered the house on Christmas afternoon, she could imagine their similar reaction.

Dinner was planned for three o'clock. The adults and children separated into three groups: Barbara and Akemi to the kitchen to make final preparations, Harrison and Isamu to the front of a glowing fireplace in the living room, and the Armstrong children taking the Tanaka children to their bedrooms to show off their Christmas presents. Keiko and James remained at the back of the group. At one point, James pulled Keiko aside and kissed her firmly on the mouth. Startled, Keiko jumped back and looked around to make sure no one was looking. When she saw that they were alone, she reciprocated, pulling James close and returning his kiss.

"Okay, everybody, it's time to eat," Keiko heard Barbara

Armstrong's voice from downstairs. She and James followed the other children down the steps.

Harrison supervised seating around the table, placing Isamu on one end of the rectangular table and himself at the other. Keiko and James were seated directly across from each other. James smiled and winked. Keiko noticed that Misaki, sitting next to James, had observed this interchange. Misaki was the only other person who knew what was going to happen. With her usual quiet and steady nature, her personality actually mimicked James's. *Either one would make a good poker player*, thought Keiko.

Keiko was nervous but felt confident that she and James were doing the right thing. They had rehearsed their speech that, after several practice runs, turned out to be quite short. They had agreed that James would do the talking at the conclusion of the meal. Keiko suggested that they wait until just before dessert. James had informed her that it would be apple pie, an Armstrong family favorite.

Keiko had been in for a surprise two days earlier when James had gotten down on one knee and made a formal request for the hand of his bride. An unexpected bonus was the ring that he had produced from his pocket, a simple gold band with a small diamond. Keiko knew that James's parents allowed him to keep his own savings account in the bank. She was about to scold him for spending money on such an extravagant gift, knowing that they'd need more practical things soon. Just in time, she managed to withhold her disapproval, realizing that this might be one time in her life when criticism was not appropriate. She wore the ring home but then hid it inside a sock at the back of her drawer.

Keiko surveyed the abundance of food spread across the table. Her mother had brought three Osechi-ryori dishes. As the meal began, Akemi explained that they were usually prepared for a New Year's celebration, but in light of this special occasion, they seemed appropriate.

"This first one is called Kuri kinton," Akemi said. It was one of Keiko's favorites; she liked anything sweet. "It's made of sliced sweet potatoes mixed together with sweet chestnuts in a syrup. The golden yellow color is supposed to symbolize prosperity."

Akemi smiled shyly, obviously unsure of how these dishes would be received. "The second one is called Datemaki. It's an egg omelet mixed with fish cake. And the third is called Nimono. It's made of taro, carrots, and mushrooms. See how the carrots are made to look like a flower?"

With the mention of fish, Keiko watched James's younger siblings for their reaction and was impressed at their response.

Mrs. Armstrong reacted immediately. "Children! Look how beautiful these are. We are very lucky today to be able to taste these genuine Japanese dishes, and we have Mrs. Tanaka to thank for this."

Mr. Armstrong picked up the slack. "This looks fantastic. I can't wait to try the Kuri . . ." He looked toward Mrs. Tanaka for help.

"Kuri kinton," Akemi replied. "I hope that you like it."

"I don't think you have to worry about that, Mrs. Tanaka. My ears perked up as soon as I heard sweet potatoes and nuts."

Keiko surveyed the rest of the table. Most of the dishes had, at one time or another, also appeared on their own dinner table. There were two types of meat: ham and chicken. She watched as Mr. Armstrong took on the duty of slicing both. Other dishes included mashed potatoes, gravy, string beans in a white sauce, applesauce, a salad made with orange Jell-O and canned fruit, and hot biscuits. Drinks consisted of water and strawberry Kool-Aid.

As food made its way around the table, Keiko checked for perhaps the thousandth time to make sure that her ring hadn't somehow escaped the confines of the tiny pocket on the right side of her skirt. She intended to put the ring on secretly as James made his statement. Although Misaki knew of their planned announcement, even she didn't know about the ring. Keiko was proud of being able to withhold at least one secret from her twin.

As the two families ate their fill, conversation covered the gamut: prospects for next year's vegetable crop, the weather, special gifts received for Christmas, then on to a general discussion of the country's future now that the United States had declared war. But no one dared broach the subject of the future of the Japanese Americans in the Bellevue community.

Keiko was pleased to see that her normally staid parents had let themselves relax a bit. They seemed to be enjoying themselves. As good as Keiko knew the Japanese culture could be in making a guest feel welcome, Keiko concluded that Harrison and Barbara Armstrong were no slouches as hosts. Keiko marveled at their various comments and gestures that made everyone feel so at ease. And even their children were polite. Keiko listened carefully, deciding that she would try to be this way after she and James wed.

Time was getting close. Mrs. Armstrong held her fork in the air, smiled, and asked if anyone wanted seconds or thirds before dessert. Masao extended Keiko's agony by asking for more ham and potatoes. Perhaps realizing that he now had an opening, the youngest Armstrong, Wally, raised his hand and pointed. "Could I have some more sweet potatoes, please?" Akemi beamed and offered to put more on his plate.

Keiko realized that she should have taken off her sweater earlier, wondering if anyone noticed the perspiration she sensed clinging to her forehead and cheeks. She looked across at James, ever cool and calm, who hadn't let on in the slightest that anything was afoot. That was one of James's qualities that she admired: remaining calm under fire. Keiko ran her fingers along her thigh to feel the impression through the fabric. *Yes, it's still there.*

While food passed around the table yet one more time, one person in the room chose to bring up the subject that everyone had avoided, and the source surprised Keiko: her father.

Isamu looked across the long table. "Mr. Armstrong, what do you think is going to happen?" A man of few words in any situation, he didn't elaborate. Everyone knew what he was referring to.

The table grew quiet. Masao stopped eating mid-bite, his eyes sweeping back and forth between the two ends of the table. Everyone looked toward Harrison, who took a moment to gather his thoughts.

"Mr. Tanaka, I wish I knew. There is so much crazy talk going on, and I am so embarrassed for all of us. I'm embarrassed for you and your family, and I'm embarrassed for my friends who are saying things they full well know better not to say. Where is all of this heading? Let's all pray that saner minds prevail."

All eyes remained on Mr. Armstrong. Perhaps realizing that his comments had deflated the holiday mood, he continued. But first, he made a point of looking each person in the eye. He then raised his glass, gesturing that everyone at the table do the same.

"Just so all of you know, the Tanaka family does not stand alone. No matter what happens in the coming weeks and months, I can assure you that Barbara and I are here to support you. We are your friends and will not desert you."

Keiko's mind whirled as she drank to the toast. Had the mood changed so much that they should consider calling off their announcement? She looked across at James to assess his reaction. His appearance had not changed. He pursed his lips and nodded. Keiko responded in kind.

"Well, I think it's time for some apple pie," Barbara Armstrong said cheerfully as she started to get up from the table.

Before she had risen halfway, James had pushed his chair back so forcibly that it made a loud screeching noise on the hardwood floor. He stood tall. "Mom, please sit down. I have something to say."

Surprised, Mrs. Armstrong slowly resumed her position. Everyone, with eyes open wide at this unexpected development, glanced up toward James.

Keiko was ready. Even before James started his first sentence, the ring was securely in place on the third finger of her left hand.

8

SAFETY IN NUMBERS

Bellevue, Washington
Christmas Day, Thursday, December 25, 1941

James cleared his throat. "Mom, Dad, Mr. Tanaka, Mrs. Tanaka—" He looked at his siblings. "Benjamin, Wally, I'm glad that you are here to hear this." Not wanting to leave anyone out, he then glanced at Misaki, Masao, and Shizuka. "I am happy that you are here too."

Tension in the room ratcheted up immediately. Harrison Armstrong turned toward his wife, who shrugged her shoulders. Isamu and Akemi Tanaka looked up casually toward James, with no idea that James's upcoming words would deeply affect both families seated at the table. Except for Misaki, the children of both families went on alert.

James continued. "I will make this short. I have asked Keiko to marry me, and she has said yes. We plan to get married before I enlist this spring."

At once, Keiko's left hand snaked from under the table to the left side of her plate. Her right hand followed quickly to remove the nearby napkin, providing adequate clearance so that all could see her gorgeous ring. Realizing that those at the ends of the table were at a disadvantage, she made a point of casually raising her hand about a foot above the table and rotating it slowly left and right. All eyes immediately shifted away from James toward Keiko's hand.

The first person Keiko noticed was Misaki. Even her eyes had grown large, a naughty smile meeting Keiko's gaze. Keiko had Misaki's support, but feared the reactions of the rest of her family. Would they be pleased? Or were they in shock at James's announcement?

James continued. "Keiko and I know how surprised you must be to hear this news." All eyes returned to the speaker. "We thought long and hard about the best way to tell you. We chose Christmas Day so that you will always associate it with me and Keiko, to our happiness."

At this point, Keiko thought she should stand as well. She reached across the table with her left hand and took his right, rotating her hand in his parents' direction. Surely, they would appreciate his sincerity when they saw this beautiful symbol of his affection. She tried to gauge their reaction. She saw surprise, but not shock. So far, so good!

Keiko felt her face flush, and she knew why. She struggled to look to her right, toward the one person at the table whose approval was paramount. What she saw was not what she had hoped for. Isamu's mouth hung open, and it looked like he was squinting. His color was gone. Fear gripped Keiko's heart. She turned farther to try to assess her mother's reaction. Unfortunately, because Akemi was looking at her husband, Keiko saw only her profile.

Hoping for better news at the opposite end of the table, Keiko turned to her left again. As she did so, Harrison and Barbara Armstrong switched their gaze from James to her. Compared to Keiko's father, their complexions appeared more normal. The younger children at the table didn't seem to know what to make of the situation. Their heads whipped back and forth from one adult to another, trying to make sense of what was obviously something quite unusual.

And then, Misaki came through. Across the table, next to James, the quiet of the room was broken by one set of hands clapping. *Misaki promised that she would support me, and here she is.* Perhaps concluding that if Keiko's twin sister thought that this proclamation was worth applause, the rest of the children clapped as well.

Regrettably, Keiko saw that none of the adults were joining this spontaneous display of approval. Isamu's back had straightened, and he was staring down the table, at no one in particular. Akemi bowed her head. Keiko hoped that James's parents had chosen not to clap with the children so as not to embarrass their other adult guests. When the kids realized that those whose opinions at the table counted most were not participating, the applause petered out.

Keiko and James had figured that this could happen. James turned first toward his parents and then toward the Tanakas. "Mom, Dad, Mr. and Mrs. Tanaka, I want you to know . . ." He spoke directly to Isamu. "Mr. Tanaka, please. I love your daughter more than anything. I promise you that I will take care of her, every bit as well as you have. You have my word."

Keiko noticed the chirp of a bird outside the window. She wondered if anyone else did, the senses of those at the table seemingly muffled by the tension filling the room. Keiko decided it was time for her to speak, and she turned to her right. "Papa, Mama." Tears began to flow. "Papa, please look at me." Another moment. "Papa, please." A bit of color had returned to Isamu's face, and he lifted his head to face his daughter.

Keiko sniffled and struggled to contain her emotions. With her left hand still in James's and wet with perspiration, she wiped at her face with her right. "Papa, I love James and want to spend the rest of my life with him. I need your blessing." Another beat of silence. "Mama?"

Please, God! Keiko prayed in her mind. With deafening silence riveting the room, from the left end of the table came a respite as Keiko sensed movement.

Mr. Armstrong got to his feet and motioned to James and Keiko. "Please sit down." As had happened earlier, Mr. Armstrong seemed to gather his thoughts. "I think that what I am about to say could be said by anyone sitting here at the table."

Keiko stole another look at her father, hoping to detect some softening in his disposition. She saw none.

"James. Keiko. What you have to understand is that Barbara and I—and I'm sure Mr. and Mrs. Tanaka would agree . . ." He gestured in their direction. "We've been absolutely blindsided by this sudden news. I guess that I blame myself for not having noticed some clue about what has obviously been going on right under my nose. You two sure have done a good job of keeping this a secret. What you've seen here"—he pointed to Barbara and then toward the Tanakas—"our reaction is what you should have expected, assuming that you had thought this through at all." He fired off a look of disapproval in James's direction. "That's not to say that we're not excited about hearing this news, but you might have given us a little warning."

Keiko knew full well what James's father was saying, but she also knew that he was wrong in suggesting that they hadn't thought it through. They had decided to do it this way because of the response they feared from Keiko's father. Safety in numbers, she had said repeatedly to James.

With Mr. Armstrong now quiet and with further conversation stalled, Mrs. Armstrong stood up next to her husband. "Well, then! This has certainly turned into a more interesting afternoon than I had expected." She grabbed her fork and lifted it high. "I'll try again. How many here want apple pie?"

* * *

In comparison to the relative joviality of the pre-announcement afternoon, the remainder of the visit turned morose. Keiko and James remained at the table after everyone else left. Keiko watched as Harrison motioned Isamu back to the living room, out of earshot. She would have given anything to listen in on that conversation.

Barbara, Akemi, and the children cleared the table. Misaki made a point of patting Keiko on the shoulder. She whispered, "It's going to be okay. I just know it."

As if by mutual agreement, the afternoon festivities broke up about five thirty. The leftover food was divided, and the Tanakas left the house with three casserole dishes full.

* * *

Safety in numbers. Keiko realized that she had lost that protection as the Tanaka family left the secure confines of the Armstrong home.

In times past, when one of the children did something wrong that might warrant punishment, the others would remain quiet, knowing that sticking out his or her own neck could result in a share of the punishment. For one person in the car, that rule fell by the wayside.

As usual, the three girls shared the backseat. First, it was Misaki and then Shizuka who reached for Keiko's hand to take a closer look at the ring.

"Papa." It was Misaki. "Why can't you and Mama be happy for Keiko? With our country going to war—and with who knows what is going to happen to us Japanese—it seems to me that we could stand a little happiness in our lives. If James and Keiko are in love, I think we should support them."

During the short drive back to the house, Misaki's editorial comments were the only words spoken. This was what Keiko had been afraid of. If only her father had started yelling at her once they left the house, she might have felt better. But that was not his way. She would be made to stew in her transgression, her parents punishing her first for going behind their backs, and second for a reason ultimately more profound, Keiko knew—a proposed marriage of one of their own outside their race.

The Tanaka's respectful third-born child (Misaki was fifteen minutes older) would be crying herself to sleep tonight, she knew. But she also knew that she had followed her heart and that she and James had accomplished what needed doing. Before James left Bellevue to go fight in the war, Keiko vowed that her last name would change from Tanaka to Armstrong.

9

DEAD END

Monterey, California
Early Wednesday evening, October 25, 2000

What do you mean, her reaction was odd?" Patrick had arrived at the house a little after seven and was installing light timers in the living room and bedroom. Kazuko had finished dusting, a chore her mother insisted be done once a week.

Following Aunt Shizuka's arrival earlier, the remainder of Sato's visit had been short. In response to Kazuko's direct question, Shizuka had explained, with some embarrassment, that Misaki's death made the pain of any memory associated with her sister unbearable—including mention of a fiancé. Shizuka said that she was sure that was why Keiko had never mentioned it either.

Following this awkward introduction, Shizuka turned polite and welcomed Sato. Sato told Shizuka much of what he had told Kazuko earlier, that he and Keiko had been corresponding and that she had invited him down from Washington. Shizuka had obviously not known of Keiko's plans.

Sato asked if he could visit Keiko. Shizuka didn't seem happy with this request and said that such a visit was pointless, that Keiko was in a coma. Sato persisted, saying that Keiko would want him to see her. Kazuko offered to meet him at the hospital in the morning, but Shizuka insisted that she would do it. Since Shizuka planned to spend much of the night with Keiko anyway, she would stay until eight, the agreed upon time when Sato would arrive.

The visit broke up when it appeared that Shizuka wasn't interested in further discussion. While Kazuko returned to her watering duties outside, Shizuka walked Sato to his car, out of earshot. Kazuko watched out of the corner of her eye, but she saw nothing unusual in the body language of either.

Kazuko shrugged. "What I mean is that Aunt Shizuka's response was unusual. She was surprised, but there was something more."

Patrick snapped on the table light by the sofa and tested the timer. He then plopped himself onto the sofa and looked across at Kazuko. "Maybe you should cut Aunt Shizuka some slack. The last time she saw this guy was almost a lifetime ago. Can you imagine the memories that came flooding back?" He paused. "Tell me more about this Mr. Sato."

"He was a pleasant man. He said he was a year older than Misaki. That means he's somewhere in his late seventies. He told me a lot we didn't know. All the way from when he became infatuated with Aunt Misaki at our family's farm, to later when all the Japanese from Bellevue got themselves shipped to Tule Lake. He started dating her there and proposed. They planned to marry after he returned from the service. While he was in Mississippi, he got word that she died."

Patrick shook his head. "But why, after all these years, did he come here?"

"It was Mom's doing. She found him on the Internet and suggested they get together. He lives in Seattle."

"Mom was just trying to reconnect with someone from back then," Patrick proposed.

"Yeah. Maybe she felt it was a way to be close to Aunt Misaki again, by reliving old memories."

"Back to what you were saying. Aunt Shizuka's reaction?"

"Yes. She recovered quickly, but there was an instant . . ." Kazuko stood abruptly. "Just forget it. I obviously overreacted. She hadn't seen the man for fifty-some years, for goodness' sake."

"What else did he tell you?"

Kazuko walked to the rear of her chair and leaned forward, bracing herself on the back. "It was fun listening to him, Patrick. I wish you'd been here. You remember how it was almost impossible to pry anything out of Mom or Aunt Shizuka about those days in the camp?"

Kazuko spent the next twenty minutes recalling the details, including Sato's friendship with their uncle Masao.

"Well, there you have it." Patrick had it figured out. "That makes more sense than his connection with Aunt Misaki. Mom was there when Aunt Misaki died but, from what you've said, Sato was the last person who Mom knew to see Uncle Masao."

Kazuko raised her finger. "Oh, and get this. Have you ever seen any photos from the camps, of Mom, Daddy, and me?"

"Nothing other than that picture over there." Patrick pointed toward the wall.

Kazuko returned to her seat and sat tall. "I haven't either. Well, here's what Sato said. He said that after I was born, Daddy came back to the camp especially to see me." As she made that statement, emotion swelled in her chest, and she blinked moisture from her eyes. "He said that I couldn't have been more than a couple months old. Daddy had finished up his training and was getting ready to ship off to war. I was obviously conceived before he left Bellevue."

"That's what I always figured."

"Yeah, but here's what's interesting. Mr. Sato asked me if I ever saw the pictures. He said that Daddy hired a professional photographer to document the occasion. And Daddy insisted that he take pictures of everybody, our entire family, including Aunt Misaki's fiancé, Mr. Sato. Mr. Sato said that if I ever ran across them, that he would pay for copies. He never had a picture of the woman who was to become his new wife, Patrick. After she died, all he had was a memory."

Patrick leaned back and folded his arms. "Didn't he ever marry?"

Kazuko pursed her lips. "Yes, but she died of cancer in her forties, and he's been alone since. He does have one son who lives on the East Coast." *Oh, that's something I hadn't thought of!* "In the same way that Mom may have been searching for a connection to her past, I can imagine how pleased Mr. Sato was when he heard from Mom too. She was the sister of his fiancé."

On the other hand, things don't add up. Why aren't those pictures a part of our family's collection, and why haven't I seen them? Kazuko turned to face the corner of the room to her left. Their amateur

47

photographer father had made it a lifelong hobby of preserving his photographs in albums—in addition to the ones he had blown up for the walls. There were dozens of albums squeezed onto the five shelves of the corner cabinet.

"Patrick! Wouldn't it be something if we could find those pictures, make copies, and give them to Mr. Sato before he went home? He'd be thrilled."

Patrick followed Kazuko's eyes to the bookcase. "Do you think they're here, and we just haven't seen them?"

"Let's find out."

It turned out to be an easy task. Each binder was labeled with the month and year of the photos inside. After ten minutes of searching, sister and brother realized that there was nothing there that they hadn't seen before. The few old pictures of the family from before the war were in the first binder, but things came to a halt in 1942. Nothing again until 1946, the year Patrick was born, following their father's return from the war.

As she thumbed through that earliest album, Kazuko turned sad. "I've never thought about it, Patrick, but these pictures with you are the first ones that ever documented my existence. I wouldn't mind seeing those pictures that Mr. Sato talked about myself. And why weren't there other pictures of me?"

Patrick smirked. "Come on now. Don't make more of this than what it is. The pictures were obviously lost somewhere along the way. Besides, there are good reasons why there aren't any others. I doubt any cameras were allowed in the camps. Remember, the Japanese were interned because everyone was afraid that they'd help a Japanese invasion. The last thing they'd allow would be a camera." He raised his hands. "Besides, if there'd been a camera, don't you think that Sato would have had a picture of his fiancée to take with him?"

"I understand, but can't you see that this makes me want to see those pictures more than ever." Kazuko hesitated. "If they're not in this house, where could they be?"

"Like I said, they probably got lost. But you make a point. If they're here, you and I should know where," Patrick said.

When their parents had downsized in 1990 and moved to Monterey, Kazuko and Patrick had coordinated the move. Kazuko had even made to-scale drawings of all the rooms, figuring out where the furniture was to go even before the movers arrived.

Patrick stood and pointed to the hallway where the fold-up ladder came down from the ceiling. "Well, then, they've got to be in the attic. Everything left over from the move is up there. You remember how Mom and Dad cleaned house big-time."

Kazuko did remember. The house they had grown up in back in Bellevue was twice the size of this downsized version, and their father had argued that it thus made sense that half of everything had to go. Especially the junk, as he referred to it. A lot of that junk consisted of boxes of lifelong mementoes they had collected.

"We threw a lot away, Patrick. What was still useful we gave to the Salvation Army."

"Yeah, we did, but I also remember looking at everything. I wasn't about to throw something away that we could sell to a collector for a fortune. There're still a lot of boxes and trunks up there."

Kazuko looked at her watch. "What do you say we go up and take a look?"

* * *

An hour later, sweating and breathing hard from the stuffy air, Kazuko sat backward on the rough floorboards, holding herself up with her arms. She stared at the last of the boxes they had rifled through and blew air upward through her hair.

"Well, Patrick. That was a waste of time."

"At least we tried." Patrick stood and lent Kazuko a hand.

As Kazuko started down the ladder, she glanced up toward Patrick. "You know what? I'm going to be there when Sato arrives tomorrow morning. I have a second question for Aunt Shizuka."

"And what's that?"

"I wonder if Aunt Shizuka remembers those pictures any better."

"Any better than what?"

"Any better than her conveniently forgetting to ever tell us that Aunt Misaki had a fiancé and planned to get married."

"In that case, count me in. I'll be there too."

10

DINNER INVITATION

Community Hospital of the Monterey Peninsula
Monterey, California
Thursday Morning, October 26, 2000

Kazuko and Patrick arrived at their mother's hospital room by seven-fifty. Shizuka was dozing in a chair in the corner. The RN at the nurse's station told them that their mother's condition remained unchanged.

Patrick stepped to the bedside, took his mother's hand, and stroked it. He and Kazuko watched for any sign of expression or movement on their mother's face. There was none.

A loud noise outside in the hallway startled Shizuka, and she opened her eyes. "I thought you two weren't coming in until later."

Kazuko gestured toward her aunt. "You need to go home and get some rest, Aunt Shizuka."

Shizuka blinked the sleep out of her eyes. "I promised Mr. Sato I'd be here to meet him."

It had been too much to hope that Kazuko and Patrick could have spent some additional time alone with him.

Kazuko looked at her watch. "It's going on eight. He'll be here—" Her words were cut short as they sensed motion near the door and in walked Sato. He nodded, acknowledged the three other visitors, and walked slowly to the head of the bed, hands folded in front. He drew close and stared at Keiko's face.

Kazuko thought to herself that an outsider might interpret what he saw as a funeral viewing, a motionless body laid out in front of mourners.

"You say it happened on Sunday?" Sato turned toward Shizuka.

What was that? Kazuko could have sworn that she saw a flicker of movement in her mother's left eye. She poked Patrick, standing beside her and motioned toward their mother.

Kazuko interrupted. "Before you answer that, Aunt Shizuka, I need to make an introduction. Mr. Sato-san, I'd like you to meet my brother, Patrick."

Sato shook hands. "I'm so pleased to meet you."

With that formality completed, Shizuka continued. "Yes, it was Sunday. I just happened to drop by the house to leave some fresh flowers, and I found her on the kitchen floor. It was about one o'clock. Since I know that Keiko comes home from church a little after noon, it couldn't have been more than an hour, at most, from when it happened." She sat forward in her chair. "When did you last talk to Keiko?"

Sato shook his head. "Actually, we never did talk. Keiko found me on the Internet earlier in the year, and we started emailing. We never sent pictures, either. I think that we were both looking forward to seeing each other again after such a long time. But to answer your question, my last email to her was Friday evening. By then I had my plane tickets and knew when I'd be arriving. She emailed back and said she'd be waiting at the airport." Sato addressed Shizuka. "She never said anything to you?"

As Sato had continued talking, Kazuko watched her mother carefully. *It must have been my imagination.*

"No, she didn't. But Keiko liked to pull surprises. She was probably planning to call us all over one night to introduce you properly." Shizuka stood. "Does Keiko look the way you expected? I guess it's been fifty-some years."

Sato smiled. "I think that we automatically age someone in our minds. To tell you the truth, she looks exactly the way I imagined in my mind's eye." He hesitated. "Of course, the person that I have aged in my mind is Misaki. Since they were twins, it's easy for me to imagine that it's Misaki lying here."

51

The room turned quiet as everyone reacted to that statement. Kazuko imagined how it would feel to have an aunt who looked like her mother.

Patrick jumped in. "Kazuko tells me that you knew Uncle Masao."

Sato smiled. "Oh, yes. We were best friends at Tule Lake and then through basic training in Mississippi. He and I were among the first to volunteer for service, I guess you know. That didn't make us too popular among some of the others at Tule Lake who thought that we were being disloyal to the Japanese predicament. We were birds of a feather, Masao-san and I."

Kazuko, still brooding over Shizuka's coolness toward Sato and her initial reaction to him the previous day, decided this was a good time to confront her aunt. "Mr. Sato-san told me something I didn't know. He said that Daddy came back to the camp from basic training to see me when I was only a couple months old. The reason I bring this up is that Mr. Sato-san said that Daddy hired a photographer to take our pictures, including him and Aunt Misaki. Mr. Sato-san said he would be particularly interested in getting a copy of the one of him and his fiancée. Patrick and I have never seen these pictures. Do you know anything about them?"

To Kazuko's disappointment, she saw nothing suspicious in the body language when her aunt replied. "It's funny you mention that. I was thinking about those just last night. Yes, James hired a photographer to have pictures taken. I vaguely remember seeing them after they were developed, but I have no idea what happened to them. That is something you need to ask Keiko when she wakes up." She nodded toward the bed. "I haven't seen them since." As an afterthought, she said, "They probably got lost after the war."

"I was thinking about those just last night." *I'll bet you were!* Kazuko couldn't help being cynical. Nothing made sense. *Those pictures would mean the world to our family, because they would have been the last ones ever taken of Aunt Misaki and Uncle Masao, except perhaps for those of him in the military. If Mom had them in the camp, there's no way that she would have lost them.*

After a few minutes chitchat skirted around nothing Kazuko considered pertinent, Shizuka started toward the door, indicating that Sato's visit had gone on long enough. He took the hint and thanked Shizuka for allowing him to visit.

Before leaving, Sato took Keiko's hand. "Keiko, if you can hear me, I'm sorry that this happened to you and that we did not get a chance to meet. When you get out of this coma, please let me know, and we'll plan it all over again."

Sato lifted Keiko's hand and kissed it before leaving the room.

Shizuka, Kazuko, and Patrick followed Sato into the hallway in the main pavilion of the hospital. They walked together toward the beautiful central visiting lounge. Lit from above by a huge circular glass dome, the lounge area consisted of comfortable sofas and chairs situated on three sides of a large square pool of water, more than fifty feet on a side. Bubblers and fountains added motion and sound to the ambience. With live plants both in the water and around the seating area, it was a pleasant spot to spend time.

The group congregated on the backside of the pool, their attention drawn to the colorful Koi fish meandering through the water. No one seemed to want to talk first. After a moment, Shizuka asked, "Are you going home today?"

Aunt Shizuka seems to be in an awful hurry for Mr. Sato to leave.

"I'll go tomorrow, I think." Sato took a card from his wallet and handed it over. "You'll call me, please, and let me know how she's doing?"

Shizuka nodded.

Suddenly, Kazuko felt embarrassed. *This is wrong!* Her mother would not have responded this way. They were showing no courtesy to a kind, older gentleman who had flown a great distance to see a woman—at her invitation—whom he had known half a century earlier. The Japanese side of Kazuko knew that more was expected. Shizuka was being rude.

Kazuko faced Sato. "Mr. Sato-san, you've come such a long way. Patrick and I have so many questions we'd like to ask you. You were there! You knew Aunt Misaki and Uncle Masao. I'd love for you to tell us more about what you remember. How was Mom different from Aunt Misaki? What was Uncle Masao like? Please! Patrick and I would love to host you for dinner tonight at Mom's house."

Sato was obviously pleased at the invitation. He bowed slightly and said that he would be delighted. However, he insisted that the conversation not be one sided. He wanted to know about their lives as well. Six o'clock was agreed on.

With this sudden change of plans, three sets of eyes turned toward Shizuka. Kazuko extended the invitation to her aunt. "Aunt Shizuka, please come too. I would think that you and Mr. Sato-san would have a lot to talk about."

Kazuko gauged Shizuka's reaction. "I've been up most of the night with Keiko, and I've got to get some sleep before I come back tonight. You three have a good dinner."

Kazuko knew Shizuka was a night owl who could get along on three to four hours of sleep. Her reply was one more indication that she was either hiding something or knew something about Sato that made her uncomfortable.

Shizuka addressed Sato. "Have a good flight home."

Sato bowed in reply.

With everything decided, the three parties separated. Kazuko and Patrick returned to their mother's room to maintain their vigil. It had been nearly four days since their mother's stroke.

* * *

The voice from almost a lifetime ago had made Keiko's heart skip a beat. Until she heard Sato's words, she had forgotten about their planned meeting this week. *Poor Takeo. He and I were so looking forward to seeing each other. I wish I could have seen what he looked like. His voice was always so soft, so caring.*

Keiko's purpose in inviting Sato to Monterey had been innocent. As the numbers of friends and family from the camps dwindled—and especially after her husband's mind began to fail—she become nostalgic for memories of her youth, difficult as they often were. When she discovered that Sato was still alive, she couldn't resist getting in touch. Keiko knew that there was no shortage of memories from those days at the camp that could be visited once again through his eyes. He was, after all, Misaki's fiancé and Masao's best friend. After he and Masao left the camp for Mississippi, Keiko never saw him again. Why would she have? The two people who were the links between them were both dead.

Keiko reflected on one other aspect of the conversation she had heard. The pictures! It was too bad that they had been lost, Shizuka had stated. Of course, Shizuka's use of the term *lost* was a convenience. In fact, Misaki had insisted that Keiko destroy them, and Shizuka had agreed. But Keiko had kept one; that one had been special indeed. *Surely there was no harm in that*, she thought. Besides, there was no reason for anyone to look in the spot where she had hidden it.

Keiko briefly interrupted the recollection of her life, reliving her personal store of memories involving Sato. Before long, she continued her reminiscence of the war.

11

STALEMATE

Bellevue, Washington
Sunday, December 28, 1941

For the three days following James's infamous Christmas Day announcement, living within the Tanaka house was not a pleasant experience. Keiko and her siblings thought they had moved into a monastery, so intense was the absence of sound. And because each of the children knew the reason for this state of affairs, none wanted to be the first to speak, for fear of reprisal. The informal rule typically ignored in happier times—children will speak only when spoken to—became the standard.

Silence compounded silence—except behind their parents' bedroom door. Night after night, the children strained to decipher words exchanged. Because of this uncomfortable situation—even though December daytime temperatures rarely reached fifty—the Tanaka children chose to spend as much time as possible outdoors.

To make matters worse, public sentiment seemed to be turning against the Japanese. What struck Keiko was that the degree of animosity increased the farther one traveled from home. Most Caucasian neighbors who lived the closest, who knew the Japanese families personally, understood them to be honest, hardworking individuals who could be trusted implicitly. They knew how ridiculous it was to think that any of them could be enemy spies.

But outside Bellevue, those in the Seattle area who knew the

Japanese only for the strawberries they grew during the summer or for the various farm products they provided throughout the year, were more affected by the ranting of individuals inclined to be suspicious of anyone with a different skin color. Out-of-state newspapers from as far south as San Francisco and Sacramento confirmed the fact that public concern about the Japanese was not limited to Washington State. Editorials were nasty.

But beyond this predicament that affected all Japanese and about which they could talk among themselves, there was no similar group in which Keiko could take comfort. There was no one she knew who had ever married outside his or her race.

Keiko's parents had not spoken to her since the Christmas dinner. Even her mother, Akemi, to whom she had always felt closer than her father, avoided eye contact and conversation. Keiko understood that Akemi was taking cues from a husband who, in a Japanese household, typically held the final word on matters of importance.

It was on the morning of the third day afterward, a Sunday, when the impasse finally broke. The family was getting dressed for church, as usual. As they occasionally did as twins, Keiko and Misaki decided to dress alike. Misaki said that it was a display of solidarity with her sister during this difficult time. They were nearly ready when there came a knock at the bedroom door. It was their mother, who asked that Keiko follow her into their bedroom. Misaki hugged her sister and told her to be strong.

Before closing the door, Akemi gestured to a chair next to the window. Isamu faced the wall opposite. Many seconds passed before Keiko's father turned around. Akemi stood alongside her husband in an obvious sign of unity. Keiko briefly held her own in the staring contest but, before long, started to tremble. To maintain control, she sat on her hands while biting her lower lip hard to suppress her emotions.

As expected, Keiko's father did the talking. Never known for raising his voice in anger or displaying outward aggression of any kind, Keiko figured she knew what to expect. Although her father was strict, everyone considered him a fair man. It was this knowledge that gave Keiko hope.

With hands rigidly pinned behind his back and feet spread, Isamu began. "You have disappointed your mother and me, Keiko. You must have known how this would affect us. Why didn't you come to us before you made this announcement? Why did you embarrass us in front of the entire Armstrong family?"

Keiko blinked. She had honestly not even considered that aspect of what she and James had done, that they had embarrassed her family. In Japanese culture, respect within a family was paramount. Keiko chose not to bring up the obvious: that it had been James, and not she, who had made the announcement. That seemed to be a point not worth making.

"Please believe me when I say that James and I did not intend to embarrass you or Mom. To tell you the truth, I didn't even think of that. We did what we did because we knew you would be displeased. That's why. If I had come to you first, would you have reacted differently?"

Isamu responded. "No. I would have tried to talk you out of it. You know you cannot marry this boy."

Keiko's heart sank. She had hoped that her father would show more flexibility. "Why? James comes from a fine family. You know he is a good person and would make a good son-in-law. I also know that you like him. I've seen you together. He makes you laugh."

It was obvious that Isamu viewed James's personal attributes as irrelevant. He came to his point immediately. "He is a Gaijin, Keiko. He's not like us. Even as we speak, the government is considering sending all of us Japanese away. What would you do then? Do you think James's parents will let him go there with you? You are being naïve."

At least we're dealing with logic and facts now. That's something I can handle. "First, we're not in camps yet. That may never happen. But even if it does, it won't last forever. Don't you remember that James is going to enlist? When the war ends, he will come back, and we will be together forever."

All the while, Akemi stood silent. Keiko looked at her beseechingly, trying to elicit some compassion.

Keiko reflected on her discussions with James over the past three days. Since their big announcement, they had had two opportunities to meet. In light of Isamu Tanaka's decision to punish his daughter with silence, Keiko had nothing to report to James. In contrast, James and his parents had had a good discussion, going over the positives and negatives of the proposed marriage. Keiko knew James's parents to be far more open to new ideas than her own.

What absolutely astounded Keiko was what James told her first. Mr. Armstrong had informed him, that if they went ahead, their marriage would be legal in the state of Washington. Incredulous, Keiko asked James the obvious. Why would it not be? As it turned out, Washington was one of only four states west of the Mississippi to allow interracial marriage between a Caucasian and an Asian. Only New Mexico, Kansas, and Iowa had similar laws. Just by the luck of the draw did James and Keiko reside where their marriage was even possible. They had unknowingly dodged one bullet.

Beyond that startling discovery, Mr. and Mrs. Armstrong emphasized to James that if he and Keiko did marry, they would be in for a rough row to hoe. As evidenced by the existing animosity toward the Japanese, James needed to understand what he would be getting himself into. He would no doubt find himself open to criticism not only from the Japanese, but even from friends and family. He would have to be strong to withstand that criticism.

Interestingly, James's mother asked him if he thought Keiko would be up to this challenge. Keiko had never felt so proud, so strong, as when James gave his response: "Mom, you don't have to worry about Keiko. She has twice the strength I'll ever have. That's one of the reasons I want to marry her." When the conversation was over, the Armstrongs gave their blessing and said they would support James's decision.

Keiko wished that she could read her father's mind. There had been no apparent body language to indicate what he had been thinking when they had pulled off the road following the news of Pearl Harbor, and there was none now. The positive aspect of such typical behavior meant that the Tanaka children rarely witnessed any displeasure from their parents. They hid their emotions well. On the other hand, what the children imagined going on inside their father's head often made it seem worse.

Keiko had asked a question, but her father did not reply. He had obviously concluded that his last statement had sufficiently defined his position regarding his daughter's ill-advised decision.

Acquiring a bit of confidence, Keiko removed her hands from under her and folded them on her lap. She had held back her two big arguments and decided that now was the time to use them.

"Father, you know I respect you and Mom more than anything, and I always listen to what you say. Do you remember what happened on December 7, how we sat around the table that night, and you reassured us kids? I remember what you said. You said, 'No matter what happens, because of this country's constitution, you are the equals of our Caucasian neighbors, just as they are the equals of us Japanese.'"

When she witnessed her father's eyes narrowing, it was obvious to Keiko that he had not expected to have a philosophical discussion with his teenage daughter. The humor of the moment was evident shortly thereafter when Akemi, for the first time, turned her head to assess her husband's reaction.

"If I am the equal of every white citizen in this country, and James is the equal of all of us Japanese, that means that we are equal to each other. And if we are equals, there is no reason why we cannot marry. Is that not so?"

Keiko knew that she had caught her father off guard. And the last thing he would want would be to lose to one of his twin daughters' clever counterarguments. He had to say something.

"This is different, Keiko, and you know it. You are twisting my words. Your mother and I know what is best for you." His rebuttal was a weak one.

Another stalemate. Keiko had hoped she wouldn't have to deploy her most powerful weapon, but her father had given her no choice. She feared his reaction.

"Father, I am not a child. You know that I am already eighteen years old." Keiko said nothing more because the implication was obvious. She and James were adults in the eyes of the law, and they could decide for themselves whether to marry.

Seemingly disoriented by Keiko's bomb blast, Isamu turned and stared at his wife for some time. Then he walked out of the room.

Akemi, left to contemplate the silence in the wake of this domestic mayhem, stayed put, and looked down at her daughter. Keiko stared back, searching for even the tiniest sign of support, of any appreciation by a mother for her daughter's predicament. Keiko understood that things had been different for her mother, and thought that she could not understand. She had never had the opportunity to marry for love. Everyone knew that she had been a picture bride, chosen by families who lived an ocean distant.

But in an instant, the clouds separated, and Keiko witnessed the miracle that she had been praying for. Had she blinked, she might have missed her mother's signal: a diminutive smile accompanied by a nod. In a previous moment of nonverbal communication between husband and wife, Akemi had obviously recognized that her husband had capitulated.

With that message delivered to her daughter, Akemi turned and left the room.

Keiko exhaled a huge sigh of relief, tears welling up in her eyes. The battle was over. She leaped to her feet and ran to her bedroom, nearly bowling over her sister waiting in the doorway.

"Tell me everything," said Misaki excitedly. "I want to hear it all, word for word."

12

EXECUTIVE ORDER

Bellevue, Washington
Saturday, February 19, 1942

even weeks had passed since that momentous day in December when Keiko realized she had won over her father, not only with logic, but through her own sheer will. At least that was the way she interpreted how it had gone down. It took a few days afterward, but household dynamics returned to normal. As Keiko expected, her father saw no need to discuss the matter further.

Akemi told her daughter that the conflict this situation had sparked in her father's mind had been huge. It was not only because Keiko wanted to marry outside her race, but also because she had chosen for herself whom she wanted to marry. Regretfully, Akemi said, he still thought that such a union would prove to be a mistake.

Akemi recounted the discussions that had raged between husband and wife. What surprised Keiko was that her mother had been much more an advocate than she expected. Although Akemi told Keiko that she wouldn't trade her marriage to Isamu for anything, she said that she fought for her daughter because she wanted her to have the choice she never had. This was the first time, Akemi said, that she had known of a Japanese woman marrying other than through an arranged marriage.

Misaki reminded Keiko that she had predicted that everything would work out. Having shared each other's private thoughts for their entire lives, Misaki pestered Keiko mercilessly to recount her inter-actions with James, verbatim when possible. And Keiko knew part of the reason. Early on, when it became clear to Misaki that James fancied Keiko over herself, Misaki let it slip that she too had a crush on James and had hoped that he would pick her. But any resentment that might have festered between the sisters faded fast.

"Don't worry," Keiko remembered telling her sister. "You're going to find someone who's perfect for you. I just know it!" With that memory in mind, Keiko recognized that God had favored her and that it would be selfish indeed if she did not share her experiences with her sister.

As much as the upcoming Armstrong/Tanaka wedding domi-nated conversation within these two families, as well as among friends and neighbors, the larger issue of the future of the Japanese in the greater Seattle area became the principal topic of discussion in the weeks following Christmas. There were so many questions and concerns, along with speculation and fear.

It was looking more and more like at least some Japanese would be forced to leave their homes. Initially, everyone thought that it would be only the Issei, those first-generation Japanese who were not citizens—aliens—who would be targeted. Keiko knew that she and her siblings had the same rights as any Caucasian citizen. As weeks passed, however, the Japanese sensed the worst: that none would be spared. Anyone reading the newspapers realized that it was the politicians who kept stirring the pot. One public official after another tried to outdo the rest in his Japanese bashing, even though there had been no documented incidents to implicate Jap-anese Americans in any reported treachery. Hysteria was driving public opinion.

"What do you think is going to happen, James?" Keiko and James were sitting on the front porch of the Armstrong residence. Ever since both families had come to terms with the upcoming nuptials, they had spent most evenings together. Still, Keiko's father had admon-ished his daughter: you may be getting married, but you're not mar-ried yet. Keiko knew exactly what her father meant. He had made a hefty compromise, she knew, and she didn't want to embarrass or question him further. However, that didn't mean that she and James couldn't sneak around the corner occasionally to kiss and touch each other as much as they could.

"Dad says that things are going to come to a head pretty soon." James took Keiko's hand and kissed it gently.

What this meant, Keiko knew, was that the government would soon make a decision regarding exclusion zones, those geographic areas considered militarily sensitive. They spanned the Pacific Coast, including all of California and most of Oregon and Washington. Politicians warned that the Japanese who lived there represented the "fifth column," loyalists of the Japanese emperor, ready to spy and provide support for a Japanese invasion. Sensitive areas should be purged of Japanese, they said.

With the upcoming marriage bringing the families closer together, Keiko and her parents knew they had no better advocate than James's father, a respected local attorney. Having resources that the Tanaka family did not, including access to many newspapers, radio news reports, and knowledgeable colleagues, Harrison kept James up to date on the latest government position regarding the Japanese; he in turn informed Keiko; she in turn her family; and they in turn many others in the Japanese community.

The senior Armstrong reported that there was much debate at the highest levels in the government. Contrary to prevailing opinion, he said there was little concern among the military or the FBI with regard to either a West Coast Japanese invasion or spying by Japanese locals. In fact, he reported that Attorney General Francis Biddle saw no need for an evacuation from the prohibited areas, and that even the director of the FBI, J. Edgar Hoover, shared that view.

It was a host of lower-level officials who kept fomenting hysteria, reporting incidents involving Japanese submarines lurking along the coast, enemy planes plying the eastern Pacific, and various other implausible incidents in which the Japanese were supposedly providing aid for an expected invasion. None of these reports was ever proven in fact, but politicians and others who harbored anti-Japanese sentiments referenced them repeatedly as if they were true. Ironically, lack of evidence of something untoward happening was proof to some that the Japanese were up to something.

Responding to this frenzy, Secretary of War Henry Stimson recommended to Biddle on January 25 that they officially define the militarily sensitive exclusion zones. Biddle interpreted this request to mean the exclusion of only aliens from these zones. However, Lt. General John DeWitt, the commanding officer of the Fourth Army and Western Defense Command, who had stoked the fires of anti-Japanese hysteria immediately following Pearl Harbor, had President Roosevelt's ear. DeWitt wanted to remove all Japanese. Things were looking bad.

To be fair, not everyone joined the bandwagon, particularly at the local level. Churches, in particular, stood up for the Japanese. When he could, usually at public meetings, Harrison Armstrong and other sympathetic locals made measured, logical arguments in support of the Japanese. More often than not, these moderating viewpoints were rebuffed as naïve and shortsighted. James told Keiko of a conversation he had overheard between his parents in which his father vented his frustration concerning the "stupidity and ignorance" of some of his friends, many of whom were professionals as well.

A few who had given the situation some thought pointed out that if the Japanese left the Seattle area, much of the fresh produce that locals appreciated would be gone. Counterarguments in the Seattle *Post-Intelligencer* pooh-poohed such talk, suggesting that other civilians could easily replace any loss in the fields. This argument ignored the reality that white farmers took little interest in working the smaller truck farms that the Japanese maintained.

When everyone in the household had finished reading the newspaper, Keiko would cut out relevant articles. One, in particular, a letter to the editor by Charlotte Drysdale of Seattle, made the racists' case: "We had gardens long before the Japs were imported about the turn of the century, to work for a very low wage (a move for which we are still paying dearly) and we can have them after we have no Japs."

One organization that promoted the Japanese point of view was the Japanese American Citizens League (JACL). Many JACL members and others, including Keiko's father, purchased Defense Bonds as a demonstration of good faith. They also promised to remain loyal to the United States and look for any saboteurs who may be hiding within their community. Their efforts had little effect and were diminished significantly when, immediately following Pearl Harbor, the FBI arrested many Issei leaders in the community. More than a few ended up sequestered in Fort Missoula in Montana, nearly five hundred miles away.

Keiko responded to James's kiss and pulled him close to her. She looked at him, longingly. "You know that we're not going to have much of a married life, at least at first."

Because of the unrest, the pace of events had accelerated, and Keiko and James were counting the days. As he had said he would, James had enlisted and was scheduled to leave by the end of April. With this firm deadline, the Tanaka and Armstrong families agreed to a March wedding. The Armstrong family left it to the Tanakas to determine the exact date. With Keiko's preference that it should be sooner rather than later, they chose Monday, March 2.

Although the early date in the month pleased the soon-to-be new-lyweds, there was another reason why Keiko's parents had chosen it: there would be a full moon on that day. Although it wouldn't be Tsu-kimi, Akemi said they would pretend that it was.

Tsukimi referred to the Japanese tradition of celebrating the har-vest moon of September, considered the brightest of the full moons. This day was considered special among the Japanese, a time to gaze at the moon, to give thanks for a successful harvest, and to celebrate that event through festivals and special foods. If Akemi had her way, the marriage would have waited until September. But under the circum-stances, a wedding six months earlier when another full moon would be occurring would have to do.

James responded to Keiko's embrace and kissed her neck. She had a sudden desire to take a walk behind the house. But she knew they had to be careful. She pulled back. "James, we have to hold out. It'll only be a few more weeks."

"I know, but I don't know if I can wait much longer. I want you so much, Keiko."

"I want you too, James, but we have to wait." As hard as it was to do, she pushed James away.

James played the game by folding his arms and doing a respect-able job of pouting. They both burst out laughing.

Keiko turned serious. "Time's running short, James. Is there anything we haven't planned for?"

"You keep asking the same question. Between the two of us, you're the organized one. Stop worrying!"

Although their mothers were coordinating the event, Keiko had her input. The two families agreed to split the costs of the wedding, a common practice among the Japanese, Keiko knew, but which she discovered was contrary to American wedding tradition, where the bride's parents usually bore the expense. James's parents, blessed with more means than the Tanakas, tried to reduce the burden on the Tanaka household. The Armstrong's church was chosen as the most economical and practical venue for both the wedding and the reception.

Keiko heard the screen door open behind her. Harrison Armstrong took a seat across from them. He didn't look happy.

"What is it, Dad?" James asked.

"It's not good news." Armstrong stared at his son. "You know about these exclusion zones they've been talking about?"

"Where the government wants to remove the Japanese from? What about it?"

"I just heard it on the radio. Today, President Roosevelt signed Executive Order 9066."

Keiko and James waited for an explanation.

Keiko's future father-in-law sat up straight. "This means that the Secretary of War has been authorized to set up those military areas."

Keiko felt James's hand squeeze hers tighter. "So what?" he asked. "That doesn't mean that the government has to do anything with them, does it?"

"I don't know, James. I just don't know." He stood and walked back into the house.

Keiko faced reality. Both James and his father knew the answer to that question, and she did too. Everyone in the Japanese community recognized that once the government took the first step of setting up the exclusion zones, there would be no turning back.

13

HONEYMOON

Bellevue, Washington
Tuesday morning, March 3, 1942

*I*t seemed as if time had stood still the previous evening, Keiko and James had been so excited. It wasn't until after nine o'clock when the last of the guests left the reception that the honeymooners could finally retire for the night.

Keiko sat up and squinted to read the bedside clock: it was four in the morning. One positive had been that the newlyweds didn't have far to go for their honeymoon. The minister and his wife, an older couple who had served the congregation for many years, had generously offered their nearby parsonage for a two-night honeymoon, temporarily relocating to another parishioner's house.

Staying close to home had been Harrison's suggestion. With the United States at war with Japan, and public feelings tense toward anyone who looked Asian—and not forgetting that a marriage of this sort was highly unusual for the times—he had arranged for the use of the parsonage.

After their brief honeymoon, the newlyweds intended to stay in the Armstrong house until James departed for the war. Once he left, Keiko planned to move back with her family until he returned.

Keiko was lying alongside James. Hand in hand, they stared at the ceiling. Through the gauze-like curtains in the bedroom of the small two-bedroom house, moonlight provided a romantic ambience for their first night together. That, together with the gentle breeze wafting through the screened window, provided a most peaceful setting.

"Do you know how much I love you?" Keiko, on James's left, propped herself up, head supported by her right hand.

James turned and grinned. "No. How much?"

With that cue, Keiko got up on her knees. She leaned forward and gave him a deep kiss. She then straightened up, opened her arms as wide as possible, chest thrust forward, and stretched hard for the walls on either side. "This much, that's how much I love you." She reached even farther, her head angling backward. She then relaxed and looked down. "Once you're headed off to fight the enemy, you won't forget, will you?"

"Not a chance, Mrs. Armstrong. Not a chance." James's thousand-watt smile added to the light from the moon. "Now come lie down."

Keiko reveled in the warmth of James's body and the security she felt with her new husband. Mrs. Armstrong. Having a new last name would take a while to get used to, and she looked forward to the transition.

The wedding twelve hours earlier had been traditionally American. They had planned the ceremony for four o'clock in the afternoon, followed by a reception that included a buffet dinner in the church's recreation room. Altogether, there had been almost one hundred family and guests, nearly equally divided between those of the bride and groom. Akemi and Barbara had drawn up the list, with input from Keiko and James. Naturally, Keiko picked her twin sister, Misaki, as maid of honor. James chose his oldest brother, Benjamin, as best man.

Toward the end of the reception, Keiko had noticed the minister walk up to Harrison and whisper something in his ear. She poked James sitting next to her, and they both observed a somber response from James's father. Something was wrong. After the guests had left for the evening, James asked him what he had heard. Harrison said that it could wait, but James persisted.

Keiko repositioned herself tight against James's left side. She could hear his heart thumping. "Let's try to get some sleep, James." Keiko knew that James was exhausted. As was she, but from what she already knew about her husband, she could function on far less sleep than he could. Knowing these kinds of things about him was important, she thought.

"Okay, if you say so." He leaned over and kissed Keiko on the forehead. "Good night."

"Sleep tight."

It wasn't long before James's breathing changed noticeably. Keiko lifted her head slowly and pulled back, once again watching her husband from the perch of her right hand. She watched as his chest rose ever so slightly up and down, again and again. Before long, his head fell to the side away from her.

Keiko knew that she should sleep as well, but was too excited. *I am Mrs. Armstrong, Mrs. James Armstrong.* She kept replaying in her mind various details from the wedding, where two sets of people from very different walks of life had come together to wish the couple well. James's parents' genuine interest in Keiko's well-being made her feel warm and secure. She had not one but two families who loved her and wanted the best for her and James.

Keiko slowly removed herself from James's body and rolled over to face the window. She needed to get some sleep too. That sleep would be marred, however, by the news that the minister had given Keiko's father-in-law.

Unbelievably, on the same day that Keiko and James had dedicated their lives to each other, General John DeWitt of the Western Defense Command had nearly spoiled it all. He had announced to reporters that all Japanese, citizens or not, would have to leave the Pacific exclusion zones.

14

SPECIAL REQUEST

Monterey, California
Thursday evening, October 26, 2000

Kazuko left her mother's room at the hospital by mid-after-noon, with Patrick agreeing to stay until five or so. He would arrive in time, he said, for their planned dinner with Sato at six.

For dinner, Kazuko looked for a solution inside her mother's freezer. She found frozen salmon steaks and took out three for thawing. Knowing that Patrick was good at broiling on their mother's grill, she called and coaxed him into coming early to do his share of the meal preparation.

With the main course set, Kazuko drove to the local Safeway and selected a vegetable: broccoli. Rice, a staple in any Japanese household, she'd make at home. She was about to head to the bakery to look for dessert when she remembered Sato's fruit basket. A selection of sliced fruit arranged on a pretty plate was always an acceptable dessert at a Japanese dinner.

"There's so much I want to ask you, Mr. Sato-san. Do you remember Aunt Misaki and Mom as being close?" The three sitting at the dinner table had finished the main course. Except for small talk, Kazuko had held back until now.

Sato rested his fork on his plate. "Oh, yes. They were twins, of course, which made them special. I remember at the farm that they would sometimes dress the same. But what you're getting at is whether

71

they were close emotionally. From what I saw and what Misaki told me, I'd say that they were very close."

"Kazuko told me that you knew about the wedding," Patrick said. "Were you invited? Did you go?"

Sato grinned and shook his head. "I only knew your family peripherally back in Washington. I fancied Misaki at their farm but only got to know her after we got ourselves shipped out of Bellevue on May 20. There were about three hundred or so of us."

"That was in 1942?" Patrick asked.

"Yes, not even six months after Pearl Harbor. That's how fast things happened. There were about sixty families." Sato paused. "Back to the wedding. As I told Kazuko yesterday, everyone knew about it. A Caucasian and a Japanese getting hitched, that was most unusual." Sato seemed to process another thought. "You, of course, know that James's father was an attorney, a well respected man in the community. Once everything started to hit the fan, he became a source of information for the Japanese."

Kazuko pointed to Patrick. "We knew Grandma and Grandpa Armstrong quite well. They didn't pass away until we were in our thirties. But, again, we didn't discuss those times. What do you mean, he became a source of information?"

Sato folded his napkin and set it by his plate. "You have to remember how difficult a time this was for the Japanese, particularly for the first generation. My parents were a good example. Their English was broken, at best, and they could read only Japanese. There were many times when my sister and I acted as interpreters."

Kazuko felt embarrassed yet again. "I'm sorry, Mr. Sato. I've been so caught up with my own family that I've failed to ask about yours. You mentioned a sister. Did you have other siblings?"

"You are kind to ask. No, it was just my older sister and me. Hiromi was her name. She passed away about ten years ago."

"I'm sorry."

Sato continued. "At the camp, your family was special to me, not only because of Misaki, but also because of their acceptance of me when Masao and I decided to join the service." He took a tissue from his pocket and dabbed at his eyes. "I'm sorry about that. My recollections are sometimes emotional for me."

Kazuko waited a moment before proceeding. She wanted to ask what it was that could cause so much pain but knew that would be prying. "You said that Grandfather became a source of information?"

"That's correct. Back in Bellevue, once your parents became engaged, the two families obviously became closer, and Mr. Armstrong kept his ear to the ground. What he learned he passed on to the Tanakas. And, of course, they told the rest of us."

Mr. Sato rubbed his forehead with his fingers. "There's something else, though, that I want to tell you, something you may or may not know but you should never forget. Misaki told me everything once we moved to Tule Lake.

"Keiko's decision to marry a Caucasian caused a lot of trouble within her household. I can only imagine her father's reaction. Not only was he upset because of her wanting to marry someone outside her race, but it was the way Keiko and James had gone about it." Sato's eyebrows rose. "You do know about the Christmas dinner, don't you?"

Kazuko and Patrick stared at each other. Patrick said the obvious. "We have no idea what you're talking about."

Sato seemed surprised. "The details are fuzzy now, but I do remember the upshot. Are you aware that your mother's parents leased the land that they farmed from your father's parents?"

Kazuko handled that one. "Yes, that we know."

"To shorten a long story, once James proposed to Keiko, they were so afraid that one side or the other would keep them from getting married, that they made a surprise announcement to both families at a Christmas dinner—a dinner that Keiko and James had arranged as a cover, in fact."

Kazuko had never heard this story.

Sato continued. "This is becoming convoluted. Sorry. I need to get back to the reason I brought this all up. Word spread like wildfire about the engagement. Everybody thought that Keiko's parents would put a stop to it. More surprising to the Japanese was that we never heard about any commotion within the Armstrong household. You've got to understand how forward-thinking that was back then for either set of your grandparents. They were all obviously tolerant, special people, and you should be very proud. Your parents' marriage could have been sabotaged so easily."

Kazuko was fascinated by these details. A true romance. "Did you know that my mom was pregnant with me on the train, on the way to Tule Lake?"

"Like I said, I didn't get close to your family until we got there. Tell me again, when were you born?"

"January 19, 1943."

"This should be easy to figure out. If we go back nine months," Sato counted on his fingers, "that puts us in the middle of April 1942."

Patrick cleared his throat. "That makes perfect sense. I know for a fact that Dad left Bellevue for basic training at the end of April. You were obviously conceived a week or so before he left town." He looked at Kazuko and winked. "What do you put the odds at that you were an accident? There's no way that Mom and Dad would have wanted to be pregnant then—with her being shipped off to who knows where, and him going off to war."

Sato smiled at Patrick's comment and continued. "So, there you have it. All of us got on the train only a month later. Keiko wouldn't have been showing yet. She may not even have known she was pregnant." He leaned forward. "Once we arrived in Tule Lake, it was a month or two before I got up enough nerve to call on Misaki." Sato looked up. "I remember now. It was a couple of months later when I began to notice your mother showing." He gestured. "And now, here you are."

Everything Kazuko had deduced concerning the date and location of her birth was being substantiated by Sato. Nothing seemed suspicious. Sato had been an on-scene observer, as was Shizuka. But try as she might, Kazuko couldn't forget her aunt's reaction to Sato. Furthermore, where were the family pictures Sato had mentioned?

Kazuko wanted more details. "Do you remember when you proposed to Misaki?"

Sato nodded. "Oh, I can tell you exactly when I proposed. It was March 21. By then, Masao and I had decided to enlist, and I didn't want to take the chance of losing her to someone else while I was gone. That would have been about two months after you were born." He smiled. "I remember choosing that date to propose because there was going to be a full moon that night. You know how we Japanese love our full moons. I was hoping that it would bring us good luck in love."

"You said yesterday that Daddy came by sometime between January and April."

"It had to be. Masao and I shipped off to Mississippi on April 26. It was a Monday." Sato rubbed the side of his face. "It's a darn shame those pictures were lost."

Kazuko nodded internally. *Yeah! A darn shame.* "Please tell me everything you remember from that day when the pictures were taken. You said that Daddy hired a photographer?"

"That's right, all the way from Klamath Falls. You ask what happened that day?" Sato thought for a moment. "I don't remember a lot, I'm afraid. What I remember is Misaki running down to get me—I lived in another part of the camp—telling me that we were going to get our pictures taken."

There's a pertinent detail, thought Kazuko. "Wait! If she came to get you for the pictures, doesn't that mean that you were already engaged? She wouldn't have come if you had been just a boyfriend."

Sato nodded vigorously. "That's a good point, Kazuko. In that case, we have the answer to your question. The pictures were taken between March 21 and April 26. You would have been two to three months old."

Sato's description of his experience in the camp continued for another hour. He described the buildings and their living conditions. He dwelt for some time on the government's Selective Service Form—something he had mentioned the day before—with the infamous question numbers 27 and 28 that had been so divisive among the Japanese.

The conversation then switched to Uncle Masao. Sato told them everything he could remember about their uncle, including a story that made the camp newspaper, when Masao nursed a bird with a broken wing back to health. Kazuko realized that she would have liked him very much had he lived.

Once the conversation waned, after Kazuko and Patrick had asked all the questions they could think of, Sato took the lead. "We've talked about everything except for you two. And could you please start with how your family ended up down here in Monterey?"

With this change in direction, Kazuko stood. "How about

dessert and tea? Patrick, do you mind filling in Mr. Sato while I go to the kitchen?"

Patrick obliged. "Compared to the stories you've been telling, our lives are plain vanilla. First, Kazuko and I are the oddballs, if you like. Neither of us is married. I work for the city of Monterey as a city planner, and Kazuko is a social worker. She works mostly with problem children and their families.

"With regard to Monterey, that all started back in the late sixties, and it snowballed. I have to confess that I'm the one responsible. After college, I came here for a job. Two years later, purely by chance, Kazuko came across a work opportunity here as well. And by the early nineties, Dad had retired. I don't know if you knew that he had partnered with Grandpa Armstrong in his law firm after the war. And then, after Grandma and Grandpa Armstrong passed away, I think our parents were getting lonely for family. When we suggested that they move down here to join us, they jumped at the chance. Aunt Shizuka, who by then had been widowed and retired early, said that she didn't want to be left behind when everybody else was leaving. I must say that it worked out well for all of us."

By the time Kazuko returned from the kitchen, Patrick was responding to Sato's question about what it was a city planner did. Pleasant conversation continued over dessert until about 9:30 when Sato looked at his watch and said that he should be getting back to his hotel. His plane would be leaving by mid-morning the next day. He thanked Kazuko and Patrick profusely for wanting to spend time with him, declaring that he had had a most splendid evening.

Kazuko responded. "You've got it backward, Mr. Sato-san. We thank you. You've given us word pictures from a period that we know so little about."

She wanted to reciprocate in some way. "Is there anything we can do for you, Mr. Sato-san? And thank you for the fruit by the way."

"Thank you for asking. I'd really like to be kept up to date on Keiko. I know that I asked Shizuka, but she might forget."

Aha! Sato doesn't trust her either! "You can count on us. Could we have one of your cards, please?"

Sato stood, took out his wallet, and presented his card with two hands. As he returned his wallet to his pocket, he looked sheepishly across the table. "Since you asked, I do have one other request. It'll cost some money, but I'll gladly reimburse you."

"What is it, Mr. Sato-san? Anything. Just name it."

Sato pointed to the picture that he had noted the previous day. "That picture that your dad took, where our Tule Lake camp used to be. Would it be too much to ask if you could make me a copy?"

Kazuko felt pleased that he had asked. She'd be able to do something meaningful in return. "That'll be easy. Daddy was the picture taker, and Mom was the framer." She waved her hand across the room. "All of these pictures were a joint effort. What's important is that Daddy insisted that the original negative stay with each picture. I'll make another print and mail it to you. Is that size okay, or do you want it bigger?"

* * *

Patrick would call soon, Kazuko knew. She looked about the kitchen. She had finished the dishes and had returned everything to its original location. It was important that all of her mother's things be in their proper places when she returned home.

Earlier, following Sato's departure, Patrick had suggested a deal. Never a fan of kitchen work, he offered to check in with Shizuka at the hospital and see how their mother was doing—if Kazuko would clean up. Kazuko had agreed but wanted an immediate phone report.

Kazuko wiped the stove with the tea towel and returned it to its hook. Everything looked clean and tidy. She returned to the living room and plopped down on the sofa. It had been a long day. A moment later she jumped to her feet, realizing that there was one more thing she could do before she left for the night.

Kazuko removed the Tule Lake picture from the wall and returned to the kitchen. Laying it upside down on a towel to keep it from getting scratched, she then located a spackling knife. It was the perfect instrument to bend back the metal tabs that held the backing in place. Behind that stiff cardboard, she knew, would be the envelope containing the negative.

Kazuko removed the backing and set it to the side. As expected, underneath lay the envelope that contained the thirty-five-millimeter negative.

Kazuko picked up the cardboard backing and was in the process of returning it to the back of the frame when the phone above the counter rang. Startled by its unusually loud shrill, she accidentally let go of the backing, which tumbled toward the floor. As it dropped, the cardboard turned upside down. As Kazuko focused on what she saw next, her eyes grew wide.

As the phone continued to ring, Kazuko bent over and picked up the cardboard. Her fingers shaking, she steadied herself against the counter and stared. It took a fourth ring before she composed herself enough to answer.

It was Patrick. "I was afraid that you had already left. Shizuka says that there's been no change." There were several seconds of silence. "Kazuko, are you there?"

Her mind working feverishly to process what she was seeing in front of her, Kazuko couldn't speak.

"Kazuko, are you okay?" he asked. "Can you hear me?"

Kazuko's heart was thumping hard. "I'm here, Patrick. You're not going to believe what I just found in the last place we would have ever looked."

15

SIMULTANEOUS JOY

Bellevue, Washington
Monday afternoon, March 30, 1942

On March 3, the *Seattle Times* printed the details of Lieutenant General J. L. DeWitt's pronouncement. The day before he had established Military Area No. 1, which included coastal portions of Washington, Oregon, and California, as well as the southern half of Arizona. Military Area No. 2 included those parts of those four states not in Area No. 1. Additionally, he defined five classes of people subject to removal from these geographic regions:

Class 1: anyone suspected of subversive activity;
Class 2: Japanese aliens;
Class 3: American-born Japanese;
Class 4: German aliens; and
Class 5: Italian aliens.

Other than the obvious Class 1, Classes 2 and 3 would be the first to leave Military Area No. 1. It didn't escape anyone's notice within the Japanese community that those in Class 3 were bona-fide US citizens.

Now that orders were being committed to paper, the Japanese in the Seattle area knew time was getting short. Who would be the first to leave? Among many obvious dilemmas the potential evacuees faced was one specific to farming, a dominant occupation among the Japanese, including Isamu Tanaka. It was spring and time to plant crops. If they weren't going to be around when harvest time came, what was the point? The government answered that question persuasively, stating that those who did not plant their fields would be doing something akin to sabotage. Because of Japanese respect for authority, all farmers planned their crops as usual that year.

As was common in the families of farmers, everyone pitched in during busy phases of the agricultural cycle, especially during planting and harvesting. Children who were still in school would work evenings and Saturdays. Although Keiko was no longer living at home, she felt obligated to help her family. Truth be told, she enjoyed working outdoors with her siblings.

As Keiko climbed onto the Armstrong porch after having spent the afternoon on her father's truck farm, she noticed the Armstrong car coming down the road. Harrison's 1939 black Buick Roadmaster was an unmistakable fixture in the local community. Four days out of the week, he made the twenty-five-minute drive to Seattle where he had his primary office. Because James had been working alongside his father since the previous summer, they traveled together.

As Keiko stood and waited on the steps, she noticed the expressions of her husband and father-in-law through the windshield. They did not look happy, and she had a good idea why. Seven days earlier, on March 23, General DeWitt had held a press conference announcing that the first group of Japanese would leave soon, under the authority granted by Civilian Exclusion Order No. 1. In particular were those who lived on Bainbridge Island to the west, across the Puget Sound from Seattle. Most everyone in the Seattle area knew that they were an important source of strawberries during the summer. The remainder of the Bainbridge Japanese were fishermen.

Although the Bainbridge Island Japanese had the worst of it, the March 2 order affected all Japanese. They now had to abide by a curfew, starting at eight in the evening and lasting until six the next morning. Further, they could not own firearms, explosives, radio transmitters, or cameras. Keiko's family had no worries there; the FBI had already confiscated those items.

In keeping with DeWitt's concern that the Japanese might interfere with military operations, newspapers reported that the residents of Bainbridge Island were chosen first because of their proximity to military bases. To the west lay the Bremerton Naval Shipyard and the Naval Torpedo Station at Keyport. To the east were the Boeing Aircraft Company and the Seattle shipyard. The only military activity actually located on Bainbridge Island was Fort Ward, a military listening post. Bainbridge Island was accessible only by ferry.

James exited the car, ran over to Keiko, and whispered in her ear that he loved her. As James backed off, and Harrison caught up, they both looked at Keiko. "It's happened, I'm afraid," began Harrison. "Starting at eleven this morning, the Japanese from Bainbridge Island were removed. First, they took them to Seattle by ferry. And now they're on a train going south. From what I hear, they're headed to California."

"Do you know how many?" Keiko asked.

"Around two hundred and fifty. Every Japanese on the island."

Harrison continued. "Keiko, I think it's time that we all sit down and talk about what's going to happen. Could you please go to your family and ask them if they would mind coming by our house this evening?"

Keiko was sensitive to the curfew. "They'd have to be back by eight o'clock."

"I know. Ask them if they could come around six or so." He turned to James and tossed him the keys to the car.

* * *

After rushing inside to check in with Barbara, Keiko returned to the car where James had the engine running. The normal fifteen-minute walk to the Tanaka farm took only two minutes by car. She ran inside and delivered her message, suggesting that her mother prepare an early dinner. Keiko said that James was waiting outside and that she needed to return because Barbara was planning dessert for everybody and needed help.

The elder Armstrongs were waiting outside when the Tanakas drove up. Having been together not that long before at Christmas, both families settled into their places around the larger dining room table. Barbara and Keiko had set the table for dessert and tea.

Since their honeymoon, Keiko had had many a meal at this table. But with all the original parties assembled at the same spot, she knew that the memory of what had occurred there three months earlier was still fresh in the minds of everyone.

Barbara had begun preparing dessert the instant Keiko rushed in earlier to tell her about the evening meeting. She decided to bake pies. When Keiko returned later, Barbara put her in charge of filling the pies. Barbara had already rolled and shaped the dough.

"Apple pie seems appropriate, doesn't it, Keiko? Do you think anyone will remember?" Barbara asked with a sly smile.

Despite her worries, Keiko couldn't help but giggle. As she smoothed out the filling in the first of two pies, James strode into the kitchen and hugged her from behind, kissing her on the cheek.

Barbara feigned disappointment. "What about me?"

With that admonishment, James reciprocated with his mother, giving her a loud smooch as well. While Keiko was adding filling to the second pie, she watched Barbara grab James's head and pull his ear down to her mouth. James listened, nodded, listened some more, smiled, and turned toward Keiko with a devilish look on his face. Keiko had gotten used to Barbara's shenanigans.

"Okay. What's going on?" Keiko asked.

"You'll see."

Harrison initiated the conversation at the table. "I'm sick with worry over what's happening to the Japanese people in our area. If you haven't heard, the authorities today removed all of them from Bainbridge Island."

Isamu spoke next. "I know something about what's happened. We have friends there."

Keiko remembered the story. When Akemi had sailed from Japan as a picture bride back in 1919, she had come with another woman, Naomi, who was slated to marry another bachelor from Washington, Haruto Yamagata. As time passed, and the Yamagata and Tanaka families grew, they stayed in touch.

Keiko knew that two days earlier, Isamu had gone to the island to ask if he could help the Yamagatas in any way. Haruto told Isamu that he appreciated his concern but that he should go home and prepare for his own family.

"Will you please tell us what you've learned from them, Isamu?"

Harrison asked. "Anything we know now will help us if and when the time comes that you have to leave."

Isamu shook his head in disgust. "As we've all heard, they got their notice on the twenty-third. Only seven days warning to leave! Each person could take only one suitcase. And . . . ," Isamu paused for emphasis, ". . . one duffel bag per family. In that duffel bag they were supposed to take all of their sheets, blankets, and pillows."

Keiko watched the reactions around the table. Masao squinted as he made his point. "They want us to put all of our bedding—for our six-member family—into one bag? How can they expect us to get along on that?"

No one at the table could argue his point.

Isamu continued. "Our friends, the Yamagatas, are better off than most. They own their own land."

Harrison pursed his lips and nodded. "Is their land in the names of their children?"

"Yes."

Wally, James's youngest sibling, looked puzzled. "Why is that important, Dad?"

Although most at the table understood the significance of what Isamu had said, Harrison explained. "That's a good question, Wally. The problem that Mr. and Mrs. Tanaka have is that they are not American citizens. And because they're not citizens, they're not allowed to own land by themselves."

"And why are Mr. and Mrs. Tanaka not citizens?" Wally persisted.

"It shouldn't be that way, but it is. It's because they were not born here. Their children"—Harrison gestured—"were, though, and they are citizens."

Keiko knew that Harrison was being purposely vague. The situation was more complicated, and Keiko was sad because of the racism it implied. Asian aliens, such as the Japanese, were ineligible for naturalization, a process in which aliens could normally become citizens. Worse, a separate law prevented these same Asian aliens from owning their own land. It was for that reason that Japanese families often put land they purchased into the names of their children.

Harrison steered the conversation back to Isamu. "Keep going. Please."

"A big problem has been everybody's possessions. The Yamagatas had friends who said they'd watch over things. And because they owned their own house, they could leave things there, like furniture and appliances. Those who rented and didn't have friends had no choice but to sell what they had. Haruto told me some sad stories. Good furniture and appliances went for practically nothing."

Harrison looked Isamu in the eye. "You know that's not going to happen here. If you end up going away, we'll be here to watch over your things. I promise you that whether you come back in one month or six months, everything will be waiting for you."

Keiko squeezed James's hand under the table. She began to tear up as she watched her father's reaction. He stared respectfully at Harrison and bowed his head. "My family will be forever in your debt."

Harrison replied in kind. "We are one family now. If the roles were reversed, you'd do the same for us." He paused. "Is there anything else that you learned? Anything at all that might be useful?"

Isamu nodded. "Their biggest issue had to do with the crops. Everybody's been told that they need to plant and tend their fruits and vegetables as usual. As you know, they mostly grow strawberries on that island. Again, Haruto is luckier than most. He has a neighbor who has agreed to harvest and sell his berries, and they are going to split the profits."

"Does your friend know anyone who leases land?" asked Harrison.

"As I said before, that's when it got bad. Anyone who rented or leased had to get rid of their farm equipment. Irrigation pipe, tractors, trucks, plant stakes, crates—all those things." Isamu looked around at the Armstrong family. "You've been to our sheds; you've seen all of the odds and ends that it takes to run a farm. And I can tell you, people are taking advantage of them. It's heartbreaking. Those who are leasing are also trying to sell their crops, but they're not getting much for them."

Harrison indicated that he understood. "Okay. That's what we're going to have to do here too. Isamu, obviously my family and I can't harvest your crops. So you and I need to start looking for someone else to do it. Although you won't be here to watch over what's going on, I will be. So you're not going to have to worry."

To Keiko's eye, her father seemed relieved. There was a

moment's silence, and then Isamu spoke again. "I need to ask you something, Harrison."

"Please, Isamu. That's why we're all here, to figure out a strategy."

Keiko noticed her father glance briefly in her direction. "You understand the law. Do you think that because Keiko is married to your son that she might be able to stay behind? She would be a big help to you in running the farm. She knows everything that I know."

Keiko's face flushed with pride. *She knows everything that I know.*

"Isamu, you're not the first person to ask this question. James has been hounding me almost every day since the wedding." Harrison took a breath. "This internment thing is so new. It's not like it's been done before, with rules and regulations that are on the books. That's what a lawyer does, you know. He looks for precedents, previous legal cases that can be used to make new decisions. So, in answer to your question, I've been looking into it, but I've come up with nothing so far. I'll keep looking."

Keiko reflected on what she had just heard. James hadn't said anything about this to her. She knew why. The chances of the government deciding in their favor were probably nonexistent. He wouldn't have wanted to get her hopes up.

But now that the topic had arisen, Keiko admitted to herself that she would have mixed feelings about staying behind. Helping with the farm would be a positive but if she did so, she'd be without not only her husband but also the family she had grown up with. That would be a difficult decision to make if the need arose.

Twenty-five minutes later, the meeting seemed at an end. Harrison looked around the table. "Does anyone have anything else to say?"

After a few moments of silence, Barbara began to stand, obviously getting ready to serve dessert.

Keiko suddenly felt James pull his hand free. He pushed his chair back noisily, stood up tall, and looked very serious. "Mom, please sit down. I have something to say."

Since those at the table had heard these identical words not that many months ago and had witnessed the firestorm set off by James's announcement, ten sets of eyes grew wide as everyone stared upward. Keiko could imagine what they were thinking. Her parents' faces turned two shades whiter, and they were looking upward with their mouths open. Harrison blinked and seemed to be holding his breath. Barbara, on the other hand, winked at Keiko.

With absolute silence in the room and following a good number of seconds during which James milked the moment, he suddenly relaxed and waved his hand through the air in a gesture of dismissal. "Oh, don't worry. It's nothing. Mom told me earlier to ask how many people here want apple pie. Could I see a show of hands, please?"

It had been a perfect set-up, and Barbara, now standing, was grinning from ear to ear.

There was a beat of silence and, at once, the room burst into laughter. Keiko looked about the table as everyone was howling. Harrison was dabbing his eyes with his handkerchief, he was laughing so hard.

But as Keiko enjoyed this singular happy moment between her two families, her eyes settled on her parents. Keiko glanced at Misaki and noticed that she saw it too.

Isamu and Akemi were looking at each other and laughing hysterically. In her nineteen years of life, Keiko had never once witnessed such spontaneous, simultaneous joy between her mother and father.

16

SHIPPING OUT

Bellevue, Washington
Early morning, Wednesday, April 29, 1942

"Once you leave here, you're not going to forget how much I love you?" asked Keiko. She and James were lying next to each other on this, their final night together.

James stared up at Keiko, his face scrunched together. "You know what? I think I have forgotten. Could you remind me again?"

For the first time since their honeymoon night, Keiko spread her arms as wide as she could. "You're hopeless, you know. You can't remember anything." She grinned. "See if you remember this." Keiko flipped herself around and went straight for the bottoms of James's feet. "Tickle, tickle, tickle, tickle."

As Keiko held down James's body by pinning his legs, he thrashed about the bed, giggling incessantly, but trying to stifle the volume. He was notoriously ticklish. "Stop it! You're going to make me wake up everybody in the house."

James had a point. Although the Armstrong parents had been kind enough to give the newlyweds the bedroom at the far end of the upstairs hallway, a reasonable distance from their bedroom and even farther from James's siblings, noise could still carry. Keiko backed off and returned to James's left side. Their quickened breathing subsided.

Keiko turned her head completely around and squinted into the faint light. The big hand on their alarm clock was somewhere around the three, but that wasn't the important one. She leaned closer. The little hand had just passed one. She was tired and wanted to sleep but knew that this was not the night for such a luxury. Tomorrow morning, James would report for duty, boarding a train out of Kirkland at ten o'clock. He would be heading south, one of Uncle Sam's newest recruits.

In the end, after considerable discussion and some coercion within the family, James had decided to enlist in the navy rather than the army—much to the relief of his parents. Depending on his aptitude and test scores, the recruiter had explained, his technical specialty would be determined later.

Keiko reflected on both the anxiety and happiness that had passed through the Armstrong home over the past week. With a dinner every bit as magnificent as the one at Christmas, both families had met for a farewell get-together three nights earlier. Everyone had wished James well. At one point after the meal, Keiko observed her father talking privately to James, out of earshot. She saw something pass between them.

After the Tanaka family went home, Keiko asked James what that had been about. James said that her father told him to return home safe. "And he gave me this." James removed what Keiko recognized to be her father's Omamori. A two-inch by four-inch double thickness of sewn cloth with Japanese symbols on the front, it was a Japanese good luck charm.

"Your Dad said that although he is no longer Buddhist, he has kept this ever since his father gave it to him when he left Japan in 1905." James took the gift from his pocket and showed Keiko. "He explained that inside is a thin piece of wood. There's a prayer written on it, Keiko, a prayer that will keep me safe from harm. He told me to never take it apart because that would destroy its protective qualities. He said that I was the one who needed it now, and that I should keep it on me at all times. It will protect me, he said."

Keiko knew that giving away such a personal item had been a gracious act toward his new son-in-law. "That's a fact, James. It will do that. Promise me you will do as he says."

"I will, but I also told him that I would give it back when I return from the war."

Beginning with the farewell dinner, Keiko sensed the anxiety level within the Armstrong family ratcheting up significantly. Perhaps not knowing what else to do, Barbara spent hours cooking and baking James's favorite foods. Harrison had taken off work and gone fishing with his son. James's brothers understood what was happening and pestered him less than usual. But Keiko wasn't worried. She believed in her heart what she had told James months ago, that he would return home safely. It was only a matter of waiting for it all to end. Surely, the war wouldn't last very long—a year at the most, Keiko figured.

Keiko was also aware that James had promised his parents that he would begin college after he returned. James's father wanted him to follow his example and become a lawyer. James wasn't so sure about that.

But during those final days before James's departure, Keiko had more than her husband to worry about. *What's to become of my family?*

To their surprise, the Japanese who lived in Bellevue were still waiting for orders from the government. Following the initial departure of the Bainbridge Island Japanese at the end of March, it had taken several more weeks before the next event occurred. That happened on April 21 when new government notices began appearing in Seattle. Instead of being sent south to California, like the Bainbridge Japanese, those from the Seattle area didn't go nearly so far. In fact, it was only a thirty-mile ride south, to Puyallup. They were to stay at a temporary processing center there called Camp Harmony until the government found a more permanent location.

In the meantime, word had gotten back from the Bainbridge Japanese. They had traveled directly to a place called Manzanar, to what was called a War Relocation Center. Located in the high desert at the foot of the Sierra Nevada Mountains northeast of Los Angeles, theirs had been a thousand-mile journey by train. Letters from internees did not speak highly of the place, saying that it was terrible, with blowing dust and sand everywhere.

There had been some good news the past week. Following the powwow between the Armstrong and Tanaka families, Harrison Armstrong had been true to his word. He helped Isamu arrange for another farmer to maintain and harvest the produce from the

Tanaka truck farm. Isamu had planted a wider assortment of fruits and vegetables than usual for the spring/summer harvest, including peas, beans, and lettuce. He also expected a bumper crop of strawberries because, two years earlier, he had increased his plantings by fifty percent.

Concerning Isamu's request that Harrison check into the possibility that Keiko might be exempt from any relocation, James informed Keiko that his father was coming up dry, that he couldn't find anyone within the government who had the authority to make an exception for her. Interestingly, Harrison reported that the West Coast was bearing the brunt of the hysteria concerning the Japanese. In Hawaii, where a much larger portion of the population was Japanese, there was no thought given to internment—even considering the sizable presence of the US Navy in Pearl Harbor.

Finally, after having explained to James her hesitancy about staying behind even if it were possible, Keiko took her father-in-law aside and told him not to spend any more time worrying about the issue. "If James wasn't going off to war, it would be a different story," she told him. "But in light of all that's happening, I think it's more important for me to stay with my family." Harrison said that he understood and admitted that, had he been in the same situation, he would do the same.

After a few minutes of quiet, as they lay close together, James turned his head. "Keiko."

"Yes, James."

"I know that we both need to be optimistic. But if something happens to me, I want you to mourn for just a little bit and then go on with your life. You're a bright, attractive girl and will be a great catch for anyone. I want you to have a happy life. That's what I want for you, Keiko."

In an instant, Keiko was back on her knees. "How many times do I have to tell you? Nothing is going to happen to you. Especially now that you're going into the Navy. What's the worst that could happen? Huh?" Keiko held up both hands, incredulous. "Your ship gets hit, sinks, and you have to tread water for a few minutes before help arrives. You're a good swimmer."

James tried to stifle his laughter. "That's the worst that could happen, is it? Well, in that case, what was I thinking? I am a good swimmer."

"Darn right." Keiko returned to James's side and pulled him close.

James let out a big breath. "While I'm away, it'll be you and your family that I'll be worrying about. All this internment crap is so outrageous."

Keiko got up on her elbow. "I don't want you worrying about that either. When you're out there on the big ocean, you're going to have to keep your head down and pay attention to what's going on. I've thought this through. At the worst, I believe it's going to be an uncomfortable, unpleasant situation. You've heard the reports from Manzanar. I haven't heard about anyone getting mistreated. Masao, Misaki, Shizuka, and I—we're going to be fine. We're young and can adapt. But it's Mama and Papa I worry about. They're getting older, and it'll be harder for them. That's why it's important that I stay with them."

"You'll write to me, won't you?"

"As often as I can. And you too."

James looked at Keiko. "Do you want to go to sleep?"

"Not on your life. You'll have all the time in the world to sleep on the train tomorrow."

"Right," James whispered as he pulled her close. "Tomorrow."

17

JUST A JOKE

Bellevue, Washington
Early Sunday afternoon, May 17, 1942

So many weeks had passed since the Bainbridge and the Seattle Japanese received their notices to evacuate that the Bellevue contingent hoped that, somehow, they might be the exceptions. After all, the Bellevue Japanese lived much farther from sensitive military bases than the others. And then there was the all-important annual Bellevue Strawberry Festival that had been a yearly occasion since 1925. Since the Bellevue truck farmers grew nearly all of the strawberries used for that event, it was another reason to leave them behind. Their wishful thinking came to a sorry end on May 15.

It was a Friday when notices first appeared in Bellevue. The single horsehair that supported the legendary Sword of Damocles that all Japanese knew was hanging over their heads had given way. And perhaps to punish them for having had additional time at home, they received only a five-day notice, compared to the seven days the Bainbridge residents had had. They were to report to the way station in nearby Kirkland on Wednesday.

The Bellevue Japanese had used the extra weeks to their advantage. Benefiting from the experiences of the two groups that had preceded them, they knew what to expect. The Tanakas were more prepared than most. The house stood ready to be secured; farm sheds, equipment, harvesting baskets were maintained and tidy; all bills had been paid and were up to date; one suitcase for each family member (purchased weeks earlier by Akemi, they were the largest she could find) lay on the floor ready to be packed with freshly washed and ironed clothing and other personal items.

In the case of the duffel bag, to make sure they had enough capacity, Akemi had purchased canvas that she used to make her own. The material had been so stiff that she couldn't use her sewing machine. Instead, she had hand-sewn the entire thing. It sat by the front door, stuffed with bedding ready for transport.

Shizuka had involved herself personally in one important detail. Princess, her loyal collie, seemed to suspect that something was up. But to Shizuka's dismay, government notices made no mention of pets.

Shizuka made her case before a local official. "Princess has lived with my family since she was born. So she's obviously Japanese—and thus a potential threat to the homeland. There should be no exceptions to the evacuation, don't you think?" Shizuka emphasized as strongly as she could.

The bemused young man nodded and agreed that she was making a valid point. "I'll for sure look into this, and I'll get back to you. I promise."

With regard to their crops, the farmer with whom Isamu and Harrison had made an agreement stood ready to take over the upcoming harvest—and none too soon. Lettuce and strawberries were nearly ready for harvest. Keiko recalled her father's melancholy as he stared across the unpicked fields he would leave behind.

Isamu feared that even with the neighboring farmer's best intentions, some of his harvest would be lost. Already word was getting around about a shortage of pickers. Most farmers who, like the Tanaka family, leased their land had struck deals with a company called Western Farm and Produce, Inc., a business encouraged by the government to make sure that the Japanese harvest was not lost. But everyone wondered where they would find workers. Keiko had rarely seen white pickers on the small truck farms typical of the Japanese. And with the war effort siphoning off many workers to factory jobs, the available workforce had diminished further. Yet Isamu knew that he was better off than most. The farmer with whom they had an arrangement had four teenagers he could press into service.

* * *

The Tanaka family was heading home after church, Keiko back to sitting between her two sisters as usual. As planned, once James left for the Navy, she had moved back into her old room with her twin sister. On this final Sunday before their own departure, the family decided that it was appropriate that they attend church one final time. After all, it was a day of rest, and some of their best friends were church members.

During the sermon, the minister went so far as to compare the Japanese evacuation to the Exodus in the Bible. Keiko considered the analogy a tad stretched, but everyone seemed to appreciate the point he was making: that God would see them through this tribulation and that they would be better for it. A meal followed, and more than a few tears flowed among those attending.

The mood in the car was quiet. Consistent with the characteristic Japanese demeanor in such situations, the Tanaka family had resigned themselves to their fate.

As in their drive home following Pearl Harbor, Masao was the first to speak. "It's not fair that I can't volunteer for the service like James did. I'm a citizen, and I'm a patriotic American. I've thought about this a lot. I know that my ancestors are Japanese, from Japan, but I'm an American now, and what they did to us in Pearl Harbor was wrong. Why can't I fight too?"

The girls in the back seat watched as both parents turned to look at their son. Keiko doubted that anyone else in the car had even thought about Masao volunteering for the military. After all, it was abundantly clear that the government considered all Japanese to be potential enemies.

Isamu, to whom Akemi deferred in public discussions, took some time to answer the question. Quick answers can always get you in trouble, was one of his admonitions to his children. Let your mind do some thinking before you open your mouth.

After a bit, he replied, "You are right. It's not fair."

Everyone in the car was aware that several local Nisei men had signed up for service immediately following Pearl Harbor. Unfortunately, their patriotic intent to support their country ended when General DeWitt relegated them to a class considered dangerous to the war effort.

Masao made his point. "If I volunteered, wouldn't that show them that we are loyal Americans? That would make a difference, wouldn't it?'

"I would think it would, Masao."

Only Masao's mother looked at her son this time. Keiko could imagine what she wanted to say to her husband: you want my son to die in a war for a country that is sending us into concentration camps?

Isamu followed up. "As time passes, maybe there'll be a change of heart."

In another minute, they arrived at the house. While Isamu and Masao went straight to the fields to make some final checks on their crops, the rest went inside. Keiko and Misaki returned to their room and closed the door. Ever since Keiko had come home more than two weeks earlier, she and her sister had returned to their old ways.

Keiko was on the floor practicing putting her clothing into her suitcase. She intended to make use of every square inch available to her. She looked up toward her sister, who was staring down at her.

"What?" asked Keiko.

"What will you do if James doesn't come back? I know how much you love him."

Keiko's eyes rolled upward, and she looked disgusted. "Again, Misaki? I've had to deal with this for weeks with James. Listen to me! Nothing is going to happen to him! I'm not worried, and he isn't either."

Misaki peered back, saying nothing.

Because Misaki did not seem to be satisfied with this explanation, Keiko chose to exaggerate. "What is it you want to hear, Misaki? Okay, here it is! If James gets himself killed in action, I'll commit hari-kari. I hadn't intended to tell you this, but James and I have sworn ourselves to a pact. If something happens to either of us, the one who's left will end it all. We love each other too much to go on." Keiko folded her arms and looked as serious as she could. "There, I've said it."

Misaki's eyes grew into saucers, and her face blanched white. Keiko realized that she had gone too far. "Misaki, I'm sorry. I'm just joking with you."

Misaki jumped to the floor and took Keiko in her arms. "Don't ever say anything like that again. I worry about you, Keiko. Promise me you'll come to me before you ever do anything drastic."

Keiko backed off, held her sister at arm's length, and smiled appreciatively. "I promise, Misaki. Until James returns, if I'm ever in trouble, you'll be the first one I come to for help."

"Cross your heart and hope to die?"

"Yes."

18

MISSING PERSON

Monterey, California
Thursday evening, October 26, 2000

What do you mean?" Patrick's voice was skeptical.

Kazuko struggled to catch her breath. "After I cleaned up the kitchen, I remembered Daddy's photo that Mr. Sato wanted. So I took down the Tule Lake picture and pried it apart to get the negative. I had the cardboard backing lying on the counter. I was returning it to the back of the frame when your call startled me, and I dropped it."

"Yeah?"

Kazuko realized the serendipity of what had occurred. She wouldn't be having this conversation had Patrick not called.

"Patrick, I almost missed it! When it fell, the backing turned over. And taped to the other side was another picture! It has to be one of those Mr. Sato was talking about, one from the camps. I'm a baby in Mom's arms. Daddy is in his Navy uniform. And in the background you can make out a building."

* * *

Kazuko awoke from a peculiarly relevant dream, one of those she wished she could have continued. She turned sideways on the sofa and, without her glasses, squinted to read the digital clock sitting on the TV. It was nearly three in the morning.

Following their phone conversation, Patrick had returned to the house to see for himself what it was that Kazuko was so excited about. He agreed that the picture was what she said it was and suggested that they discuss it further when they met at the hospital in the morning. In the meantime, he reported that nothing had changed with their mother. Shizuka was again standing night watch.

Because it had been late, Kazuko decided to stay the night on her mother's sofa, sleeping in her clothes.

To the questions that had plagued her mind earlier, a new one had come to the forefront. Why would her mother hide such an important photo? Had it not been for Sato's request, it could have lain there unnoticed forever. But Sato claimed that the photographer had taken many pictures. Where were the ones of him and his fiancée, their own Aunt Misaki? What about Uncle Masao who died in the war? Grandma and Grandpa Tanaka?

And, for that matter, Aunt Shizuka? *They probably just got lost after the war.*

If there's one picture, maybe there's more! Kazuko leaped from the sofa, stubbing her toe on the coffee table as she made her way to the light switch. She next searched for the thermostat. The cool Monterey night had made the house chilly.

Kazuko set up an assembly line to examine each of the framed photographs. She started to the right of the entry to the kitchen and proceeded clockwise. From the combined living/dining area, the pictures stretched down the hallway and through two bedrooms. The procedure was the same as before, kitchen counter serving as workbench, soft towel and putty knife at the ready. Lifting off the cardboard backing from each one, she began the inspections.

Kazuko also examined the envelopes containing the negatives. Occasionally, she found more than one negative. In all cases, each was merely an additional shot of the same scene.

Finding nothing unusual after dismantling the first six pictures, Kazuko arrived at the Tule Lake photograph that had started this entire adventure. Accordingly, she gave it extra attention, disassembling the entire package, from the backing through to the matting, to the protective glass. She had already removed the envelope and negative. Nothing else looked unusual.

Kazuko looked at the clock above the sink. It was 3:35. Seven pictures in thirty-five minutes meant that it had taken five minutes to pull apart and reassemble each picture. A quick count showed twenty-six remaining. What were the chances she'd find yet another picture stuck to the backing—particularly since there were no other photographs associated with the internment experience? Still, all that would be lost would be a little sleep, Kazuko reminded herself.

It was nearly six when Kazuko finished the last one. Nothing. It had been a futile exercise.

Disgusted and tired, she padded back to the sofa. Before heading off to the hospital, she needed a little more sleep. Before long, she did something quite unusual. She returned to the same dream that had haunted her three hours earlier.

* * *

Kazuko found herself back at the Tule Lake internment camp. Taking in the sight of block after block of drab structures, she was walking down the muddy lanes between them. Knowing that she didn't have much time, she moved quickly. It was cold, and her short-sleeved shirt didn't offer much protection. Everyone else wore jackets or coats.

"Does anyone know the Tanaka family?" she asked repeatedly in both Japanese and English.

Finally, a man pointed into the distance to the far end of the camp. "Over there, I think. I think there's a Tanaka family down there."

Kazuko began to shiver. As she approached what appeared to be the last set of buildings before a fence, she picked a young man at random among a group heading toward a larger building. "Can you help me please? Do you know anyone in the Tanaka family?"

He looked at Kazuko, obviously confused by her appearance. "Who are you, and why are you walking around in those clothes? You'll catch your death of cold!" He took off his jacket and draped it over her shoulders.

Kazuko ignored his questions. "I'm looking for anyone in the Isamu Tanaka family."

The young man's head snapped back. "Well, you've found one. My name is Masao. My father is Isamu Tanaka."

* * *

Kazuko gasped and sat bolt upright. But just as quickly, she lay back down on the sofa, pulling the afghan tightly around her neck. Her clothing was wet with perspiration. Before it escaped her memory, she relived the seemingly real experience of what had just transpired in her mind. She had come face to face with her mother's only brother. If only she could have stayed a little longer to meet the rest of the family, to have asked Masao a few questions.

It took a good ten minutes in her mother's shower before the last chill evaporated from her bones. After drying off, she realized what she needed to do. She ran barefoot through the hall to the kitchen to look at the clock. It was after eight already. Kazuko recalled Sato saying that his flight left mid-morning. It was probably already too late.

* * *

Kazuko drove faster than she should have on Fremont Boulevard, on the way to the Highway 68 cutoff that would take her to the airport. The Monterey Peninsula Airport was small but did a good job of serving central California. More often than not, passengers from Monterey shuttled to San Francisco to the north or to Los Angeles some 300-plus miles to the south. Chances were good that Sato would be on one of the short twenty-minute flights to San Francisco, where he'd fly directly to Seattle.

Kazuko pulled into the small lower lot directly across from the airport entrance. It was 8:45. Grabbing the hardback book she had borrowed from her mother's living room to protect the photo en route, she dashed across the street and into the area where both the United and American counters were located.

Seeing nothing of Sato, she raced to the United counter and stared at the flight schedules to San Francisco. There had been one at six, with another at eight-fifty. If that had been Sato's flight, she had just missed him. The next flight wasn't until 11:20. Kazuko's heart sank. Sato would not have called an 11:20 flight a mid-morning flight.

Kazuko was cursing her luck when she realized that she had not yet checked the American schedule. She ran to that counter. They too had an early morning flight to SFO, leaving at 5:50. But there was one more at 9:30. There was still hope!

Kazuko whirled and scanned the area a second time. Nothing. People were entering the security checkpoint. She rushed to the large glass wall that separated her from the secured area and peered inside. A few passengers were already seated. But none looked like Sato.

Kazuko faced the waiting area, not wanting to accept the reality that Sato had already left. If he had a ticket for this American flight, he would have arrived at the airport by now. Before giving up, she walked to the entrance to security and watched as passengers passed through the metal detectors.

Kazuko had given up hope when she caught movement out of the corner of her eye. Sato was walking directly toward her! He had been in the restroom. They saw each other at the same time.

"Kazuko! What are you doing here?"

She got to the point quickly. "How much time do you have? I need to show you something."

Sato set down his tiny carry-on bag and looked at his watch. "My plane leaves at nine-thirty. I have maybe five or ten minutes."

Kazuko hurriedly gestured Sato toward the waiting area. He walked slowly in front of her and sat down. She joined him and quickly opened her book, removing the photo. "Does this look familiar?"

Sato examined the solitary picture for some seconds. When he finished, he looked up, his face radiating pleasure. "You found them! You found the pictures I told you about."

Kazuko hated what she had to say next. "I'm sorry, Mr. Sato-san. This is all I found. But do you recognize it?"

"Of course!" He pointed. "Here's your mother, father—and you. Just like I told you. Are you sure this is the only one?"

"It's all I've come up with so far. But if it hadn't been for you, I would never have found even this one. It was inside the backing of the picture that you wanted a copy of. But there were no others, I'm sad to say."

Sato continued to stare at the picture. "This brings back so many memories, Kazuko. I was standing off to the side with Misaki, behind the photographer. I can picture in my mind each of us standing there."

Sato then replicated what both Kazuko and Patrick had done. He turned the picture over. But the back was blank.

What about the man who took the pictures? Kazuko realized she should be asking. "I don't suppose you remember anything about the photographer?"

Sato shook his head. "I don't remember his name, that's for sure. I do recall that he wasn't a young man. He walked with a cane. And the only reason I remember that is that when he took his pictures, standing behind his tripod, he'd hang his cane on one of the legs of the tripod. He had special hooks to hold it there. The cane would hang down straight while the tripod legs went off at an angle. Isn't it funny how I remember such a silly detail like that?"

In the background, the PA system came alive. "We are in the final boarding stage for American Flight 1105 to San Francisco. Any passengers booked on this flight need to proceed through security at this time."

Sato rose slowly to his feet. "I'm glad that you found one of the pictures. At least you have that to carry on the memory of your family."

Kazuko's mind spun, trying to think of any other question she should be asking. "You say that you can picture everyone standing beside you. Please tell me who was there."

"Well, I think you know the answer to that. Besides your parents and you, there was Misaki and me, of course. Your grandparents, obviously. Masao." He nodded. "I can picture all of us standing beside the photographer and then taking our turns in front of the camera."

"Aunt Shizuka?"

Sato blinked. "Of course! Shizuka." A frown followed. "I'm sorry about that. I had completely forgotten. Something was going around the camp at the time we took these pictures, and Shizuka was very sick in bed. I remember everyone being disappointed that she couldn't be in the pictures."

19

UNCOMFORTABLE JOURNEY

On a train heading south from the state of Washington
Saturday afternoon, May 23, 1942

On this, their third day away from home, Keiko sat next to Misaki and across from the rest of the Tanaka family. The hard benches facing fore and aft made everyone feel uncomfortable, stiff, and grumpy. Someone in their car claimed that this train had been used for troop transport back during World War I. It certainly looks that old, thought Keiko.

Keiko felt sorry for her parents. Like everyone else, they had had to sleep in a sitting position for the past three nights. Worse, there had been no opportunity to bathe or change clothes. She looked across at her father, arms folded, head slumped down on his chest, eyes closed, dozing. At fifty-six, Isamu was ten years older than Akemi and not a young man anymore. He and his wife had spent their entire adult lives building a home and family back in Bellevue. Now it had come to this.

Surprisingly, it was the younger Nisei who seemed to take the situation the hardest. Masao joined others in the car deriding their situation. "What good is it to become an American citizen if this is the way we're going to be treated?" they asked. Shizuka, at sixteen, the youngest in the family, took this banter in stride but said nothing. In fact, Shizuka had said nothing since they had boarded the train, and the entire family knew the reason.

* * *

Of her three siblings, Shizuka could be the most annoying. Keiko had read somewhere that it wasn't unusual for the baby in the family to be the spoiled brat, and Keiko decided that whoever had written that definition must have known her sister. Still, as was true for all the Japanese, Shizuka didn't deserve what was happening to her, and the final straw had come a day before their departure.

The government official whom Shizuka had talked to was true to his word; he came by personally to the house. With the entire family standing by, he gave Shizuka the news. "I did what I could, Shizuka, but my boss insists that pets aren't allowed." Distressed by Shizuka's deflated look, he tried to give her some hope. "Depending upon conditions in the camp, you might be able to send for her later. Okay?"

What struck Keiko was what happened next. The man walked over to Isamu and talked slowly, simultaneously shaking his head. "I tried, Mr. Tanaka. I did my best." Keiko swore she saw a tear.

Isamu then placed his hands on the man's shoulders. "I know you did, Anthony. I know you did." Hearing the name, Keiko's brain snapped to attention. The depression-era story her mother had told came back to life: how her father had forgiven—and made a lifelong friend of—a terrified teenager caught stealing vegetables for his family. *Now I understand.*

With that door blocked, Shizuka searched for an alternate solution. She acted quickly and soon located a neighbor friend who agreed to look after Princess until the Tanakas returned. The entire family felt her grief as they watched her say good-bye to her dog.

* * *

When the Bellevue Japanese boarded their train at Kirkland, on Wednesday, May 20, most assumed that they would be having their first meal that night at Camp Harmony, located in Puyallup, Washington, to the south. After all, that was where the Seattle Japanese had gone. Why would the government treat the Bellevue folks differently? It wasn't long, however, before everyone realized that, even with the slow speed of their derelict train, they had proceeded much farther than the thirty-some miles that trip would have taken.

More than three hundred people from Bellevue, consisting of about sixty families, had boarded the old train, one that still burned coal. During the days, temperatures inside the cars were nearly unbearable, even with the windows open. But if the windows were open, black smoke from the locomotive stack would blow down and coat everyone and everything with soot. The heat affected them especially because they were used to the moderate Seattle temperatures.

To make matters worse, no one would tell them where they were going. The accompanying soldiers dictated when the window blinds could remain open. At night they were always drawn, for fear that enemy planes would spot their lights and bomb them. During the day, blinds could remain open, but only while they passed through countryside. Anytime the train neared a town where there might be something interesting to look at, the soldiers ordered the blinds drawn. The Japanese knew that there were two reasons. First, to keep them from knowing where they were going. But there was a more dire explanation: to keep townspeople from knowing that the trains transported Japanese.

As the days passed, and the morning sun continued to rise off the left side of the train, it was obvious they were headed south. One passenger who had made frequent trips on the railroad recognized the route and said there was no question that they were headed to California.

Once the train bypassed Camp Harmony, conversation revolved around speculation and rumor, most of it bad. "They intend to shoot us all." "They'll take us deep into the desert and abandon us to the wild animals. Why, otherwise, would we be traveling so long?" The appearance of the military policeman riding along at each end of the car did nothing to allay such fears. Incredibly, their rifles sported bayonets, hardly a calming sight to the nervous passengers. On the positive side, once some time had passed, most of these same soldiers became friendly and helped as best they could.

To counter pervasive fears of what might happen, more rational minds instilled calm, pointing out that such far-fetched ideas made no sense. Their group was no more a threat to national security than any of the Bainbridge or Seattle Japanese, they said. And why else would they have gone to the trouble of assigning each family a specific number if they intended to kill them later? Even their baggage, packed together in a separate car, had a tag with a corresponding number.

In addition to the discomfort, sleeping upright on the hard seats was dangerous, particularly when the cars were moving slowly in stations or on side rails. Bumps and jerks were so common that nearly every night someone slid or fell out of his seat while sleeping.

If the Kirkland train had traveled straight through, they would have arrived at their destination long ago. But it happened regularly that they stopped and went nowhere, typically on a siding off the main route, and usually during the day. Such delays occurred because their train had no priority. Trains carrying troops or war materials or even other passenger trains had the right of way, making the painful journey even more frustrating. On the second day out, a fellow passenger noticed a cattle car chugging along as they waited on their siding. "Even the animals are more important than we are," he joked. Few appreciated the humor.

Accordingly, their train traveled mostly at night. The benefit of riding during darkness was that it was cooler, and the motion of the train was conducive to sleep. That minor benefit was more than offset during the day, when boredom and stifling heat affected everyone, whether they were moving or not. At first, the accompanying soldiers refused to let their charges out during long waits on a siding. But it wasn't long before they relented. Everyone who wanted could stretch their legs, always preferring the shady side of the train. The first time this happened, the dining crew distributed box lunches. Eating outside was an unusual occurrence.

During the hours of heat, boredom, and physical discomfort everyone endured, Keiko would cope by mentally reliving those pleasant days back in Bellevue that began when she married James. Once the government set the departure date for the Bellevue Japanese, Harrison and Barbara held another going-away dinner, just as they had for their son three weeks earlier. Harrison again reassured the Tanakas that he and Barbara would look out for their interests. They should spend all of their energy looking after themselves and getting back home safe, he stressed.

Of her new family, except for her husband, Keiko treasured most the times she had spent with her mother-in-law. After the honeymoon, when the newlyweds had moved into the Armstrong house, it wasn't long before Barbara took Keiko aside. "My name is Barbara," she said. "Your name is Keiko. If you call me Mrs. Armstrong one more time, I'm going to scream. Mrs. Armstrong is my mother-in-law. I don't want to be reminded of that woman any more than is necessary. Do we have an understanding?"

Two people couldn't have been more different, Akemi and Barbara. While her own mother was typically Japanese, quiet and reserved, Barbara was the opposite. In private, she'd say the darndest things, statements that would make Keiko either blush or laugh out loud, and often both. When Keiko heard the intro "This is just between you and me," she knew that she was in for something special. Keiko figured that after years of having only boys around the house, Barbara had finally found someone she could talk to.

On Wednesday, when the entire Armstrong clan bade farewell at the train station, it was Barbara who had hugged Keiko the longest. And, as was typical for her, she whispered a truly outlandish statement: "You're the best thing that's happened to this family in a long time."

* * *

For perhaps the hundredth time since they had boarded the train, Keiko reached down under her seat to remove the letters from her bag. In the three weeks that had passed since James's departure to the military, Keiko received five letters. They had all arrived during the final two weeks at home.

Most important, Keiko now had an address in California to which she could write, and she did so immediately. Until her family departed Bellevue, she had written every day. And to make sure there was no lapse in their frequency, she had written three extra. Showing her mother-in-law that she had numbered each letter consecutively—a technique she and James had invented to help the receiver know if any had been lost—Keiko handed them over, along with strict orders to mail them one at a time over the coming days. "You can count on me, Keiko," was her mother-in-law's reply. "I'll make sure to mail them in order."

In those final weeks, James's letters came not only to Keiko but to his parents and siblings as well. Keiko and Barbara compared notes to supplement information they had received personally. The basics were the same—and frustratingly vague, at least as far as James's exact physical location and his duties were concerned. All he said was that after basic training, the Navy would send him to school. Eventually, he'd be assigned to a ship. Keiko and Barbara agreed that the longer he spent in school, the better. With a little luck, the war would be over before he finished.

Since boarding the train, Keiko had written three more letters, two to James and one to the Armstrong family. Barbara had insisted that her daughter-in-law keep them updated on their situation. The letters were sealed, stamped, and ready to go. On their second day out, when she asked one of the soldiers at the front of the car where she could mail them, he said that wasn't allowed.

Why not? What military secrets could I possibly be carrying? Keiko persisted. "Two of these letters are going to my husband. He's just joined the Navy."

The soldier's eyes opened wide, and he cackled. "Do you take me for a fool? You're lying. There are no Japanese serving in the US Navy."

"I'm not lying! My husband's not Japanese."

With this additional information, the young man's head snapped backward and, at the same time, he pulled on his left ear.

Keiko continued. "Look on your list if you don't believe me. My name is Keiko Armstrong. Here, look at the letters. You'll see that they're addressed to James Armstrong. See this military address in California?"

"Wait here." The soldier walked to the opposite end of the car and spoke to the guard there. Together, they checked a clipboard and simultaneously looked back toward Keiko. They talked some more, and Keiko saw the second soldier shake his head.

The first soldier returned. "That's your name, all right. And you say that you're married to this guy?"

"On June 2, it'll be three months." Keiko held up her hand to display her wedding band. Back in Bellevue, she had asked her mother-in-law to safeguard her valuable engagement ring until she returned.

The soldier faced away from his partner and spoke quietly. "We're not supposed to let anyone mail anything, but I don't see what harm it would do. Besides, my mother always tells me that I never do what I'm told." He smiled and held his hand down in front of him, out of sight. "Give them to me, and I'll mail them the first chance I get."

* * *

Misaki broke the silence. "Does your head still hurt?"

Keiko touched the area gingerly, in the middle of her forehead. "It's going to be fine, Misaki. It looks worse than it actually is. I barely notice it anymore."

Besides the mental anxiety affecting everyone in the Tanaka family, Keiko was actually worse physically. On their second day out of Kirkland—when they had finally been given the opportunity to walk outside during a layover—Keiko tripped as she boarded her car. She blamed the incident on a temporary bout of nausea and dizziness attributed to motion sickness, having never ridden on a train before. Others on the train had been sick as well.

Keiko tried to catch herself as she fell, but her forehead struck one of the angular metal supports holding up the seats. A soldier standing nearby came to her assistance and requested a clean cloth from the dining car. Her wound had bled profusely at first. But after steady pressure from a compress Akemi had fashioned, the bleeding stopped. Fortunately, the cut, about three-quarters of an inch long, was only superficial.

Keiko didn't want to think about her head; she wanted only thoughts of her husband. She opened the first of his letters to read it again. As she began, she glanced sideways and caught Misaki looking. She quickly turned the letter over. Misaki knew she had been caught.

Keiko made her point compassionately but firmly. "I know that, up until now, I've shared almost everything with you. But these letters are mine. Right now they're all I have of my husband, and you can't read them."

Misaki nodded. "I understand. I promise not to do that anymore."

Keiko reread James's first letter:

Dear Keiko,

As I write this, it is Thursday, April 30, and we're still traveling south on the train. So that you know, we've been told that we can never say exactly where we are or what we're doing. If the enemy somehow intercepted our letters, they could use this information to their advantage. So please don't be upset with me when I don't give you those kinds of details.

Other than still riding on the train, there's nothing else to report. Our train has a dining car, and we get fed really well. This morning I had eggs, bacon, and pancakes, with lots of coffee. If I continue to eat like this, you may not recognize me when I get back. Ha ha!

Keiko, I can't believe how much I miss you already. We no sooner left the station than my heart began to ache. I miss my family too, but not a tenth as much as I miss you. Do you miss me?

I wish I knew when your family is leaving and where you are going. My guess is that you'll go to Puyallup like the other locals. That won't be too bad because Mom and Dad will still be close. It would be easy for them to help you if you need things. Of course, that won't last forever because Dad says that Puyallup is only a temporary location. Only God knows where they'll send you next! Oh Keiko, I can't believe the world is so crazy that the government would send you away like this. Mark my word! It won't be long before President Roosevelt realizes that he's made a BIG mistake.

In the meantime, I'm counting on you to take care of my new family. It still feels odd for me to think that I now have a whole bunch of in-laws—mother, father, sisters, and brother. You have the same. Does it seem strange to you too?

I've been rambling and need to stop. We'll soon be eating dinner and then trying to sleep.

I wish you were here to show me how much you love me. For the life of me, I keep forgetting how much that is. Ha ha!

I'll write again tomorrow.

Your loving husband,

James

Keiko blinked back tears as she realized that her husband had probably ridden over the same railroad tracks that her family was riding over now.

"Please, God, keep him safe," she mouthed to the air in front of her.

20

THE RABBIT DIED

Pinedale Civilian Assembly Center, California
Tuesday afternoon, July 7, 1942

They had arrived on Sunday, May 24. It had taken four days on their Godforsaken train for the Bellevue Japanese to travel a mere 930 miles. In the final days on the train, word got around that their destination was the Pinedale Civilian Assembly Center, located six miles north of Fresno, California. Geographically, Pinedale sat very near the center of the state. The Assembly Center would be one of fifteen temporary facilities used to house the Japanese before the War Relocation Authority (WRA) completed the ten permanent Relocation Centers.

No one on the train had ever heard of Pinedale. The guards told them that they were among the lucky, that Pinedale had been built from scratch and was brand new.

Those on the train already knew that the Seattle Japanese who had been transferred to Camp Harmony in Puyallup, Washington, had to make do with cowsheds, horse stalls, and other structures associated with the huge fairgrounds located there. If Pinedale was built especially for them, maybe the Bellevue Japanese had finally caught a break. But as they climbed down from the train and boarded the trucks that took them to their new temporary home, they began to question their luck.

The first thing they noticed was the heat. The sun was so strong and the temperatures so stifling that the Bellevue group thought they had been dropped off in hell. When they arrived at the facility, the surroundings looked like a desert, although most had never seen one up close. The facility was enormous: ten blocks with twenty-six buildings in each, designed to house nearly 5,000 internees. An eleventh block consisted of buildings for administration and security. The remainder of that first afternoon at Pinedale consisted of standing in line—in the oppressive, airless oven of an environment—for registration and receiving assignment of an "apartment."

The structures looked like barracks, which was what they were: cheap, hastily built wood-framed, wood-sided structures covered with tar paper. The carpenters among the group soon pointed out the huge gaps that were showing up between the boards on the walls. The green wood that the builders had used was shrinking fast in the dry, kiln-like temperatures of that Fresno summer.

Each barracks building consisted of four apartment units, typically twenty by twenty feet, each with one small window. Although solid vertical partitions separated the four apartments, those separations did not extend to the roof, which meant that the gabled area above the living spaces was open—open to bugs that managed to enter any of the apartments, open to dust and sand that blew in from outside and, most noticeably, open to traveling sounds. A conversation held in the middle of the night by one family became common knowledge to everyone in that barracks. Children who lived there soon discovered one glorious advantage to the open gables. Tossing anything that resembled a ball back and forth over those walls became a source of entertainment any time, day or night.

In general, one family occupied one apartment. Accordingly, each could house as few as three people and as many as eleven. The six-person Tanaka family was better off than larger families. The government-issue blankets, of no use during the summer, were soon adapted to provide another function: room dividers, hung from a stretched rope. The Tanaka family created three rooms: the smallest for Masao, a slightly larger one for Isamu and Akemi, and the largest for the three girls. Shizuka, having been used to her own room back in Bellevue, had the most difficulty with the new arrangement and complained frequently. Keiko and Misaki made it clear to her that they weren't pleased with the situation either.

With no moving air and sweltering temperatures, sleeping at night became a miserable proposition. Walking around outside provided temporary relief—and allowed them to see the lights of Fresno in the distance—but there was nowhere comfortable to sleep. Each member of the Tanaka family said more than once that he or she wished they had brought along their electric fan. The outlet used for the single light bulb hanging from the ceiling could have been adapted to run the fan. Accordingly, anything light in weight and having suitable surface area became the makings of a hand fan. Women were constantly fanning themselves.

After their first night's stay, the Tanaka family noticed that their apartment had one serious flaw beyond the obvious ones. Instead of concrete, theirs sat on asphalt. This tar-like surface had two serious deficiencies. First, it became much warmer than concrete, making their apartment even less pleasant to live in. At night, a second problem arose. The standard issue GI cot with its metal legs would sink through the warm asphalt until the legs reached the underlying ground. For this reason, the search was on for stones or blocks of wood to place beneath the legs. At least their cots had mattresses. Some of the later arrivals had to make their own using straw.

In the center of each barracks block stood buildings common to all internees: mess hall, latrine, and washroom. Each of those spaces was disliked to varying degrees. Having arrived at Pinedale only four weeks before the summer solstice meant that they could not have come at a hotter time of year. While standing in line for meals, those who had umbrellas used them to block the sun's fierce intensity. Not a day went by when someone didn't faint.

Initially, there was a lot of grumbling concerning the food. The Japanese diet, particularly for those from the Pacific Northwest, consisted of fresh vegetables and rice, together with seafood when available. At the camp, rice was not a staple, and fresh fruits and vegetables were rare. Mutton and Vienna sausages, foods the Japanese didn't eat, were served often. Many became sick. Breakfast became the favorite meal among many, especially the children, when eggs and hotcakes were available in abundance.

After food, latrines produced the most complaints, at least among the Japanese women, typically modest and accustomed to being by themselves there. Privacy was in short supply because of the open nature of both the men's and women's bathrooms: two lines of open toilets back to back, with no partitions either to the rear or to the side. To avoid embarrassment, many made it a point to use the bathrooms either early in the morning or late at night. A second advantage of using the latrines at those hours was to avoid the stench caused by the daytime heat. Shovelfuls of lime tossed down through the holes helped somewhat.

For the washrooms, the open bay of showers caused similar privacy gripes. Many Japanese had never taken a shower. They were used to baths instead. One positive was the availability of both hot and cold running water.

When Keiko arrived, she expected to see the Army running the facility. But it wasn't long before calls went out for help from the internees in nearly every operational area involved in running the camp. Masao, who as a teenager had had some experience working for a restaurant in Bellevue, volunteered for service in the mess hall. Akemi encouraged him to do this, figuring that her growing boy would get enough to eat if he worked where food was being prepared. Masao came home the first evening and reported that the chief cook in their block had been the same person he had worked for back in Bellevue.

Somewhat to Keiko's surprise, all jobs were paying jobs. Because of his previous experience, Masao qualified for a cook's position. The thirteen dollars-per-month salary was a lot better than the eight dollars he would have gotten as a dishwasher.

It wasn't long, however, before Masao came home and announced that he had made a big mistake. "Work as a cook is too hard. If I ever have the opportunity, I want to transfer to the Fire Department."

"Why?" Akemi asked.

"There are never any fires."

Having had some instruction in first aid and feminine hygiene back in high school, Keiko and Misaki volunteered for work in the "hospital." Calling the place a hospital was generous considering that there was only one doctor and minimal facilities. Still, it was somewhere anyone could go if he or she was injured or became sick. Before long, Keiko was vaccinating people for typhoid and smallpox. With minimal equipment, but with books and some instruction, they also did blood counts and urine tests.

Akemi and Shizuka took on the tasks of running the household. Among those was washing the family's clothes in the washroom basins. Sweeping out the apartment became a daily chore as wind blew in dust and sand through the openings in the siding. Plugging cracks and gaps became an ongoing task.

With few jobs available for the older Issei men, they found living at Pinedale humiliating. Compared to their status as head of their households back home, they felt unneeded. Isamu was among them. He spent much of his time commiserating with other men from the Bellevue area.

By the end of June, when the heat was at its worst, word got around that they would be leaving soon. Later, announcements made at the Fourth of July celebration stated that transfers would happen before the end of the month. It was on the morning of July 7 that the Tanaka family received their specific orders: they would be departing Pinedale on July 16, headed to the Tule Lake internment camp in northern California. On that day, they were to report to the Visitor's Building, at the southeast corner of the Center, at eight o'clock in the morning. Hand luggage and bedding needed to be tagged and ready for pickup outside the apartments by six. Their instructions included warnings to turn in their federal blankets, to avoid a charge on their account.

Standing in line for dinner on the afternoon they received their orders, the Tanaka family knew that their days at Pinedale were numbered.

Masao had the evening off. "From what I learned at lunch, it looks like all of us Bellevue people are going to Tule Lake. We'll be able to stay together."

Of the family, Shizuka had the least tolerance for the heat. "At least we're going north and not south. Thank goodness they're not sending us to Manzanar."

Keiko was thinking about James. "Do you think they'll know to forward our mail to Tule Lake? That worries me a lot."

Chuckling, Masao replied, "If they don't, they'll have more than enough paper to stuff all of the cracks in the walls."

With her tin cup grasped firmly in hand, Keiko took a big swing at her brother's head. "Funny! Very funny!"

But it was true. Compared to her siblings and parents, Keiko received more mail by far. Misaki, Shizuka, and Masao had each received a letter or two from Caucasian friends back in Bellevue. Isamu and Akemi received biweekly letters from Harrison, providing updates on the status of their crops. But it was Keiko who received the preponderance: three to four letters a week from James and weekly letters from Barbara Armstrong.

Keiko had done her share in supporting the financial viability of the post office. She hadn't missed one day in writing to James. And once Barbara had started to write to her personally, Keiko replied. Truth be told, Keiko felt embarrassed about her close relationship with her mother-in-law. In her letters, Keiko told her things that she would have had difficulty discussing with her own mother. Perhaps it was because Barbara had been so open with Keiko that it had become easier for Keiko to reciprocate.

James's letters often came in bunches. Several of James's that Keiko was sure had gotten lost in the mail—because of their numbering scheme—eventually showed up. They happened to be the last of the ones sent to Bellevue and then forwarded by Barbara.

Keiko had received James's latest letter a day earlier. Although he missed his family and especially his wife, Keiko sensed that he was adjusting to military life reasonably well. The food was good, he said. He had made many good friends, several of whom hailed from the Southeast. Except for the fact that they talked funny, they were good people, he said.

But besides all these goings-on, Keiko had much more on her mind than the upcoming move. When she missed her first period, she chalked it up as an unusual aberration. With the excitement of the marriage, it made complete sense to her that her emotions had somehow disturbed her cycle.

Keiko continued to apply this same logic when she missed her second period. But in the back of her mind, she knew that something was wrong. *Have I contracted some serious illness?* With this abysmal thought in mind, she had lost sleep and kept the secret from everyone, even from Misaki. But when she missed her third period in a row, it finally hit her like a ton of bricks. *How could I have been so stupid?*

A baby. We're going to have a baby.

* * *

The reason that Keiko had obstinately avoided the obvious was because she had faithfully followed all of the advice she had been given. Keiko stifled a giggle as she recalled her mother's instructions in the days leading up to the wedding.

Once the two families had accepted the fact that the marriage was going to happen, Keiko learned that both mothers had a special interest in the reproductive aspects of their progeny. First to speak was Akemi. She took Keiko aside and asked if she had given any thought to birth control. During the twins' teenage years, their mother had not been shy in explaining the facts of life, and it appeared that this was still the case. Keiko's eyes opened wide indeed when her mother presented her with a rubber bag contraption with a hose on the end.

"All you do is mix lemon juice or vinegar with water," Akemi said. "But make sure to use it within five minutes after intercourse," she cautioned, "or it might not work."

Armed with this new information and her new rubber apparatus, Keiko practiced a few times until she had the procedure down. She felt extremely enlightened with her newfound knowledge. But then, about a week before the wedding, her future mother-in-law made her own contribution to the topic as she took Keiko aside one afternoon when they were alone together in the house.

Not wanting to embarrass Mrs. Armstrong by boasting that she already knew everything, that her mother had explained things in detail—thank you—Keiko forced herself to be polite. When Mrs. Armstrong asked Keiko if she had given any thought to family planning, Keiko played it cool, confidently saying that she knew that the way to keep from getting pregnant was to irrigate afterward with either lemon juice or vinegar.

To Keiko's utter shock, Mrs. Armstrong waved her hand in dismissal. "That doesn't work, I'm here to tell you. People think that it works, but they're wrong. My firstborn, your future husband? He's a good example of what you get after you use lemon juice."

Mrs. Armstrong had then gone on to explain that there were several reliable methods of birth control. Armed with this knowledge, although slightly amazed that people had even thought of some of the methods, Keiko had felt more confident on her wedding day.

* * *

It was the evening of the seventh, and everyone was in bed; the building was quiet. *I still can't believe it*, Keiko thought to herself. *James and I were so careful!* Still, thinking back, Barbara had told her that the birth-control gel was not perfect.

Tomorrow, she'd sit down to write a letter to James and inform him of this important development. He needed to be the first to know. Two days later, another letter would go out to Barbara and Harrison, breaking the news to the Armstrong half of the family. A day or so later, but definitely before they headed to Tule Lake, Keiko planned to tell her own family—outside, in the dark, where no one else could hear.

Keiko and James would be having a baby. Keiko wished that she had been able to tell her husband to his face. The words in her letter would have to do.

21

VISITORS

Tule Lake Relocation Center, California
Tuesday morning, August 18, 1942

With her siblings and parents standing nearby, Keiko waited anxiously, staring out through the metal links in the fence to the left of the camp entrance. Her family would be receiving visitors today, the first since they departed Bellevue.

A month had passed since they and the other Bellevue residents had arrived at the Tule Lake Relocation Center in northern California, ten miles south of the Oregon border. The Tanakas had departed Pinedale on July 16 after more than a seven-week stay at that temporary facility. On the ride north, Keiko swore to Misaki that they were riding the same train as had brought them south from Washington. She proved it on the afternoon of the second day when she showed Misaki dried remnants of her blood at the base of the metal bench where she had fallen back in May.

Their latest train ride took two days rather than four—a quicker journey, but once again preposterous considering the mere 480 miles traveled. As before, waiting on sidings was the reason for the long journey. Everyone aboard the train complained about the food, which consisted of sandwiches for every meal. Many found it ironic that they would think back fondly to the mess halls at Pinedale.

Keiko learned that construction of the Tule Lake camp had begun more than a month before the Bellevue Japanese departed

119

Washington. The Tule Lake Relocation Center was one of ten permanent facilities built to house Japanese Americans. Keiko's new address was Newell, California. Of the ten, only Tule Lake and Manzanar were located in California, with one each in Colorado, Wyoming, Idaho, and Utah, and two each in Arizona and Arkansas.

Several of the men on the train who had been fishermen in southern California before their incarceration looked forward to fishing in Tule Lake. When they arrived, they were sorely disappointed. To create fertile farmland, the original lake had been systematically drained, starting in 1907. The upside was that the surrounding land was conducive to farming.

As they had disembarked from the train, the internees peered at what again looked like a desert, with not a tree in sight. But this time, they were in for a pleasant surprise. Replacing the 100-degree-plus extremes endured at Pinedale were temperatures fifteen to twenty degrees cooler. Masao, who had excelled in high school science, explained why. He observed that their train had done a lot of climbing on their trip north. "The higher you go, the cooler it gets," he said.

Masao's family discovered how right he was: at just over 4,000 feet in elevation, Tule Lake was 3700 feet higher than Pinedale. But the few locals who worked in the camp told them not to celebrate too soon, that there was a cost: "With the more moderate summer temperatures you're going to get cooler winters," they said. To a person, the internees said that they would gladly accept that trade; no one wanted to experience the scorching heat at Pinedale ever again. Nighttime temperatures were finally conducive to a good night's sleep.

Designed for over 18,000 Japanese Americans, the Tule Lake camp had the capacity to house more than three times that of Pinedale. Interestingly, word got back that once the internees left Pinedale, that facility had taken on another role—as an Army Air Force training facility for signal technicians. "They can have it," was a common refrain.

Defined by the government as a permanent facility, more thought and preparation had gone into the construction at Tule Lake, and things were more organized. The tar paper–covered barracks were the same, but there were more windows. This time the floors were concrete. After a while, plasterboard became available and the men, some with little experience as carpenters, covered the interior walls. Although often crudely done, this refinement helped keep out the dust and dirt and provided some insulation against outside temperatures.

By the time they arrived at the end of July, they were among the last to settle in. Half of the Bellevue families, including the Tanakas, found themselves living in an area some distance from the main gate, to the rear of an irrigation ditch—an area called Alaska.

The *Tulean Dispatch* (Volume III, Number 15), the official newspaper for the camp, provided a humorous account of their residences:

Across the Ditch Is Isolated Alaska

Remote from the "mainland" and secure in the feeling that they are exclusive, a peaceful contingent of colonists have established themselves away from the noise and humming activities of a busy city.

These colonists arrived from Pinedale on July 19 and consolidated their position by occupying the barracks on the other side of the irrigation ditch.

Day by day, the foothold was enlarged. Today the whole block comprising Blocks 56 to 59 has been unofficially labeled "Alaska" because of its distant location, and its separation from the rest of the Project by the ditch.

The name is now being rapidly popularized. Such conversations as "I'm going home to Alaska" or "So you're from Alaska," are becoming more frequent.

In retaliation, the Alaska residents claim their blocks to be the exclusive residential district, separated from the "common people" by the river as yet unnamed.

Residents living at the other extreme end which includes blocks in Ward VII, prefer to call their area, the exclusive Country Club district . . .

It was in Block VII, the Country Club District, where the remainder of the Bellevue families found themselves living.

By early August, Keiko gave up trying to hide her pregnancy. According to her calculations, she was about five months away from giving birth. Because her last period had occurred on time, back in Bellevue at the end of March, she concluded that she had gotten pregnant about two weeks later. Accordingly, she explained to James in her first letter that she expected to give birth around the middle of January 1943, give or take a few days.

Following her letters to James and to the Armstrong family, Keiko awaited their responses, particularly James's. How would he react? The two had talked about starting a family but had agreed that they would wait until after the war. Would he be disappointed? Would he be mad at her for being careless? When his response came ten days later, Keiko's fingers shook as she read his reply:

> *Dear Keiko,*
>
> *I don't have much time to write this evening, but I wanted to get this out right away.*
>
> *Oh, Keiko! What wonderful news! I swear that my heart almost stopped beating when I read your letter. WE'RE going to have a baby!*
>
> *Have you written Mom and Dad? What was the reaction of your family? Are you okay? Do they have the proper doctors for you at Tule Lake? Are you eating good foods?*
>
> *My only regret is that I'm not there with you now, holding you and telling you how much I love you. This is so wonderful!*
>
> *I'll write more tomorrow.*
>
> > *Love,*
> >
> > *James*
>
> *P.S. I hope it's a girl, so that there will be someone else just like you for me to love.*

While none of the Bellevue contingent was surprised at the news of her pregnancy, explaining the situation to the others living at the camp proved more taxing.

"Where is your husband?" "Why isn't he here?" "What do you mean, he's in the Navy?" "Quit kidding me. That's not possible." After a significant pause following Keiko's explanation, there would be one final word before the person walked away. "Oh!"

Reactions from her own family were supportive, as Keiko expected they would be. Her loyal twin, Misaki, promised to do whatever was needed to make sure Keiko had a healthy pregnancy. The lightest moment followed Keiko's announcement to the family, when Akemi took Keiko aside. "Didn't you use the lemon juice like I told you?"

Having timed the letters to make sure that James would be the first to know, Keiko waited next for her mother-in-law's response. It arrived the day after James's. As she read the first sentence, she could imagine the droll look on Barbara's face had she made the statement in person.

"Well, you and I both knew this could happen." Barbara would have held out her hands, palms up, and said, "What can you do?" She would then have smiled and taken Keiko in her arms and told her everything would be all right. In effect, that was what the rest of her letter said.

It was what her mother-in-law had written in her last paragraph that surprised Keiko. "Harrison and I will be down as soon as we can. You may not know it, but with the war and the ongoing rationing, it's getting harder and harder for us to get some things. Make a list of what you and your family need and get it to us soon. We'll be able to hand carry much more than we could mail."

In the three months since the Tanakas departed Bellevue, Harrison and Barbara had mailed several packages, first to Pinedale and then to Tule Lake. Many of these contained toiletries and other personal items difficult to get at the camp exchange. In light of the approaching winter, new requests included winter clothing from the house.

* * *

Keiko pointed into the distance. "That's got to be them."

The others looked and saw dust trailing behind a single automobile. Barbara had written a week earlier to say they would be making the trip by train. They would have preferred driving, but she said the ongoing gas rationing made that option out of the question. Keiko concluded that they must have hired someone to drive them from the train station.

As the car approached the entrance, the gate guard motioned their vehicle to the side. Harrison and Barbara exited the back doors. Their driver opened the trunk, and Harrison removed two huge bags. Barbara carried a separate cardboard box.

The Armstrongs were within shouting distance, and Keiko yelled through the fence to get their attention. At once, Harrison and

Barbara began waving excitedly. The entire Tanaka family waved back. Keiko was so thrilled to see friendly faces. She watched as they approached the gate guard, who pointed toward the fence.

Keiko understood what was happening. Visitors could not enter the compound. Their visit would have to take place on opposite sides of the fence.

Harrison, who had been holding his two bags, set them down abruptly. Keiko couldn't hear his words, but she could tell that her father-in-law was not happy. The volume of the discussion intensified to where Harrison pointed past the guard to the interior of the compound. There was a brief standoff, after which the guard returned to the guardhouse. Through the window, Keiko could see that he was making a telephone call.

Before long, a jeep with someone more senior showed up. The guard and his superior headed back toward the Armstrongs. Harrison's hand gestures made clear what it was he wanted. After this second flare-up, the superior returned to the guardhouse and made yet another telephone call. He then exited the guardhouse and pointed to a soldier, this one armed with a rifle, motioning him to accompany him back to the Armstrongs.

Please, God, no! Will they send her in-laws away by force? Halfway back to the Armstrongs, their intentions became less threatening. The superior motioned for them to come forward. After a brief conversation, he pointed to an administrative building sitting between the gate and where Keiko and her family were standing.

Once it became clear what was happening, the Tanakas and Keiko headed toward the building as well. They all met at the entrance. At this point, there were tears on both sides, as if the two families hadn't seen each other in years. The guard with the rifle broke up the meeting and pointed to the door. Before entering, he took possession of the two large bags, presumably to inspect their contents. He also took a quick look inside the cardboard box, but then indicated that Harrison could take that one with him.

Inside, the guard took them to a private room that had only chairs and a desk at the front. It appeared to be some sort of training room. He pointed to the chairs and then at his watch, and said that he would be waiting outside the door.

Harrison opened his arms. "First of all, how are all of you? We've been so worried."

Keiko felt obligated to answer for the family. "It's been sort of hard, but we're making do." And after a pause, she said, "We can't believe that you've come all this way to see us."

"You are our family," Barbara responded. "Why wouldn't we come? Besides, unless I've misinterpreted your letters, Keiko, I think that I'm going to be a grandmother. You couldn't keep me away."

Harrison held up his hands to get everyone's attention. "Before we go any further, we need to be aware that we have only one hour together."

"One hour?" asked Masao.

"If you were watching what happened outside, we're lucky to be inside here at all. So, let's make the most of our time together."

A lot of communication occurred over the next sixty minutes. Harrison and Barbara gave a quick summary of events back home. With a few setbacks that Harrison said he didn't want to get into, the produce from the Tanaka farm was making its way to market. The Tanaka house and its contents were safe. This latter assurance was not trivial; many internees were receiving letters telling them that their homes had been ransacked and their belongings stolen.

Most of the information flow occurred in the reverse direction, responding to Armstrong questions. "Are they treating you well?" "Are you getting enough to eat?" "What are your accommodations like?" "Are you warm enough at night?" "What are you doing with your time?" "Do they make you work?" "What is it you need?"

Toward the end of the hour, Barbara got up and motioned Keiko to the corner of the room where they could speak in private. "Are you really okay?"

"I'm doing all right, Barbara. I had some morning sickness in the beginning, but that's gone now. As far as I can tell, everything's fine. You can see that I'm starting to show."

"What about the hospital here? Are you going to have proper care?"

"Like we did at Pinedale, Misaki and I volunteered to work in the hospital. There are two Japanese doctors here from San Francisco, and they seem to be very good. I had my first examination after I wrote to you, and he says that everything's fine. Please, don't worry."

Keiko reached into her pocket and removed the letter. "Barbara, here is James's first letter to me after he learned I was pregnant. I want you to read it."

Barbara read the letter, dabbed at her eyes, and handed it back. "That's my James. You married a good one, I can tell you that."

By then, the door to the room opened, and the guard returned, setting the two bags on the floor. Everyone looked in his direction, not wanting to believe that their time was up.

Harrison grimaced and pointed. "We've got to go. Those bags are filled mostly with the clothing you wanted."

Masao pointed to the box. "What's in there?"

Barbara walked over and put her hand on his shoulder. "Why don't you take a look? There are two things: one you asked for, and one you didn't."

Masao lifted the cardboard flaps and peered inside. As he removed what looked like two pies, a big smile came over his face.

Barbara apologized. "They're a little worse for wear, so I'd eat them soon if I were you. I seem to recall that you all like apple."

Masao removed the second item, holding it up for all to see. Keiko and her family smiled at the sight of their old electric fan and then broke out in spontaneous applause.

22

BURIED GUILT

Monterey, California
Friday morning, October 27, 2000

Kazuko lingered behind and watched Sato exit the terminal and walk toward his plane. He turned, looked back through the partitioned glass, and waved.

In the car, Kazuko leaned back in her seat, closed her eyes, and replayed Sato's words. "I was standing off to the side with Misaki, behind the photographer . . . Something was going around the camp at the time, and Shizuka was very sick. I remember everyone being disappointed that she couldn't be in the pictures."

This was new information. Aunt Shizuka had not participated in the picture taking! Why hadn't she mentioned this yesterday at the hospital? Had she forgotten? An unforeseen illness was certainly no reason for embarrassment.

But that oversight on Shizuka's part made no more sense than her mother losing those precious pictures. Or, even more puzzling, why she would have hidden one away.

Kazuko returned home, changed clothes, and headed back to the hospital to meet Patrick. By then it was past ten o'clock, and he called on her cell to ask what was keeping her. When she arrived, she intercepted him heading back to their mother's room, coffee in hand. Instead, they returned to the lobby where Kazuko elaborated on her decision to intercept Sato before he left town.

She detailed his recollections about the day when the photographer took pictures.

Patrick's reaction mirrored Kazuko's. "Why didn't Aunt Shizuka just admit that she'd been sick?" On the other hand, he pointed out the obvious. "None of what Sato's told us is of any real significance. Just let it go, Sukie. Mom simply lost the pictures."

It was easy for Patrick to make light of her suspicions. He hadn't been there to witness Shizuka's response when she first saw Sato.

* * *

Sister and brother remained at their mother's bedside until late in the afternoon when they left to visit their father. As Kazuko had hoped, he neither asked about his wife nor wondered why she hadn't visited recently.

After five days, neither parent's condition had improved. Kazuko couldn't decide between the two who was in worse shape: their comatose mother or their father who, day by day, was becoming more withdrawn from the outside world.

And yet Kazuko couldn't shake from her mind the complete serendipity and irony of the information she had stumbled upon, beginning with Sato's revelations about his life at Tule Lake, including the initial surprise that their Aunt Misaki had had a fiancé. Why couldn't Sato have arrived a week earlier? On the other hand, had he met up with Keiko as planned, there'd have been no guarantee that Kazuko would have had the opportunity to meet him. But it was what it was, and the information uncovered since Sunday was unsettling. Kazuko found it disheartening that all of this had taken place at precisely the moment when her mother was incapable of adding her perspective.

Kazuko felt an urgency to solve these puzzles while her mother still lived. Accordingly, she decided it was time to up the ante. It was time to have a serious conversation with the sole person still alive who had a ringside seat to the saga of the Tanaka family at Tule Lake.

* * *

Kazuko left Patrick, headed home to grab a quick bite, and returned to the hospital to meet with Shizuka. Although there was no sign of her when Kazuko arrived in her mother's room, she did meet Keiko's neurosurgeon who was just leaving.

"Doctor Siradnamalah."

"Kazuko. The nurses tell me that you've been here most of the day."

"Patrick and I have been doing day duty, and Aunt Shizuka nights."

Kazuko sensed movement down the hall. It was Shizuka. "Here she is."

Shizuka joined the duo, and Dr. Siradnamalah addressed them together. "If you have a few minutes, maybe we can talk." He pointed toward the lobby.

Kazuko and her aunt took seats facing the doctor. From earlier conversations with him, Kazuko understood the medical details of what had happened to her mother. A hemorrhagic stroke, the kind that results from bleeding in the brain, was the culprit. Dr. Naresh Siradnamalah, a highly respected local neurosurgeon, had repaired the burst aneurysm, a weak spot in one of the small arteries inside the brain. Apparently, this had all occurred somewhere near the brain stem—about the worst place it could happen because both heart and lung functions are controlled in that area.

Dr. Siradnamalah began. "I thought I'd bring you up to date, although there's not a whole lot to say."

Kazuko remembered Dr. Siradnamalah showing her Keiko's first CAT scan. The white areas on the film signaled the existence of fresh blood, proof of a stroke caused by bleeding. There were two ways to repair it, he had told them, but using a catheter and doing it remotely was not an option. He had had to operate, tying off the leak using a metal clip.

"As I told you earlier, our goal has been to drain away the blood that has pooled near the brain stem. It's that pressure that put your mother into a coma in the first place. Since Sunday, we've done two scans to see how it's going, to see if the hematoma, the blood pool, is decreasing."

"And what have you seen?"

"It's definitely shrinking, but we certainly don't have anything to show for it, except for some normal involuntary responses. The truth is that we don't know how much damage has already been done to the brain." The doctor's face registered concern. "But there is another risk.

Statistically, twenty percent of the aneurysms that we repair bleed again. And if that happens, we are at a huge disadvantage because we have no way of knowing when that's occurring—unless we just happen to be doing a scan right after it starts."

Shizuka hadn't said anything so far. "So what do we do?"

"All we can do is to keep monitoring your sister's condition and hope that decreasing pressure will bring some function back to the brain. I wish I could offer more encouragement."

Kazuko stared at her aunt. Neither could think of any more questions to ask. "Thank you, Doctor. Please call right away if anything changes."

"Of course." The doctor nodded and left.

The two sat quietly, digesting what really wasn't anything new. Kazuko imagined what Dr. Siradnamalah wanted to say, but had not: *You've got to realize that the longer things go on, the less hope we have.*

With concern evident in her eyes, Shizuka asked, "How are you and Patrick holding up?"

"We're okay, Aunt Shizuka. We went to see Daddy this afternoon and, afterward, I asked myself who was better off. At least Mom doesn't seem to be in any pain. If it has to end like this, I hope that it comes soon. Mom has told me more than once that the last thing she wants is to linger or to be a burden on us."

"She's told me that too, Kazuko."

Kazuko decided that this was as good a time as any to confront her aunt. "Aunt Shizuka, can we talk a little bit?"

Shizuka leaned forward and nodded. "Of course, Kazuko. What is it?"

"Back in the camps, were you close to Mom and Aunt Misaki?"

Shizuka seemed surprised at the question, but after a moment shook her head. "Not really. Remember that I was three years younger and, of course, Misaki and Keiko were twins, practically inseparable. I was the odd one out. I remember how upset I was when I had to share a room with them, first at Pinedale and then at Tule Lake. I was a spoiled brat, and they knew it." She laughed. "They told me so."

It was time to ask the pertinent question a second time. "What do you think happened to all those pictures Mr. Sato talked about? I refuse to believe that Mom lost them. They're the only pictures of our family at the camp. And the only ones of me as a baby."

Shizuka waved her hands in the air. "You've got me. I remember them being taken and then seeing them later. But don't forget that I left for Chicago in the fall of 1943."

Kazuko had forgotten that. She had left camp to take a job.

Kazuko thought that if she provided more details about what happened that day, it might jolt Shizuka's memory. "Mr. Sato said that Daddy hired a photographer who took pictures of everybody. And it happened sometime between March 21 and April 26 in 1943. The twenty-first was when Mr. Sato proposed to Aunt Misaki, and April 26 was when he and Masao left for the service. It had to happen then because Mr. Sato said that he and Aunt Misaki had their picture taken together, and that wouldn't have happened if they weren't already engaged to be married." Kazuko tried to read her aunt's face. "You don't remember anything about that day?"

Shizuka shifted uncomfortably and shook her head. "It was so long ago."

Is Aunt Shizuka lying or does she truly not remember that she had been sick?

Kazuko opened her mother's book, removed the photograph pressed between the pages, and held it up for Shizuka to see. "Does this look familiar? It's me, Mom, and Daddy. You don't remember this?"

Shizuka's eyes grew wide. "Where did you find this?" She grabbed the picture, took off her glasses, held it to her face, and looked at it closely.

"Do you remember the Tule Lake picture that Daddy took and that Mom framed? It's in Mom's living room?"

"Of course!"

"At dinner last night, Mr. Sato asked me for a copy. As you know, Mom made a habit of always including the negative inside the frame. So, after he and Patrick left last night, I took it apart. You can imagine my surprise when I found this picture taped inside."

Shizuka asked quickly. "Were there others?"

"Nope. This was it." Kazuko paused deliberately. "Which makes me wonder why Mom would save only one picture."

Shizuka seemed confused, searching for an answer.

Kazuko pushed further, turning her statement into a specific question. "Do you have any idea why Mom would have hidden away this particular picture?"

Shizuka looked up slowly and shook her head. It was obvious to Kazuko that she was avoiding the question. This thread of conversation was going nowhere.

Kazuko chose to play her ace and was anxious to witness her aunt's reaction. "I learned something else from Mr. Sato. He told me that you were sick that day and that you didn't even come out for the pictures. You don't remember that either?"

The look on Shizuka's face was telling. Something was wrong! A sudden blush of color accompanied a look of disappointment. Her hands were clenched. The blush turned into crimson. And then Shizuka did something Kazuko had never seen her aunt do. She buried her head in her hands and began to cry.

After a week of suspicions, Kazuko suddenly wished that she hadn't said anything. "Aunt Shizuka, what is it?"

Shizuka straightened, tears washing over her face. The words erupted from her mouth. "Yes, I was sick! Now you know it! That's why I didn't get my picture taken. I had been sick inside our apartment for nearly a week. I've been hiding that fact for more than fifty years."

Hiding? "Aunt Shizuka! Why?"

"Why? It was because of me that Misaki got sick. I am the one responsible for your Aunt Misaki not being here today! I lived, and she didn't."

23

INFORMERS

Tule Lake Relocation Center, California
New Year's Eve, December 31, 1942

Summer had transitioned to fall, which too soon became winter at Tule Lake. The payment they had postponed for their cooler summer temperatures by moving from Pinedale came due—in the form of colder winter temperatures. A neighbor to the Tanaka family fancied himself a weatherman and kept daily records of temperature, as well as measurements of rain and snow from a tin can he checked every day.

He said that the lowest temperature he measured during December was ten degrees Fahrenheit, and the highest fifty-five. On average, he said, the lows were in the twenties and the highs in the forties. Compared to Bellevue, winter temperatures were some ten degrees colder. To further remind them that they weren't back in the Pacific Northwest anymore, they had experienced six inches of snow during the month.

Keiko and her family had adjusted to their new, more permanent home, yet they lived only marginally better than they had at Pinedale. Their basic accommodations and monotonous lives, together with the fences and guard towers, left no doubt in anyone's mind that they were in prison—a large open one, but a prison nonetheless.

The world war continued to terrorize the planet. Along with the Allies' struggle against Hitler's maniacal push to dominate Europe, all evacuees in the camps anxiously followed the war in the Pacific. By May 1942, Japan had advanced rapidly—invincibly it seemed—taking Burma, Malaya, the Dutch East Indies, Singapore, Rabaul, and the Philippines. In addition to inflicting major losses on the Allies during these invasions, the Japanese added several punishing naval victories.

But in June, a significant turnaround occurred. The Battle of Midway resulted in a decisive victory for the American Navy. By the end of 1942, the Americans gained additional momentum by turning back the Japanese on Guadalcanal. Still, the war that everyone had hoped would be over in a few months had passed its one-year anniversary, with no end in sight.

Except for Shizuka, everyone in the Tanaka family had jobs. The WRA defined three classes of wages: unskilled labor, $12/month; skilled labor, $16/month; and professionals, $19/month. Keiko realized the gross inequity of their pay scale when she heard that a civilian WRA librarian at another center was making $167 a month. Of course, Keiko joked to her family, the librarian's wages did not include their camp's opulent life style.

Crediting their previous experience at Pinedale for giving them an edge, Keiko and Misaki snagged positions at the Tule Lake hospital and received the wage for skilled labor. Akemi was particularly keen on their working there because it meant that Keiko would be under constant surveillance—although Keiko's pregnancy had proceeded normally, with no reason for worry. At Christmas, Keiko's supervisor ordered her to stay home for her remaining month. With the cold weather and the long walk from Alaska to the hospital, he thought it would be safer. Keiko agreed but dreaded confinement inside their tiny apartment.

Akemi, with an eye toward Keiko's projected January delivery, took a job as the block mother, attending to the needs of newborns in their section of the camp. Because there was no running water in the apartments, her duties, among others, included sterilizing baby bottles in the mess hall, mixing formula, and distributing baby foods. She also coordinated the monthly truck that transported pregnant women to the hospital. There the expectant mothers received checkups, got weighed, and received calcium tablets and vitamins to supplement their diet.

Masao, who had eventually concluded in Pinedale that working in the mess hall wasn't all that bad, accepted the same job at Tule Lake. But it was her father whom Keiko felt most proud of. After his initial reaction to Pinedale, where he had felt demoralized over what had happened to his family, Isamu came into his own when he took on the post of Block Manager, a position usually assigned to a respected Issei.

Isamu's position paid $16 per month and included an office located not far from the Tanaka apartment. One benefit was a telephone, the only one available for the block. With that prestigious position, however, came numerous headaches, many of which involved handling complaints. Still, no one became more popular to the women under his charge than Isamu after he acquired scrap wood and had carpenters construct partitions between the toilets in their washrooms. As word spread, other block managers were besieged by requests from their women: "If Alaska can have partitions, why can't we?"

Shizuka was the only one of the Tanaka children who hadn't yet graduated from high school. That problem was addressed by late fall when schools were formally established at Tule Lake, resulting in four levels of education: nursery school, elementary, high school, and adult education. On her first day, Shizuka reported that classes were being held in unpartitioned buildings identical to the one they were living in. There were no chairs initially, and the children had to sit on the floor. To make matters worse, books and qualified teachers were scarce. But with time, conditions did improve. Shizuka told her family that the most comical situation occurred when they attended typing class. Because there were no typewriters, students practiced by pressing their fingers on sheets of paper made to look like keys on a real typewriter.

Having skipped a year in grade school, Shizuka enrolled as a senior. Back in Bellevue, she had completed most of the coursework for her junior year and needed only a few credits more. She triumphantly proclaimed that she would still graduate on time in the spring.

It was New Year's Eve, and the family huddled together around their potbellied stove. Fueled by coal, it was Masao's job to haul buckets from a common pile outside. Because even the heaviest clothing that the Armstrongs had delivered from Bellevue wasn't warm enough, everyone wore the wool government-issue navy blue peacoats. Because these nondescript plain coats did nothing to enhance the human figure, the Recreation Department challenged seamstresses to use their skills to improve them. Military personnel on the grounds were amazed to see the results and wished that they could have worn such streamlined, stylish variations, some of which included colorful sewn-in linings.

The Tanaka family had already eaten dinner and was planning to attend the New Year's party sponsored by the Recreation Department. That same department had done a commendable job of hosting activities over Christmas. And considering their dire situation, families with children soon discovered that they had not been forgotten by friends, including those in various Christian organizations, other service groups, and the Japanese American Citizens League (JACL). The December 22 *Tulean Dispatch* reported that some 2,500 gifts had been donated to Tule Lake—everything from model airplanes, puzzles, crayons, and games to towels and pajamas and even macaroni. Shizuka volunteered to help the Recreation Department staff that worked overtime to wrap these presents in time for Santa's arrival. In addition to gifts, money came in to supplement the Christmas fund used for decorations, parties, and special foods.

Owing to the artistry of many of the internees, craft making produced many of the gifts exchanged during the holidays. Tule Lake, having once been an actual lake, provided an important raw material—seashells. Digging for the most intact and beautiful shells soon became a competitive enterprise. With a little glue, a safety pin, and nail polish for lacquering, rather attractive pieces of jewelry were the result. Shizuka had secretly made one for her mother and each of her sisters.

Following dinner on this last day of 1942, Isamu had asked his family to gather to ask for God's blessings as they readied themselves for the New Year. "God has tried our souls over the past year, but we are still together as a family, and we are healthy. That's more important than anything. God willing, next year the war will be over, and we can go home."

That they were still together as a family was no small accomplishment, Keiko knew, and something all Japanese valued highly. For various reasons, some families had split up, not even going to the same camp. In other instances, one family resided in different apartments. But more commonly, the camp atmosphere led to artificial separations. Demeaned and discouraged by the humiliation of their situation, many Issei fathers lost control of their children, who ran wild and found friends in other blocks, spending time there and eating separately from their parents. Through all of this, Isamu was proud that his family still ate their meals together.

Isamu reached out, suggesting that everyone gather hands. "Masao, would you please say a prayer?"

Through all that had happened over the past year, Masao seemed to have matured the most. As the oldest, and only male child in the family, Keiko figured that he had realized that it was his place to appear strong and support his father.

Masao closed his eyes. "Dear God, as we head into 1943, please watch over our family here at Tule Lake. Give strength to our military to conclude this terrible war. Although we don't have much, we thank you for what we have. Thank you for the Armstrong family, who worries about us and supports us every way they can. And as bad as we have it, it's nothing like what is being endured by our soldiers in Europe and in the Pacific. Watch over them and, especially, keep an eye on James in the Navy.

"Dear God, please watch over Keiko too. As you know, she will bring a new member into our family very soon.

"And finally, please do not allow the troubles at Poston and Manzanar to come to Tule Lake. In Jesus's name we pray, Amen."

"Amen."

All hands returned to coat pockets to stay warm.

Keiko knew that Masao's final request came because of two incidents that had happened just within the past two months. The first was at the Poston, Arizona, camp on November 1 when someone beat up an informer. Two suspects were caught and held responsible, but this led to internee strikes in support of the very men accused of the beating.

A month later, on December 5 at Manzanar, a more serious confrontation occurred. Six masked men assaulted another suspected informer, again resulting in discord. In defiance, an angry crowd vowed to search out other informers and do the same to them. Tear gas quelled the riot, but in the resulting scuffle, military police killed two internees and wounded nine.

The "informers" to whom the crowds were responding had come about because of the unfortunate position into which the government had placed many of its Japanese-American citizens. Following Pearl Harbor, the JACL, a community-based organization that advocated for the rights for Japanese Americans, found itself to be the official liaison between the Japanese community and the government. Founded in 1929, the JACL encouraged and fostered relationships for Nisei within the larger Seattle community; as such, it also created cooperation and socialization within their ethnic group.

But with the JACL's association with the government came resentment. One reason was that JACL members did not include Issei, the older, more respected members of the Japanese population. As a result, the JACL was hardly representative of their community. A second, more condemning reason, was that the JACL fully cooperated with the government in the internment of its own people and reported troublemakers to the FBI. And at the camps themselves, JACL members often assumed powerful positions. It was at Poston and Manzanar that these tensions led to violence.

The situation involving the JACL had led to some interesting discussions. In general, the family had a common opinion, but Masao occasionally took the opposite side. "If trouble comes here, maybe we should support the protesters? What the JACL did was wrong. If they had stood up for our rights back in Washington, we wouldn't be here."

Keiko knew that her father, in his position as block manager, had listened to many of his neighbors debate the merits of the JACL. "We shouldn't support either side," he said. "That's what I tell everyone who asks me. It'll lead to nothing but trouble."

It had been Keiko and Misaki who had been the debating champs back in Bellevue. Misaki could invariably win an argument on any topic through logic and clever thought. She jumped right in. "And so, Masao, you think that we'd be better off if we had fought back?"

Masao was always at a disadvantage arguing with his sister. "Most of us here are citizens. It's wrong what they've done to us."

Isamu threw in his own logic. "Sometimes even when you know that you are right, it's better to back down, to live to fight another day."

Masao was getting worked up. "So are you saying that is what we should have done after Pearl Harbor, Papa? We should have turned the other cheek? We didn't, Papa! President Roosevelt took no time at all to declare war."

Keiko outlined in her mind how she would have responded, but deferred to her sister. "You can't compare the two, Masao. It's a faulty argument." Misaki raised her index finger, an indication that she was on the attack. "Back at the house, when the FBI men came to look through our things, you knew that what they were doing was wrong, didn't you?"

"Of course, I did. I am a citizen. Mama told them so. They had no right to go through our possessions, let alone take our radio and other things."

"So why didn't you fight them when they came? You could have used Papa's rifle to drive them off."

"Because we would have lost! They would have come back with reinforcements. They have bigger guns than we have."

Misaki lowered her voice. "I think that's what Papa is saying, Masao. Sometimes it's smarter to back down, to wait until you have the advantage."

"So you're saying that if one of us knows about an informer, we should keep quiet?"

"Masao, a lot of people hate the JACL because they cooperated with the authorities. But the JACL is made up of people like us. Maybe the way they handled things back home wasn't the best, but they did what they thought was right at the time. And if they had resisted and made it hard on the government, I'd wager that we'd still be here at Tule Lake. Then even more of the public would hate us. They'd have validation that we couldn't be trusted, that we'd help Japan defeat our country."

Misaki continued. "As terrible as things are for us now, I know it's going to work out. Already we're reading about how the government is working on programs to let us leave the camps. We all know people who have been let go to help farmers with their beet crops. Do you think this would be happening if we had all risen up in protest back in the beginning? Papa is right. It's best that we stay neutral."

Keiko looked around at the faces of her family. Misaki's logic had had its effect. Everyone, including Masao, nodded in agreement.

At that point in the conversation, Masao noticed that the fire in the stove was low. He knelt down and threw in more coals.

24

NEWBORN

Tule Lake Relocation Center, California
Saturday, January 30, 1943

Keiko's doctor, a kindly, middle-aged, Japanese-American man from San Francisco, had agreed with her that she would give birth sometime during the second half of January. As she got bigger and bigger, Keiko tired of everyone in her family asking if she thought it was time. "You'll be the first to know," she told them.

In the latter months of her pregnancy, her boss at the hospital insisted that Keiko work shorter days. Starting at Christmas, because he had ordered her home permanently until the baby arrived, she remained confined to the Tanaka apartment. During the day, when the sheets that separated their living space into bedrooms came down, the area became a larger living area. Still, there was no kitchen or bathroom. Tiny under even the best of circumstances, the apartment seemed to grow smaller and smaller as the days wore on. With everyone in her family either working or going to school, Keiko found herself alone for a good part of the day, her primary duty being to add coal to their potbellied stove.

Occasionally, when afternoons were pleasant, Keiko would take walks about the compound. But with January's weather and the ever-present mud, those days didn't happen often. Besides, standing outside three times a day to get fed in the mess hall was difficult enough for a pregnant woman. Those waits, together with additional treks to the bathroom and shower, gave Keiko more than enough appreciation for the wintry outdoors. Keiko vowed to herself that if she and James had a say in any future pregnancy, it would result in a birth in a warmer season of the year.

With little to do outside of writing letters, Keiko read. One of Misaki's jobs was to keep her supplied with books from the camp library. Toward the middle of January, Misaki informed her sister that there were no more to bring. Keiko had read every book available, numbering well over one hundred, including seven new titles donated earlier in the month.

Thus, when Keiko's water broke at twelve minutes after one in the morning on Tuesday, January 19, she knew not to get excited. From the two medical books available in the hospital, she had learned that when this happened, labor would not start immediately. She crawled quietly out of bed, careful not to wake her sisters, lifted the dangling sheet to enter her parent's bedroom, and whispered to awaken her father. He became far more agitated than necessary and succeeded in waking everyone in the building.

Isamu ran to his office and, for the first time since working there, used the phone to make a personal call, requisitioning the Army truck to transport his daughter to the hospital. Ten hours later, Keiko gave birth to a healthy baby girl on a cot identical to the one she had slept on back at the apartment.

In the hospital, newborns stayed separate from their mothers and were brought to them only during feedings. Because it was customary for a mother to remain in bed following childbirth, Keiko stayed in the hospital for more than a week. The irony of this tradition, she told her doctor, was that she was feeling weaker every day. He told her that was normal, but did acquiesce to her request to walk around the open bay.

Following that initial week, when she would normally have gone home, the doctor prescribed six additional days of hospital stay. He did this as a favor to Keiko—because it was January, and it was winter. Keiko appreciated his concern. Although she looked forward to having her child by her side at all times, returning to their apartment and once again standing in line three times a day for meals was not something she looked forward to.

During this second week in the hospital, with her doctor's approval, Keiko added minor exercises to her walking regimen. In between these and feeding the baby, she did not want for visitors, although rules restricted visiting hours and then to only two at a time. Her family visited as often as allowed. Having never been a grandparent before, Akemi no sooner came in the door than she wanted to hold her new grandbaby.

"You're going to spoil her to death," Keiko told her mother.

In an unusual display of humor, Akemi grinned and replied, "That's my job."

In addition to family, visitors included other Bellevue natives. With each came gifts for the newborn and mother. These ranged from baby clothes, to dried flower arrangements, to special food treats. Aside from missing her husband, Keiko could not have felt more loved had she been at home back in Bellevue.

A topic for discussion on which Keiko stood her ground concerned the feeding of her baby. At the time, the accepted way to feed a newborn was with a bottle and formula. In fact, the medical establishment supported this approach. Keiko overruled her doctor, saying that she couldn't imagine that formula was superior to mother's milk. "Throughout history, there wasn't any such thing as bottles or formula." He wisely backed down when presented with her forceful arguments.

One task in which Keiko did not fall behind was in her letter writing. Except for the day of her baby's birth, Keiko continued her letter regimen to James and her in-laws. The man in charge of postal services for Tule Lake told Keiko's father that no one even came close to sending or receiving as much mail as did Keiko. Of course, he wasn't telling Isamu anything he didn't already know. One of Isamu's jobs as the block manager was to sort incoming mail into cubbyholes located in his office.

During the months leading to the birth of their child, Keiko and James had worked out choices for their baby's name. Entering this negotiation, they had agreed that if their offspring were a girl, she would have a Japanese given name; if a boy, an English one.

The winners were Kazuko and Patrick. Keiko had explained to James that the name Kazuko referred to a harmonious, obedient, or peaceful child. For Patrick, James chose to honor his grandfather on his father's side, a man with whom he had spent time as a child and admired greatly.

Accordingly, Keiko announced the name of her baby the very afternoon of her birth. Having not been privy to the parents' letters, everyone was amazed that this important decision had been made so quickly.

It wasn't long before Keiko recognized that she and James had chosen well. When brought in for her feedings, Kazuko almost never cried. She was indeed the peaceful, obedient child.

Not long after giving birth, Keiko wrote to inform James and his parents. Her letter to James was the first:

Wednesday, January 20, 1943

Dear Precious James,

You got what you wanted! We have a daughter. She arrived yesterday, Saturday, at thirteen minutes after eleven o'clock in the morning. Kazuko is beautiful, James, and looks more like you than me, I think.

Our daughter weighed seven pounds, eight ounces, and was nineteen and a half inches long. She already has a full head of hair and is remarkably mellow. And guess what? She has your blue eyes! I swear that when I was holding her for the first time, my heart skipped a beat. When she opened those big eyes, it was as if it was you there looking up at me.

Don't worry. Everything went fine. I was in labor for just two hours. It wasn't bad at all. It's standard procedure for me and the baby to stay here in the hospital for a while. So I'm under good care.

I've got to go. It's coming up on Kazuko's feeding time.

I'll write tomorrow.

Love,

Keiko

Replies from James and Barbara came quickly, James's with a surprise. Barbara Armstrong's letter accompanied a box filled with clothing and diapers. In addition to being overjoyed at the new addition to

their family, both husband and in-laws expressed relief that everything had gone well despite the trying conditions in the camp.

From James's letters over the preceding months, Keiko had pieced
together more about what he was doing for the Navy. She was pleased
that he had not yet left the United States proper. After attending
boot camp, he had spent six months in specialized training schools
around the country preparing him to work with a new radar system.
In the process, he had worked aboard ships operating in and out of
Long Beach, California, testing equipment and designs.

But the writing was on the wall, James had told his bride about
a month earlier. His permanent assignment would be a new light
cruiser, USS *Santa Fe*, commissioned the previous November. It was
being built on the East Coast, in Philadelphia, Pennsylvania. If everything progressed as scheduled, the *Santa Fe* would leave dry dock
by late February or early March and sail to the West Coast before
departing for the Pacific. That ship would be his new home.

Along with that news, James had a surprise for Keiko that warmed
her heart to no end. James had received permission to visit his wife
and new baby. As best he could tell, he would arrive sometime in late
March or early April.

Keiko began counting the days. It had been nine months since
they had seen each other.

25

YES/YES OR NO/NO

Tule Lake Relocation Center, California
Thursday, February 25, 1943

After two weeks in the hospital, Keiko returned home on Tuesday, February 2. The family's previous nighttime living arrangements remained unchanged. Keiko continued to share her room with her two sisters, albeit with one new piece of furniture crowding their already tiny space: a baby crib, which Isamu and Masao had built with scrap lumber and the help of a neighboring carpenter. Keiko admired its clever design—a curved bottom that allowed for easy rocking.

Continuing her sweet disposition, Kazuko rarely cried and fussed only when hungry or in need of changing. Akemi, as block mother, kept Keiko supplied with clean diapers. But in an attempt to maintain her sanity as harsh cold weather kept everyone indoors, Keiko convinced her boss to allow her to return to work part time. In fact, at the time, there was a shortage of nurse aides at the hospital, and her boss acquiesced quickly to Keiko's request. Akemi endorsed Keiko's return to work. Except for Keiko's need to return periodically to the apartment to nurse her baby, Akemi would have gladly babysat all day, she enjoyed it so much.

The cold wintry days that confined everyone to small spaces made everyone grumpy. During warmer months, sports had kept people active and dominated their time outside of work. Many of the men

146

and boys especially enjoyed baseball. Marathon races had featured teams from different wards. Also popular was hiking to a nearby rock formation called Castle Rock. Equipped with a sack lunch, some went every weekend. Keeping an eye out for rattlesnakes was the only requirement for an enjoyable day.

But as the winter mud and cold restricted outdoor activities, indoor functions prevailed. Keiko was pleased to see Masao, Misaki, and Shizuka enjoying themselves at weekend dances. With tables and chairs pushed to the side, mess halls provided an ideal location for dancing. All that was needed was a record player.

The recreation department, numbering well over one hundred volunteers, worked hard to keep internees' interests satisfied. In fact, many of the Issei and older Nisei, stripped of mundane duties they would have had back home as working men and women, took up hobbies they would never have had time for otherwise. Acting in plays, singing in choirs, learning embroidery and sewing, making jewelry, playing *Shogi* (a game similar to chess) and Monopoly, taking English classes, playing Ping-Pong—all of these activities and more drew many participants. Talent shows became extremely popular. Those who had experience or talent in writing worked on the staff of the *Tulean Dispatch*, a three-column mimeographed newspaper.

Other than the birth of Keiko's baby, another happening that had received some notice since autumn was that Misaki had a boyfriend, a young man named Takeo Sato, whom Keiko remembered helping her father sell produce back in Bellevue. The two were spending more and more time together. In the same way that Keiko had shared her experiences with her fiancé with her sister, Misaki reciprocated. She described Takeo as reserved, but one who could always make her laugh. Above all, he had a way of making her feel special, more than anyone had before, Misaki said. From Keiko's point of view, it was clear where this relationship was headed.

But there was one huge impediment standing in the way of Misaki's romantic future. At the same time that Sato began dating Misaki, he also became a close friend of Masao. That was good for Masao, but unfortunate in that their relationship fed off one another in one aspect: they had both decided to join the military at the first opportunity. As his family knew, Masao had thought about joining the service ever since Pearl Harbor and had been hugely disappointed when his military classification made him ineligible for the draft. Keiko reminded Misaki about her experience with James; she told her not to be disappointed if her efforts at discouraging Sato came to naught.

And so it was with considerable excitement that Masao and Takeo greeted the news that came from Secretary of War Henry L. Stimson at the end of January: "The War Department announced today that plans have been completed for the admission of American citizens of Japanese ancestry to the Army of the United States." In addition to removing those obstacles for serving in the military came a simultaneous decision to allow loyal Japanese civilians to work in war-related industries.

To many Japanese Americans, this new policy signaled that the government had realized its mistake in incarcerating them in the first place. But a significant complication arose almost immediately. To leave the camps, either for military or civilian work, the government handed out applications in the form of a questionnaire. For male Nisei seventeen or older, this document was called Selective Service Form DSS 304A. A similar form, the War Relocation Authority Application for Leave Clearance (also called the Loyalty Questionnaire), applied to Issei and female Japanese citizens. Most of the questions on these forms were routine. Two, however, Numbers 27 and 28, single-handedly erased any goodwill that the government had created in its attempt to redress the abuses Japanese Americans had borne because of their internment.

As Keiko read these questions on her form, she wondered what the government was thinking. Couldn't they have anticipated the irony these questions elicited—specifically for the Issei—but also for all internees?

Question 27: If the opportunity presents itself and you are found qualified, would you be willing to volunteer for the Army Nurse Corps or the WAAC?

Question 28: Will you swear unqualified allegiance to the United States of America and forswear any form of allegiance or obedience to the Japanese emperor, or any other foreign government, power, or organization?

Questions 27 and 28 from the Selective Service form for Nisei men were similar:

Question 27: Are you willing to serve in the armed forces of the United States on combat duty, wherever ordered?

Question 28: Will you swear unqualified allegiance to the United States of America and faithfully defend the United States from any or all attack by foreign or domestic forces, and forswear any form of allegiance or obedience to the Japanese emperor, or any other foreign government, power, or organization?

Isamu, as block manager, soon found himself at the receiving end of intense arguments. Painful feelings that many had repressed came boiling to the surface. The government had forcibly taken everyone in the camps from their homes and interned them without legal process. For that same government then to ask them to fight for the United States was, for some, too much to bear. Emotions ran raw, particularly among the Kibei, those Japanese Americans born here, but who had temporarily returned to Japan for an education. To them, voting yes/yes was unforgivable. Members of the JACL, when they tried to organize discussions regarding these questionnaires, were labeled as *inu*, or dogs. So as not to anger anyone who came to vent, Isamu again did his best to remain neutral in the heated discussions.

Knowing that everyone in his family would soon have to make his or her own decision regarding the disputed questions, Isamu asked them to join him after dinner for a private discussion. Owing to Misaki's interest in Sato and the real possibility that this relationship might evolve further, Isamu invited him to participate.

With everyone gathered around the coal stove, once again sitting bundled up in their coats on one of three chairs the family had acquired or the edge of a bed, Isamu began. "You've all read the questionnaires that we need to sign, one way or the other. I think that it's important that we discuss how we're going to vote—and what the implications might be, either way."

Her hand on Kazuko's crib, rocking it gently, Keiko looked about the room. When no one volunteered to speak, Isamu gestured to his son.

Masao took the hint. "I have mixed feelings, Papa. As you know, from the beginning I've been anxious to join the Army. But to do that, I would have to vote yes/yes, and that would not be fair to you."

Isamu nodded. "You should answer the questions as you see fit, Masao, not as I would. Besides, you do not know how I will vote."

"But how could they ask you and Mama to swear allegiance to the United States when you can't even be citizens? If you vote yes on Question 28, you'd be rejecting your birth country. Technically, you'd be a person without a country. You should vote no/no."

Isamu reacted. "That's all true, Masao, but if I do that, there'd be no guarantee that we'll stay together as a family. There's already talk that the no/no people will be sent back to Japan. I've spent most of my life here. I'm too old to go back." He gestured back to Masao. "But, like you, your mother and I have mixed feelings about how *you* should vote. Do you think that we want our only son to go off to war? But I also understand your wanting to show your patriotism. You *are* a citizen of this country."

Everyone pondered these thoughtful words from the family elder. Misaki, standing by Sato, spoke next. "Did you see the *Dispatch* from last week? It said that thirty percent of the eligible Japanese Americans in Hawaii had already volunteered for the service. Over 7,000 volunteers, it said."

Masao snapped back. "Yes, but it's been a lot easier over there. Nothing ever happened to them. They never got sent away to camps like we did."

Keiko knew that this was a sore point for the Japanese Americans who lived stateside. The percentage of Japanese Americans among the Hawaiian population was so large that it had been impractical to intern them, and it was never even considered. Why had those on the West Coast been treated so differently?

Isamu turned to Sato. "What do you think, Takeo? Masao tells me that you also want to join the service."

Sato paused for a moment before standing, perhaps surprised that he had been called upon. He cleared his throat. "I think that it's important that I demonstrate to our government that I am a loyal American citizen. That's what this has all been about, you know. We've been sent here because too many people think that we can't be trusted." His face turned sad. "I've already talked to my parents about this.

"My father is very bitter and says that he will vote no/no, and I understand why he would do that. My parents lost almost everything back in Washington. They aren't as young as you, and I fear for what is going to happen to them. But I also believe that it is my duty to bring honor to my family, to our people. That is why I want to volunteer, but my parents are against it."

Keiko watched as Misaki listened intently to her fiancé. Misaki reached up to take Takeo's hand in a show of support. Over recent weeks, Keiko had watched their affection grow. They were a good match.

Isamu spoke sincerely. "You speak very well for yourself, Takeo. Despite what they're saying now, your parents will be very proud of you." His eyebrows rose. "By the way, isn't it time that we meet your family. Misaki tells me that you have an older sister too. Hiromi? Is that her name?"

Sato nodded, seemingly embarrassed by the suggestion. From Misaki's reports and her own assessment of Sato, Keiko knew him to be a private person. In fact, Misaki herself had only recently met his family.

Isamu motioned to his daughters. "These questionnaires affect all of us. You also will have to fill them out if you want to leave for a job. Would you like to say something?"

Misaki turned toward Keiko, wondering if her sister wanted to talk instead. Keiko gestured for Misaki to go ahead. They were of the same mind. Shizuka hadn't voiced much of an opinion.

Misaki stood, her hands stuffed inside the pockets of her coat. "Keiko and I have talked about this, and it's as clear as day what happened here. Whoever wrote this questionnaire wasn't thinking. Anyone with half a brain could have forecast the problems these questions would cause. By releasing these questionnaires the government has, in effect, called into question the legality of our internment. I'd wager that there were many who understood this and argued against it. But they were obviously overruled."

Isamu held out his hands. "So what are you saying, Misaki? Which way are you going to vote?"

"Keiko and I have decided to vote yes/yes. The sooner that we Japanese integrate ourselves back into society and prove that we are loyal Americans, the better. We have to put ourselves above some dumb politicians. And, if we do this, I think that it will all work out."

All eyes turned toward Isamu, who was looking intently at his daughter. After a moment, he nodded and responded softly. "I agree with Misaki. For us to cause trouble would only make things worse. I have decided to vote yes/yes, and I know that this is not going to make me very popular."

As Keiko listened, she felt so proud of her father. When push came to shove, he was showing integrity and honor, responding exactly the way he had taught his children. But with his next words, he also revealed that he hadn't given up.

"With time, I believe that this country will accept even me as a citizen. I will just have to wait my turn."

26

BAD ODDS

Monterey, California
Saturday morning, October 28, 2000

er Uncle Masao looked so young. From the picture Kazuko remembered of him on her mother's dresser, she pictured him as more mature. It was probably the military uniform. In her previous night's dream, she had wanted to spend more time with him. Now, remarkably, she had been given a second opportunity.

Kazuko talked fast. "You say you're Masao Tanaka?" *I have to be sure.*

"That's what I said." Masao winked. "You have a good memory."

"Your father is Isamu, and your mother is Akemi?"

"Tell me again who you are."

"My name is Kazuko—" Kazuko caught herself barely in time. She had nearly stated her last name. "But if I told you who I really am, you wouldn't believe me. Please! I don't have much time."

"What a coincidence! I have a brand-new niece whose name is Kazuko. She's only two months old." Masao seemed genuinely concerned. "Are you in trouble?"

Kazuko! He has a niece named Kazuko! "Yes, but not the kind of trouble you could ever imagine. Could I ask you some questions, please?"

"Well, before we freeze to death, let's go back to my apartment. The wind is terrible today." He gestured. "Come on."

Kazuko pulled her jacket—Masao's jacket—tightly around her neck and picked up her stride. From her experience the previous night, she knew that her time travel could end at any moment.

Kazuko looked about, taking in her environment. What she saw, as far as the eye could see, was row after row of colorless buildings covered in black tar paper, identical to those she had seen in pictures from the camps. There was no paving, only paths of dirt and mud.

They arrived at a building that looked no different from the rest. Masao opened the door and motioned her inside. "If you had hoped to meet my family, your timing is bad. No one's here. Most of us are working; I was on my way to the mess hall. Shizuka's in school. She's my baby sister."

Two windows added only a touch of light to the dreary-looking room, and it didn't seem much warmer inside. The apartment was small, and Kazuko found it hard to imagine that two adults, four almost-grown children, and a baby called this place home. The space appeared simultaneously both sparse and congested. Beds, chairs, storage boxes, and other pieces of simple furniture crowded the floor, with narrow paths marking boundaries to what appeared to be different bedrooms. Ropes coiled up on the walls adjacent to the pathways obviously got stretched across at night to support blankets or sheets for privacy. In the middle sat a potbelly stove. Clothes hung from the walls. A few brightly colored wall posters provided some relief to the meager surroundings.

"Would you like to sit down?" Masao rubbed his hands together and made his way to the stove. He put his hand into a large glove, reached into a metal bucket, took out a lump of coal, and added it to the fire.

"Thank you, but I won't be staying long." *Time's running out.* "Besides Shizuka, you have two sisters, twins, Keiko and Misaki. Is that correct?"

"How do you know all this? From your hair and the way you're dressed, you don't look like you're from around here." He looked at Kazuko closely. "And where did you get those glasses?"

"Please, I don't have much time."

Masao slammed the door shut on the stove, startling Kazuko. He stood tall. "Okay. What is it you need to know? How can I help you?"

"What is the date, please?"

Masao appeared perplexed.

"Please bear with me."

"All right. It's Wednesday, the seventeenth of March, 1943."

Only four days before Sato proposes to Aunt Misaki! "Do you know Takeo Sato?"

Masao's eyes widened. "Yes, he's dating my sister, Misaki. And he's a good friend of mine too."

Where do I go from here? Kazuko had verified all of the members of the family, including Aunt Misaki's fiancé. Except one! "Do you know James? Keiko's husband?"

"Of course I know James. He's joined the Navy and is in training in California somewhere."

Kazuko, facing opposite the door, heard it open behind her. Masao, looking over Kazuko's shoulder, stared past her. "Keiko! You won't believe it! We have a visitor whose name is also Kazuko. Bring my niece over here so that we can show her off."

Kazuko's heart was thrashing. She would soon see her mother as a young woman! *And herself!* She leaped to her feet and turned to look.

* * *

But it was too late! Kazuko's eyes flashed open, her heart pounding so hard she thought it would explode from her chest. "No!" She turned over and smothered her face in the pillow. In another second, she would have seen her mother. She cursed aloud, regretting not taking the time to give Masao some important advice: begging him not to join the army.

The dream had been *so* realistic. As her breathing quieted, Kazuko pulled up the covers and commanded herself to calm down. She understood, disappointingly, that the reality she had experienced in her mind was no supernatural event. Her dream was simply a manifestation of her existing knowledge. But continuing a dream from a previous sleep—for the second time in as many nights—had never happened to her before.

For that reason, Kazuko chose to believe that there had been a higher purpose to her experience. She had met Masao and verified the names of her relatives. *But so what?* She had learned nothing new.

Was she subconsciously searching for an unknown truth, not knowing where else to turn other than the unconscious reaches of her own mind? Or, more realistically, as Patrick had suggested, had she simply driven herself into a frenzy because of a few factual inconsistencies uncovered since her mother's stroke?

From beneath the sheet, Kazuko checked her bedside clock. It was nearly five o'clock and that meant it was almost eight on the East Coast, specifically in the state of New Jersey. On her return home the previous evening, after another uneventful day at the hospital, Kazuko remembered that there was one other family member still alive who might be of help: Uncle Wally, the younger of her father's two brothers.

Her grandparents Harrison and Barbara Armstrong had passed away some decades earlier, having survived one of their three sons. Tragically, Uncle Benjamin, who had survived World War II fighting in Europe, died in a car accident not long after he returned home. Compared to James, Uncle Wally still possessed his faculties. But he and his wife were in fragile physical condition and had recently moved into an assisted-living facility.

Kazuko padded down the steps of her two-bedroom condo to the kitchen, turning up the heat on the way. After two cups of coffee had sufficiently defogged her brain, she dialed the number. It was early in New Jersey too, but Kazuko knew Wally to be an early riser.

"Uncle Wally, this is your niece Kazuko calling from California."

Wally had known of Keiko's stroke, and Kazuko brought him up to date on her condition, as well as her father's deteriorating mental state. It was not a happy conversation.

Finally, Kazuko decided to broach the subject of the pictures, the real reason for her call. She figured that, if anyone else in the family had kept photographs from the 1940s, it would have been her Grandpa and Grandma Armstrong. Especially since Kazuko had been their first grandchild. Surely, James would have given a second set of the Tule Lake photos to his parents.

Kazuko felt the hairs on her neck stand straight when Wally said that he remembered the pictures. They had been part of his parents' personal items, he said, distributed to family members after Barbara, who outlived her husband, passed away.

Kazuko recalled going to the funeral with the rest of her family.

"Did you see the photographs, Uncle Wally?" Kazuko blurted out.

"Of course! As I remember, James had them taken during a visit there while he was in the service. There were several of you. You were just an infant." A pause on the line. "You haven't seen them? I had assumed that you'd be the one who had them now."

Why would he think that? "Uncle Wally, why would you think that I had them?"

Again a delay, this one longer than the last. "I would assume that because I gave them to your mother at the funeral." A shorter pause. "I gave the pictures to her because they were from your side of the family."

* * *

Ten minutes later, Kazuko had nearly worn a path between the kitchen and the front door as she digested this new piece of evidence. *Although it is remotely conceivable that Mom lost the original photos at Tule Lake, there is no way that she could have misplaced a second set given to her some thirty years later!*

Boxed in by facts that painted further evidence of a cover-up, Kazuko retrieved the book she had thrown onto the sofa the previous evening. She took it to the kitchen and removed the photo that was the basis of so much turmoil in her mind. She examined it closely. The picture looked old, mostly because it was black and white. Beyond that, it had obviously been handled a lot; the edges were frayed and curling. It measured three inches by three inches, all within a white border.

Recalling the suspicious manner in which her Aunt Shizuka had examined the photograph the previous evening, Kazuko located her magnifying glass to take a closer look. First, she pored over the backside. It would have been too much to hope that there had been writing, or a stamp perhaps, to indicate the name of the photographer or his business.

The photographer had framed the photograph well, with only a blurred hint of the drab buildings to the rear. Because Keiko appeared in what looked to be a long heavy coat, Kazuko concluded that it was a cold day, not surprising considering the late March or early April dates when the photograph likely was taken. Her father looked handsome in his uniform and hat. All that was visible of the baby was a plaid blanket and a tiny splotch that could have been hair and a face. As Keiko had done with her husband's pictures, Kazuko wished that her mother had included a negative. An eight-by-ten blowup would have revealed more of the baby's face that Kazuko knew to be her own.

Kazuko sipped her coffee, agitation building. *Where else can I go for information?* Abruptly, she remembered something. Sato said that her father had hired a professional photographer from . . . from . . . Klamath Falls! That explained, of course, why there was no negative. Even back then, professional photographers likely did not relinquish their negatives.

Kazuko sprinted upstairs to her office, the second of her two bedrooms, and flipped on her computer. While it was booting up, she reached for her AAA map of the western United States to confirm the location of Klamath Falls. It was the nearest large town to where Tule Lake had been located back in the 1940s, the camp's official post office address being Newell, California.

Kazuko typed quickly. Combining *Klamath Falls* and *Photography* on Internet Explorer, five entries popped up: John Matthews Photography, Sherman Photography, BP Photography, Jessica's Photography Service, and John Clayburn Photography. Kazuko considered the odds, knowing that they were long. First, what were the chances that even one of these studios had existed some fifty-seven years earlier? And even so, how likely was it that someone from that studio had taken the pictures, and further, that he would have saved negatives from a project so old? Kazuko uttered an expletive as she remembered that Sato had described the photographer as an older man.

Kazuko turned toward the clock on her desk. It was 5:35 a.m. It took only seconds of internal debate before she made up her mind. Her father had always complained that she was too impulsive, making snap decisions that weren't always the most logical. Ignoring that criticism, she did a quick Internet search, determining that what she had in mind was feasible. She made online reservations, first for air and then for a car. Flying at the last minute was expensive but, under the circumstances, Kazuko decided that cost was irrelevant.

Kazuko had to hurry. The flight to San Francisco from Monterey left at 7:30, connecting to Klamath Falls, Oregon, arriving at 11:15. There'd be a rental car waiting, leaving her the remainder of the morning and the entire afternoon to do her research. Her departing flight at 5:45 p.m. would put her back in Monterey before midnight. Before leaving her desk, she printed a list of the photographers.

Kazuko sprinted upstairs to the shower, details of her trip spinning through her mind. She could be out of the house in forty-five minutes. Except for the picture and the stack of cash she kept for emergencies like this, there was no need to pack anything. There was no time for breakfast; she'd grab something at the airport. From San Francisco, she'd have time to call Patrick to let him know of her plans. He'd call her crazy.

No matter. This was a long shot, but one that Kazuko knew she had to take.

27

MISSED COMPANION

Tule Lake Relocation Center, California
Sunday Morning, March 21, 1943

For the past week, Keiko had been giddy with anticipation. James would be coming to visit as part of a twelve-day furlough. He would stay five nights at Tule Lake. From there, he would go to Bellevue for another three nights with his family. It had been eleven months since Keiko had watched him head south on the train from Kirkland.

With her mind pulled in so many directions and knowing that she couldn't possibly give God much attention, Keiko had begged off going to church. With the rest of the family gone, Keiko relaxed as she nursed Kazuko next to the warm potbelly stove. Her half-day afternoon work schedule at the hospital had been particularly strenuous this past week.

A portion of everyone's duties at the hospital included prevention work, warning residents of potential dangers to their health. Because the Tule Lake camp lay within a defined plague area, medical personnel warned residents to stay clear of chipmunks, ground squirrels, and rats. Another infectious disease, Tularemia (named after Tulare County), also called rabbit fever and spread through ticks and deer flies, was a concern. In addition to getting the word out to all block managers, Keiko had arranged to have an article written for the *Tulean Dispatch*—all this on top of one duty she shared with Misaki—soliciting donors and running the hospital blood bank. There had been more donors than usual this past week.

Two days earlier, the Tanaka family had celebrated the two-month birthday of their new addition. Following the hourly feedings that had dominated her first month, Kazuko had settled into a three-hour cycle that made for an easier time of it, particularly after Keiko returned to work in late February. Misaki, as well as colleagues at the hospital, urged Keiko to transition Kazuko to formula, but Keiko told them, emphatically, that she wanted to nurse as long as possible.

The past month-and-a-half had seen many changes at Tule Lake, all beginning with Secretary of War Stimson's end of January announcement. Revised edicts and rules came frequently, mostly supporting changes all Japanese wanted: increased rights that would lead to their release from camp. The first step involved registration, using the Loyalty Forms. However, deadlines for their completion came and went because of the lack of response. Camp officials were concerned.

Still confused and irritated by Questions 27 and 28, many Issei refused to sign. Worse, several weeks earlier, thirteen agitators found themselves in jail after beating others with whom they disagreed. Many suspected the Kibei to be the troublemakers, who thought that the only proper response to the inflammatory questions was a no/no vote.

Aside from those troubles, there were many progressive pronouncements. Solicitations went out to both citizens *and* aliens who were especially fluent in Japanese and English to apply for positions at the Military Intelligence Language School in Camp Savage, Minnesota. And a recruiter from the Women's Army Auxiliary Corps (WAAC) came calling; other than nurses, females serving in the WAAC were the first women to serve in the Army. Also, especially welcome to families who had inadvertently split up during the initial internment sweep, a new policy allowed evacuees to transfer to other camps. And those Nisei who volunteered for duty in the Army, but failed to be inducted for any reason, were given indefinite leaves. They did not have to return to camp. At the national level, a naturalization bill for Orientals was introduced in the House of Representatives.

Surprisingly, the Nisei at Tule Lake displayed the least patriotism of any of the Japanese-American internment camps. Percentage wise, Minidoka in Idaho had the highest percentage of volunteers for the Army. True to their word, Masao and Sato followed through on their convictions. By the end of February, they had registered and were waiting for orders. If accepted, they knew that they would be headed to Camp Shelby in Mississippi where they'd join the newly designated Japanese-American combat unit.

With restrictions easing for everyone, many at Tule Lake applied for civilian jobs outside the camp. Some jobs were temporary and others permanent. Sugar beet companies were actively recruiting workers. And as had been true since the threat of internment first arose, churches continued to do more than their share to support the Japanese. As Japanese headed east to take civilian jobs, the Church of the Brethren established a relocation hostel in Chicago, with capacity for up to ten evacuees per month from Tule Lake. Word getting back from that city suggesting that jobs were plentiful encouraged others, mostly the young, to transfer there. In another gesture of accommodation, the government allowed those leaving to take their ration books with them.

Along with these improvements to the lives of the interned Japanese came hardships identical to those affecting the nation as a whole: shortages and rationing. Mess halls declared that meals on Tuesdays and Fridays would be meatless. Sugar, butter, and coffee were other food items impacted significantly. No one went hungry because fish, eggs, and cheese were still plentiful. Rationing of nonfood items such as rubber, tires, and gasoline had less impact on those inside the camp. One rationed item, shoes, created overflow work for shoe repair shops.

Keiko looked down at her daughter. She was asleep. With that cue, Keiko placed her in her crib, rocked her for a minute to make sure she stayed asleep, and then added more coal to the fire.

As Keiko lay down on her bed for a moment of quiet peace, a luxury rarely afforded a new mother, she reflected on her family. She was proud of them, the way each had tried to make the most of their trying situation. Unfortunately, there were many in the camp who let their circumstances control and define their outlook on life. Sato's parents were a sad example.

Sato's parents' frame of mind had affected him markedly, especially when they told him they were considering repatriation, an
option offered by the government to Issei who wanted to return to
Japan. Spurring many of the Issei in this direction was their belief
that Japan would eventually win the war. Sato tried to convince them
otherwise, reminding them that the Battle of Midway (the previous
June) had done irreparable damage to the Japanese fleet.

Although Sato was determined to join the Army, he told Misaki
that he questioned that decision every day. He begged his parents to
remain in the United States and promised that, once the war was over,
he would return home to get them back on their feet.

Aside from Sato's—and thus Misaki's—worries, the Tanaka
family had much to be thankful for. Keiko had observed a perceptible
change in the household's mood after mother and daughter returned
home from the hospital. In particular, Kazuko's presence energized
Isamu and Akemi. When this was all over, and Kazuko had grown
up, Keiko wanted to tell her daughter how much of a blessing she had
been during this difficult period in their lives.

Among Keiko's siblings, all were making plans. Masao's mood
improved dramatically after he volunteered for the service. "It's as if
I now count for something, that my country appreciates me," he said.
That pride rubbed off on his father.

As for Keiko's twin, Misaki was floating on a cloud over her relationship with Sato. But Keiko knew that elation wouldn't last because
of his commitment to the military. In light of that inevitability, Keiko
wondered if Sato would pop the question before he left. More than
one conversation between the twins focused on the possibility. Misaki
was ready, she told her sister. She jokingly said that she wished her
engagement announcement could have some drama, like Keiko's had.

Keiko glared at Misaki. "No, you don't! I don't think Papa's heart
could take it."

Shizuka, a reserved young woman of few words, was the most
difficult of the family to read. They could never be sure of her mental
disposition. She had studied hard and was assured that she would
graduate from Tri-State High (thus named because most internees
had come from Oregon, Washington, and California) at the end of
the school year.

It was obvious to Keiko that, after Masao, Shizuka would be the next to leave the camp. Several of Shizuka's friends had applied for work in Chicago, and she seemed excited about such a prospect. But beyond her solemn, sometimes moody, existence, there had been one occasion two weeks earlier that had raised Shizuka's spirits significantly.

That incident occurred when Harrison and Barbara Armstrong visited a second time, their first trip to Tule Lake since the previous August. Barbara was desperate to see her new grandchild.

Compared to the tensions caused by the military during their August arrival, this visit went far more smoothly. Keiko suspected that Harrison had made arrangements or pulled strings beforehand to make sure there were no impediments this time.

Over a two-day period, during which the Armstrongs overnighted in neighboring Klamath Falls, the families spent quality time together, including visits to the apartment and having lunch together. Masao used his position in the mess hall to make special arrangements. All during their stay, Barbara wanted to hold Kazuko. Watching both grandmothers vie for her daughter's affections warmed Keiko's heart.

As with their earlier visit, the Armstrongs came weighted down with bags packed with clothing and other necessities. They brought something for everyone, including a box of chocolates big enough so that each member of the family could have two pieces. For Kazuko, they had brought a special gift: a high-quality plaid wool blanket, with muted colors of pink, green, and purple. Keiko immediately retired the old brown one she had received at the hospital after giving birth.

But it was Shizuka whose eyes were the first to light up upon the Armstrong arrival. Keiko had told the rest of the family what would happen, and they had agreed to keep it a secret. Isamu had made sure that their plan was acceptable to the camp administration.

Standing this time unattended in front of the gate outside the compound as the Armstrong car arrived, the Tanaka family stood back and waited. When Harrison opened the door to the car, Shizuka's collie, Princess, jumped out. It took a moment for Shizuka to realize what was going on.

"Princess, it's you!" shrieked Shizuka. It took only a moment before the eyes of loyal dog and mistress locked together, and they ran flat out toward each other.

As Shizuka and Princess hugged, kissed, and frolicked, both families converged quietly on the happy scene. There wasn't a dry eye to be found among them.

FINAL REQUEST

Tule Lake Relocation Center, California
Saturday morning, April 3, 1943

Keiko awoke and stared at her sleeping husband. From the first hint of light creeping through the window, she knew that it was about six thirty. She could have slept longer, but couldn't bear not spending as much waking time with James as possible. After all, in little more than twenty-four hours, he would be boarding a train to spend the remainder of his twelve-day furlough in Washington. Keiko couldn't complain: she had gotten the lion's share of his time, five nights. Because of the distances involved, four days were lost to traveling.

Kazuko had been easy on her parents during the night, requiring only two feedings. After three nights of James's getting up with Keiko for each feeding, Keiko told him to stay in bed and get some rest on this his next-to-last night at Tule Lake. Looking back, Keiko had to admit that having him assist had not been without benefit. Having been unacquainted with the process of nursing an infant, James took particular interest and tried to help as much as possible.

Keiko ran her finger along the back of James's ear. He stirred, looked up, and smiled his usual broad mile. "How did you sleep?" she asked.

"Just like my daughter over there, like a baby. It's been a long time since I've had this peaceful a night's sleep. It certainly is quiet here." He paused. "Of course, your lying here next to me might have had something to do with it." With that sentence, the expression on James's face became somber, as if another competing thought had spoiled the moment.

Keiko chose not to remind James that the Tanaka family's apartment shared the same building with three other families and was rarely quiet through the whole night. Nor the fact that Kibei who opposed the loyalty questionnaires had recently caused ruckuses and loud demonstrations well after dark. "Not always. But you're right. Most of the time."

The reason their night had been so serene was that the three-person Armstrong contingent happened to be the only family residing in a four-family structure. As block manager, Isamu had arranged some privacy for Keiko and James during their short stay together. A recent exodus of families leaving for work on beet farms had left one building empty. Other than two cots pushed together, Kazuko's rocking cradle, their potbelly stove, and a few personal items, they were alone.

Suddenly, without warning, James's face flushed scarlet, tears formed, and he began to cry.

"James, what is it?" Keiko didn't understand. Her husband had been upbeat over the past three days, and not once had she seen him this way.

James had trouble getting the words out. "Keiko, I had no idea that the camps were as bad as they are, that you'd be stuffed into these little apartments, that you'd be stuck out here in the wilderness, and that you'd be treated like prisoners. I feel so sorry for your family, and I hate the people who put you here." In frustration, he pulled his arms slowly toward his chest.

James had not known these details because Keiko had taken care in her letters to hide the dismal particulars of camp existence. Apparently, James's parents had done the same.

Keiko was up on her knees in a second. "Listen here, young man!" Realizing that she might wake Kazuko, she quickly lowered her voice. "In all our lives, a little rain has to fall." She held up her hands. "You're right! We don't have the most luxurious of accommodations, and we don't get out much. But you know what? We stay dry, and we don't go hungry. I read about what's going on in the Pacific, and what we have here would be like the Ritz Carlton to our soldiers there.

"There's no question! We shouldn't *be* here. It was stupid. But it's not going to last. It didn't take long before the government realized its mistake. People are leaving this place every day, heading all over the country." She paused, catching her breath. "And another thing, Mr. James Armstrong! The war will soon be over, and we'll spend the rest of our lives together."

At this point in her lecture, emotion was getting the best of Keiko, and her lips began to quiver, her voice trembling. She knew she was going to lose it, but she had one more thing to say.

"And you know what?" Keiko wiped repeatedly at the flood of tears, her cheeks soaked with liquid. "I have the most wonderful husband in the world, and I have a healthy baby girl that we made together." Keiko's chest heaved as she struggled to make her last point. "When you leave here, I want you to take this thought with you. I've never been so happy in my entire life!"

With that, Keiko couldn't go on any longer. She fell into James's arms and sobbed uncontrollably.

In the background, Kazuko started to whimper.

* * *

James's arrival the previous Tuesday morning had not gone unnoticed by the camp's population. While it was becoming a common sight to see Japanese men in uniform visit relatives at Tule Lake, it was quite another to see a uniformed Caucasian—this one in a Navy uniform that most of the population had never seen—who was not part of the military contingent controlling the compound. There had been more double takes than Keiko could count.

For some time, it had been known around the camp that Keiko's surname was not Japanese. But not until James arrived in the flesh, and everyone saw him and Keiko walking hand in hand, did they actually believe that Keiko had married a Caucasian. The irony of what they saw, together with the fact that he was sleeping and eating with all of the Japanese Americans at Tule Lake, was not lost on anyone.

After dinner on that first night, James and the rest of the family returned to the Tanaka apartment to talk. There was a lot to discuss, and James said that he'd prefer more privacy than the mess hall could provide. "Besides," he told his family, "I've seen my share of mess halls, and I can tell you that most of them aren't any better than what you have here." This statement surprised Keiko.

With everyone sitting around their trusty stove, including Princess curled up and sleeping, Isamu stood and spoke for the family. "James, we are so happy to receive you in our humble home. It's been almost a year, and you look much better for the experience, I have to say." Isamu clenched his fists and flexed his arms in a gesture of strength.

In fact, the first thing that Keiko had noticed when she first saw James was how much leaner he had become. From 180 pounds, he had reduced to a trim 165. It didn't take long under the covers before she realized that the fat she had remembered in certain places on his body was not to be found.

James seemed embarrassed. "Thank you. I can't say that what happened was on purpose. We get a lot of exercise, but a lot of good food too. Most of the weight came off during basic training."

Isamu continued. "We've been surprised—and pleased—that you're still here, that you haven't had to go out on a ship yet."

"Well, that's going to change soon. Time has gone by so fast. But other than basic training, I've been in school these past eleven months." James raised his finger to make a point. "Sorry. That's not quite right. I did spend a couple weeks on ships as part of my training."

Keiko watched Masao strain to catch every word. It hadn't been long after James arrived when Masao began bragging that he too would be joining the service. "You must be really smart for them to give you that much training," said Masao.

"I don't know about that. In basic training, we had to take what they called aptitude tests. That's where they decide what it is you would be good at." James gestured toward Masao. "I wouldn't be surprised if you end up taking those same tests.

"In any event, they decided that I would be good working with radios. I wish I could tell you more about what I do, but I can't. It's all secret. I'd love to brag to my father about what I'm working on, but I can't." James held out his hands, shook his head, and smiled deviously. "Ask me again after the war. I'll probably talk then."

Everyone laughed.

James continued. "But, for sure, I am now headed to sea. In fact, I'll no sooner get back to Long Beach next week than I leave for Honolulu where I'll be meeting up with my ship. We'll be based there. Keiko may have told you that my ship is called the *Santa Fe*, and it's brand new. It's what is called a light cruiser. It was built in Philadelphia, and it left there in late February. It got its name from Santa Fe, New Mexico."

James looked around the room. "Any questions?"

Misaki raised her hand. "What's a cruiser?"

"That's a good question. Before I left for the Navy, I didn't know either. It's a medium-sized combat ship with a lot of guns on it to shoot at ships and land locations. It can't carry airplanes like a carrier does. It's not as big as a battleship; those are the ones with the really big guns. Because of its smaller size, though, it can go pretty fast and for longer distances."

Masao raised his hand. "Are you allowed to tell us where you'll be going?"

James winced. "If I knew, I couldn't tell you. But, truthfully, I have no idea. I'm just one sailor on a big ship. I can only presume that we'll be sailing all around the Pacific. I'm sure you've read about all the islands where we've been fighting."

Isamu this time. "You won't have to get off your ship to fight, will you?"

"No. That's the job of the Army and the Marines. We're there to support them."

James looked around the room. "Well, that's about it for me. Like I said, all I've been doing is learning how to be a sailor. But what about you? Tell me the latest here at Tule Lake. Keiko told me in her letters about the questionnaires and the problems that caused."

For the next hour, the family brought James up to date, and he asked question after question. A few times Keiko noticed him looking sideways at her. He apparently realized that she hadn't always told him the full story, that she had purposely left out some of the more unpleasant details. To counterbalance those disagreeable aspects, Misaki jumped in and recited positive changes that had occurred since General Stimson's January announcement.

James reflected on what he had heard. "So people are allowed to leave for jobs. Have you thought about how this is going to affect you?"

Isamu summarized. "Yes, we have. Masao is obviously going to be the first one leaving, heading off to Mississippi. Shizuka!" Isamu pointed. "Why don't you tell James what you're planning?" As Isamu looked at Shizuka, he blinked. "Shizuka, are you okay? You don't look so well."

Keiko hadn't noticed until then either. Shizuka looked pale.

In a weak voice, Shizuka spoke. "I'm sorry about that. I must be coming down with something. But Papa is right; I do have news. I don't know if Keiko told you or not, but a lot of the young people here are headed to Chicago where there seem to be a lot of jobs. There's a hostel there where we can stay. I'll be graduating from high school soon, and I'm thinking about going there. Thanks to Keiko and Misaki, I've being working some hours at our dental clinic, and the dentist thinks that I would make a good assistant. And I sort of like that kind of work. Dr. Sasaki—he's the dentist—he says that if I move to Chicago, he'll make some inquiries and put in a good word for me."

James seemed impressed. "Good for you, Shizuka, good for you! And I'm sorry that you're not feeling well. Get better, okay?"

"Thanks! It's been great seeing you. But if you'll excuse me, I'm going to go to the washroom."

Akemi stood and placed her hand on her daughter's forehead. She then reached for Shizuka's coat and walked her to the door. Princess got up to follow, but Shizuka told her to stay. Mother and daughter spoke briefly.

Isamu had a big smile on his face. "But in addition to Masao and Shizuka, we do have a special announcement to make. Do you want to tell James what it is, Misaki?"

Misaki turned toward James, blushing. "I asked Keiko not to tell you in her letters, that I wanted you to hear it in person. This happened just a little more than a week ago." She held out her hand and displayed the engagement ring Sato had given her. "I'm engaged to be married."

James beamed, walked over, and gave Misaki a hug. "Wow! Congratulations! Who is the lucky guy?"

"His name is Takeo Sato. And, believe it or not, he actually lived not far from us back in Bellevue. What's more, he and Masao are good friends now." Misaki grimaced. "Too good of friends, actually, because they're both going off to Mississippi. That's something I'm not happy about but, like Masao, Takeo's determined to join the service. Because there is so little time, we've decided to wait until he gets back before we get married."

"That's wonderful, Misaki. When do I get to meet him?"

"I'll make sure he comes over tomorrow."

Isamu raised his hand. "Before I forget, there is one more thing that you need to know, James." He paused, as emotion affected his speech. "Your parents . . . your parents, they've done every conceivable thing they can to make our lives better here at Tule Lake. They've been here twice and could barely carry all the bags of supplies and gifts they brought for us. And, of course, you see Princess here. I wish you could have seen Shizuka's reaction when she arrived."

Hearing her name, Princess looked up.

"They've mailed us package after package of things that we need. You need to know that we'll never forget—or ever be able to repay—these kindnesses. And that doesn't even include your dad's work keeping our farm going."

James looked around the room and saw everyone nodding their approval.

The rest of the evening's discussion addressed the obvious: when would the Tanaka family and the two Armstrongs return to Bellevue? Those who were leaving the camps for jobs could go only to locations outside the critical military areas from which they had been ousted in the first place. For that reason, there was no point in looking for a job back in Bellevue because they would not be allowed to return there.

With this in mind, Isamu told James that he felt they had no choice but to wait it out, that the only place they wanted to go was home. In the meantime, they'd wait for the war to end, at which time James, Masao, and Sato would return to the family.

Following this sobering discussion, Keiko remembered that there was something else. "Tell them, James! Tell them what it is you planned for Saturday."

"Oh!" Everyone stared at him. "I do have a surprise. I've arranged for a photographer to come. From Klamath Falls. We're all going to get our pictures taken."

In the background, Kazuko started to cry.

James smiled. "Perfect timing, Kazuko. You tell them. I want to have a picture of my little daughter to take with me."

Everybody laughed.

After a moment, James looked at Misaki and added, "Takeo's soon going to be part of our family. Please tell him that we want him there too."

* * *

Saturday came and went. The session had gone as planned. The photographer, Leonard Marks, together with his teenage daughter who helped carry equipment, arrived at the camp by mid-morning. He suggested that the pictures be taken outside the compound facing Castle Rock, with the camp out of sight. Isamu asked James if he would mind if the camp was used as a backdrop instead. He made the astute comment that, fifty years from now, it would be important that anyone seeing these pictures know the context within which they were taken. James agreed completely.

Keiko counted about twenty pictures taken. The only disappointment—and it was a big one—was that Shizuka was not in any of them. She was too sick and had been in bed for the preceding twenty-four hours. The day before, Keiko had talked her into stopping by the hospital. The doctor diagnosed the grippe and told her to rest, saying that it would eventually pass. Except for Shizuka's absence, the picture taking session went well.

James paid the photographer for two sets of pictures and asked that he send them to Keiko. She was to keep one set and mail the other to his parents in Bellevue. He also asked Keiko to pick out one picture of them and the baby and send it to him on the ship.

* * *

It was past midnight on this, their last night together. Kazuko was sleeping quietly just feet away. Having been intimate one last time, Keiko and James held each other close. It was time to sleep. There would be an early wake-up call.

They were almost ready to drop off when James started to say something.

"What?" asked Keiko.

"Oh, it's silly. Forget about it."

"No. What is it you wanted to say?"

"Just one more time would you please show me how much you love me? I want to freeze that image of you in my mind and take it with me. Who knows how long it will be before we see each other again?"

29

A SOLDIER'S SORROW

Tule Lake Relocation Center, California
Monday afternoon, May 3, 1943

It was a fairly large group standing outside the gate. Keiko, her family, Takeo's parents and sister, and the relatives and friends of six other Army volunteers watched as a big Army truck pulled up. Eight soon-to-be soldiers were saying their good-byes to their families and their temporary home at Tule Lake

There had been happy occasions at that location, Keiko recalled, particularly when the Armstrongs came to visit. If one imagined a ledger, the sadness of this day balanced out the joy of those times. Masao Tanaka and Takeo Sato were leaving for the Army.

"You'll write as often as you can?" Akemi implored her son, her hands gripping him firmly by the shoulders.

Masao looked sad. "I'm sorry that I'll miss your special day this year. But, even so, you'll remember that I love you, won't you, Mom?"

Keiko had almost forgotten. Sunday was Mother's Day.

"I'll always remember that, Masao. And you promise to keep your *Senninbari* by you at all times?"

"Of course, Mom."

"I'm serious! Promise me that."

"I promise."

Akemi and her only son embraced for the final time. Masao then faced his father.

"We're counting on you to make us proud," Keiko overheard Isamu say.

"I'll do my best. You can count on that." They shook hands, and Keiko watched as Isamu drew Masao close and they looked at each other eye to eye.

Finally, in a three-way hug, with Keiko's left arm cradling Kazuko in the middle, trying to keep her from being squashed, she and Shizuka held their brother tight. Keiko whispered for him to be careful. Shizuka said that she loved him and told him to come back as soon as possible. Kazuko made her usual noises, and Masao kissed her good-bye.

Misaki had already said her good-byes to her brother, asking him to keep an eye on her fiancé. She was standing nearby, embracing Takeo. Takeo's parents and his sister, Hiromi, had already bade their farewells and were looking particularly downcast.

Each volunteer carried one suitcase as he boarded the back of the Army truck. As the vehicle drove off, hands on both sides of the invisible divide waved their wishes and good-byes. The new recruits were headed first to Fort Douglas in Salt Lake City, where they'd be formally inducted into the Army. From there they would travel to Camp Shelby in Mississippi, where they'd become part of the 442nd Regimental Combat Team, the special unit formed in January specifically for Japanese Americans.

As the truck drove out of sight, the various families dispersed as they walked back to their apartments. All had known that this day would come soon when, a week earlier, the Army had sent a medical team to conduct the physical exams required before induction. More than one volunteer's mother could have been forgiven for taking a closer look at her son's lower appendages, hoping for a diagnosis of flat feet, known to be a reason for disqualification. But none of the eight failed his medical exam.

But aside from the initial sadness at their sons' departure, the families also carried some newfound pride, knowing that they were making a statement to the country, to the government, that they were no different than those American families who lived on the other side of the camp fences. Their sons would defend the United States of America. With each family's sacrifice, they hoped that the government would finally accept them for what they were—loyal citizens and loyal aliens, the latter perhaps being allowed to attain citizenship one day.

The Tanaka, Armstrong, and Sato families walked together. When they arrived at the junction where the Sato family headed off in a different direction, Keiko and her family waited silently. Misaki said her good-byes and returned to her family.

"Are they going to be okay, Misaki?" asked Akemi. She knew that Sato's parents disapproved of his joining the army.

"I don't know. They're still planning to return to Japan, and that's killing Takeo. He's tried to talk them out of it, but they're stubborn. I don't know what's going to happen."

"How are you holding up?" Keiko had been trying to assess her sister's mood.

"I'm okay, Keiko. I've watched all along how you've handled James's leaving, and I'm trying to be as brave as you've been."

Keiko wasn't so sure how true that was. She had put up a good front, but it had been easy as long as her husband remained stateside. With him soon heading into harm's way, those worry-free days had passed. Worse, she now had one additional—and another upcoming—family member who needed her prayers.

As they continued walking toward their apartment, the remaining contingent stayed quiet, each left with his or her own thoughts. Even Kazuko, awake with eyes open, seemed to sense the solemnity of the situation.

Akemi turned right to look at her husband. "The *Senninbari* will keep him safe, won't it?"

Isamu reached over to touch his wife. "It certainly will, Akemi. There's no doubt about it."

* * *

The *Senninbari*, or the "Thousand Stitch Belt," to which Akemi was referring, had taken nearly a month to complete. In fact, the last of the required stitches had been finished only days earlier.

Keiko had only recently learned from her mother that the custom of the *Senninbari* belt was not that old. It had originated in modern Imperial Japan, a period of history that began in 1868. The belt was an amulet, a good-luck charm, presented by a woman to a man going off to battle. That woman could be any female relative. The belt, if kept in the possession of the warrior, was believed to offer protection from harm because of the love and effort that went into its creation.

Once Akemi knew that there was no turning back, that Masao was leaving, she began the process of creating the *Senninbari*. First, she obtained a length of material; for this *Senninbari*, the cloth had modest beginnings, originating as a large white bag used to transport rice. Before proceeding, she washed it several times. From that base material, she cut a length measuring a little more than a yard long and twelve inches wide.

The initial steps Akemi completed rather quickly. First, she hemmed the edges to keep them from fraying. Then, with a ruler and pencil, she marked off an area ten inches wide in the center. In this area, she placed two inscriptions, written in black ink: marked vertically on the left side was the soldier's Buddhist name, and on the right, a patriotic slogan. Akemi had chosen *bu-un cho-kyu* for "eternal good luck in war."

Between these two vertical captions on three horizontal lines, using red ink this time, Akemi wrote in English, "MASAO TANAKA" "FROM" and "MOTHER." Japanese considered red to be a lucky color.

Having finished that, Akemi moved on to the areas adjacent to the center inscriptions. On each side, she placed sixteen rows of dots, evenly spaced. Added together, there were one thousand.

What followed was where the real work began. Each of those pencil markings required a stitch, a different woman for each. No men could contribute. Typically, that stitch took the form of a French knot. Again, Akemi insisted on using red thread.

After Akemi had made use of her friends and acquaintances, she stayed in the mess hall night after night soliciting strangers to make their knots. Once there were no more women left in her mess hall, she moved to another one. One allowed exception to the process helped speed things along. If a woman happened to be born in the Year of the Tiger, she could sew either twelve stitches or a number of stitches that added up to her age. This custom helped considerably, and she found eight women who met this criterion, born in 1902, 1914, and

1926. So as not to impose on their generosity, she asked for only the minimum of twelve stitches.

Without complaint, women in the camp accommodated Akemi's requests. In fact, Akemi had provided a stitch for several of the other inductees. Nonetheless, it had taken more than three weeks to achieve the requisite number. In the end, nine hundred and twelve separate women had projected their best wishes and prayers toward the safety of Masao Tanaka.

* * *

Akemi brought her hand to her mouth, gasping, realizing that she shouldn't have mentioned the *Senninbari*. She added quickly, "Don't worry, Misaki! I'll help you."

Keiko looked at her twin sister. Takeo's pain had left its mark on Misaki, and Keiko sensed it. With determination in her voice, Misaki made her point. "No! I'm the one who now has to take on this responsibility. I'll have it done in no time."

The rest of the family understood that there was no rush. There'd be plenty of time for Misaki to make the *Senninbari*, to get the required one thousand stitches, and to mail it to Takeo in Mississippi before he faced the dangers of combat.

That wasn't the point! What was, was that it would be his own fiancée who would be making the *Senninbari* for him. That fact had devastated Takeo. He had left camp knowing that his own mother had abandoned any thought of keeping him safe from harm.

30

RELEVANT DETAIL

Klamath Falls, Oregon
Saturday morning, October 28, 2000

During her one-hour layover in San Francisco, Kazuko called her brother. Even after telling him what she had learned from her early-morning phone conversation, Patrick still thought that there had to be a logical explanation and that she was wasting her time. *Didn't he hear anything I said?* To Kazuko's thinking, Uncle Wally's statement about the pictures was unmistakable proof that their mother was hiding something.

Rather than spark an argument, Kazuko cut the conversation short. "Please tell Aunt Shizuka where I am and that I'll come by the hospital when I get back. I land before midnight."

As advertised by United Airlines, at 11:15 a.m. Kazuko's plane touched down at the Klamath Falls airport. Having no checked baggage and carrying nothing more than her purse, she headed straight to the Avis car-rental booth. After waiting twenty minutes while three other customers completed their rentals, she left the airport with local map in hand.

Kazuko glanced at her watch. It was noon. Plenty of time to find and check out the five photographers.

Scarcely a mile later, Kazuko cursed aloud, having forgotten that it was Saturday. Not all businesses of this sort stayed open for the weekend! *Why didn't I think of that before I left Monterey?* Still, it didn't matter. Stubborn as she was, Kazuko took some consolation in knowing that she wouldn't have taken her own advice to wait until Monday, even if she had remembered what day it was. If the proprietors weren't in their places of business, she'd track them down at home if necessary.

* * *

Three out of the five photographers listed for Klamath Falls had addresses on Main Street. From a nearby parking lot, Kazuko began her quest. Within a half-block's walk, John Clayburn Photography came into view. With her hands cupped to the window looking in, Kazuko could see that no one was inside. Fortunately, there was a phone number below the *Closed* sign. Kazuko dialed her cell phone and was relieved when someone answered.

"I'll be in after three this afternoon. Can you come by then?" the man who answered as "Clayburn" asked her.

"I'll see you then. Thank you."

Kazuko checked her list again. The two remaining establishments on Main Street were Sherman Photography and Jessica's Photography Service. Her luck changed; these stores were open.

The conversations at both began in the same way. "Hi. My name is Kazuko Armstrong, and I've flown here from Monterey in hope of finding a photographic studio that may have been in business during World War II."

"World War II?" responded the perky blond proprietor of Jessica's Photography. "I wish I could help you, but I opened up only about a year ago. And I moved here from Los Angeles. But I'll tell you what." She pointed left. "Sherman Photography is over there. I think they've been here for a while."

"Thanks!"

Sherman's Photography was more than a photographic studio. The storefront advertised prints in one hour, sold cameras and other photographic needs, and was open until six on Saturdays.

"World War II?" the middle-aged man responded identically. He had introduced himself as the proprietor, Jim Sherman. "That's a ways back, I don't have to tell you."

Kazuko removed the photograph from her purse and handed it

over. She explained that her picture was one of several taken fifty-some years earlier outside the Tule Lake internment camp. "I need to find the rest of those pictures, sir. If I could find the studio, I'm hoping that they might still have the negatives."

Sherman whistled. "Good luck with that! Could the photographer still even be alive? And if he isn't, what are the chances that someone saved the negatives?" He paused and reflected, perhaps realizing that he shouldn't have been so negative to someone who seemed so serious. "I've heard stories about that camp." He pointed to the picture. "Are those your relatives?"

"Yes. That's my mom and dad. And that's me too, as a baby."

Sherman shook his head. "My parents moved here from Memphis back in the sixties. It wasn't until I returned from college in 1984 that I opened this business. I can tell you for a fact that, of the photographers here today, the only one who was already in business when I started was John Clayburn. He's just up the street, but I don't think he's open on Saturday."

"That's encouraging. In fact, I already called him, and he'll be in after three."

Kazuko started to go but turned back. "You say that your parents were here in the sixties. Do you think they'd remember anything from back then?"

Mr. Sherman leaned against his counter. "They probably would have, but they've passed away. Sorry."

"Thanks. You've been a big help."

Kazuko realized that John Clayburn might be her best hope. So far, the others were too young to remember anything from that long ago.

Kazuko checked the time. Sherman's advice notwithstanding, she felt obliged to cover all her leads. There was time to visit the two others on her list, one on Washburn Way and the other on 6th Street.

* * *

Two hours later, Kazuko returned downtown. The two other proprietors, like Sherman, thought that her mission was hopeless. In addition to making Kazuko feel even worse, neither John Matthews Photography nor BP Photography provided any additional leads. Bruce Phillips of BP Photography had been at his studio, and she had had to call John Matthews. Again, neither had grown up in the area, and their collective historical memory went back only eighteen years. *Patrick was right. I've been on a fool's mission. What was I thinking?*

Kazuko parked her car in the same spot she had used earlier and headed back to John Clayburn Photography. It was almost three. Having been on her feet the better part of four hours, Kazuko took a seat on a bench not far up the street. *There's still hope.*

Watching people stroll the sidewalk, but with her mind swirling with thoughts that aggravated her even more, Kazuko realized, belatedly, that her strategy had been all wrong. A better tack might have been to ask people at random going down the street—particularly anyone who looked over seventy years of age—whether they had lived here early in their lives and whether they remembered any photographer from that period. *Why didn't I call the Chamber of Commerce? I'm such an idiot!*

In that canyon of despair, it took three rings from her cell phone before Kazuko noticed.

"Hello."

"It's Patrick."

Kazuko chose to cut him off. *I don't want to hear it.* "If you're calling to tell me how stupid I've been in coming up here, I now agree. I'm running into dead-ends right and—"

"Kazuko! Stop talking!"

It wasn't Patrick's nature to speak that way. "Patrick! What is it?"

"Mom's had another stroke. Thirty minutes ago, they did another CAT scan, and it looks like there's been a rupture somewhere near where the old one was. Dr. Siradnamalah wanted to go back in and do surgery, but Aunt Shizuka said no."

I should have never left this morning!

"Kazuko, can you hear me? Are you there?"

"I'm here, Patrick."

"You need to come home. With the new bleeding, Dr. Siradnamalah doesn't know how much longer Mom can hold out. It might be only a few hours, a day at the most, he says."

Kazuko checked her watch. "Patrick, my plane leaves in two and a half hours. I'll land at the airport before midnight, and I'll come right to the hospital."

Kazuko walked around the corner into an alley, proceeded far enough away from the street so that no one would hear, and broke down against an old brick wall. The cold hard surface seemed to commiserate with her dilemma.

Please, God, don't let Mom die before I get there!

* * *

Shaken by Patrick's unexpected news, Kazuko walked slowly back toward John Clayburn Photography, drying her eyes with a tissue as she approached the store. There were lights on inside. She walked in and observed a man, somewhere in his fifties, arranging the background in front of a photographic set.

"Mr. Clayburn? Thank you so much for coming in."

"You must be Ms. Armstrong. I had to come in to do some paperwork anyway. How can I help you?"

"Mr. Sherman up the street says that you've been here longer than any of the others and might be able to help me."

Kazuko showed her picture and told her story. Clayburn listened politely, took the photograph to a desk in the corner of the room, sat down, removed a large magnifying glass from a drawer, and pored over the surface, both sides.

"I've already done what you're doing Mr. Clayburn. There's nothing there that *I* could see."

Clayburn looked up, seemingly deep in thought.

Kazuko continued. "What year was it when you started your business here?"

"It was the late sixties. I may have been here before Sherman opened his studio, but not by much. I'm thinking hard, but I'm afraid I can't help you, ma'am. Like many who live here, I'm a transplant. I can't even remember whether there was another studio in town when I got here. I'm sorry."

A double veil of fatigue and despair settled over Kazuko. She couldn't remember a time in her life when she felt so defeated. It was time to go home. Her mother was waiting.

* * *

By the time Kazuko left John Clayburn Photography, it was 3:45. As she walked back toward her car, she realized how famished she was. Fueled only by adrenaline and her mistaken belief that she could somehow find the information she needed within the span of a few hours, she had forgotten to eat. Coffee and peanuts on the San Francisco-Klamath Falls leg had been her only nourishment since leaving the house. Her plan to grab a bite at the Monterey airport got delayed until San Francisco, and from San Francisco until Klamath Falls. But once she arrived there, lunch was a luxury she didn't have time for.

Kazuko did the math for her 5:45 flight departure. Allowing time to return the rental, there was plenty of time to grab a bite before heading back. On her walk from the car earlier, Kazuko had noticed the coffee shop ahead. She stared through the window and saw an array of sandwiches and desserts under refrigerated glass. *A sandwich will do just fine.* Inside, she pointed to the biggest sandwich and dessert she could see. "Give me a large coffee too, please."

Kazuko carried her food to a corner booth that provided a good view of both the inside of the coffee shop and the sidewalk outside. She wolfed down what turned out to be a roast beef and cheddar cheese sandwich and returned to the counter for a coffee refill. She slowed down to enjoy her dessert, bread pudding, one of her favorites.

With that physical need attended to, Kazuko looked around the coffee shop. There were two other customers: a man in a suit reading the newspaper and a young woman nursing a coffee, engrossed in a book. The female teenager behind the counter was busy, industriously cleaning various surfaces with a spray bottle and cloth.

Beyond the people, Kazuko noticed an establishment that had obviously been around for a while: an old, creaking wooden floor, wooden chairs and corresponding tables, large old windows with wavy glass, a bar front that looked like it might have once graced an expensive hotel, and an old cash register that wouldn't have been out of place in an antique store. All of this together created an inviting presence: a warm comfortable spot to take a load off, to relax, to sip one's favorite hot beverage, all the while pondering the day's events.

But the single feature that gave the establishment so much character was what hung on the walls. There were dozens and dozens of old photographs. Most of the pictures appeared to have been taken locally. There were pictures of the downtown, of the surrounding area when the town had not been as large, and many, many pictures of people, some going back perhaps a century, judging by clothing and hairstyles. Kazuko turned around to look at one behind her. It had an inscription: *Klamath Falls, circa 1933.* The walls provided a veritable visual historical record of the city.

Kazuko snapped to attention, checked the time, and realized that she needed to get a move on. She approached the old cash register and waited patiently for the girl behind the bar to respond. When she didn't, Kazuko cleared her throat. "Sorry, but I need to get going. Can I have my check, please?"

The skinny, pig-tailed girl smiled pleasantly. "Not a problem."

While Kazuko waited for her to tally the numbers, she looked at even more photographs hung on the wall beside the espresso machine. More pictures of people.

At once, Kazuko stepped backward and felt blood drain from her face. *THERE HE IS!* "I can't believe it!"

The cashier flinched at Kazuko's outburst. "Are you okay, ma'am? What's wrong?"

Kazuko pointed. "I need to buy that picture from you!"

"I don't think the pictures are for sale. They all belong to the owner."

Kazuko realized there was little time, and she needed to act fast. "Can you please call him or her? Tell him I'll pay whatever he wants."

"Which one are you talking about?"

"The one with the man standing beside the tripod.

Without asking, Kazuko ran behind the bar and leaned over the back counter to get as close as possible. The cashier, now on the phone, watched nervously.

Kazuko stared, her eyes inches from the picture.

This wasn't just any photographer posing beside his camera. This one had something special: hanging vertically on the side of the tripod was a walking cane.

To complement this detail that Sato had mentioned just two days earlier, there was a penciled inscription. It read, *Leonard Marks, 1947.*

31

SERENDIPITY

Klamath Falls, Oregon
Saturday afternoon, October 28, 2000

Given the significance of the photograph, together with the hand-written name, Kazuko considered fifty dollars a bargain. She rushed into the street but stopped short. What should she do? It was 4:15, only ninety minutes before her plane's departure.

Kazuko needed further information fast. Looking down the street, she took off at a trot, hoping that John Clayburn was still at his store. He had been the most knowledgeable—and sympathetic—person she had talked to. A hundred feet away, she could see him locking the door.

"Mr. Clayburn!" Kazuko yelled as she sprinted to catch up.

Clayburn turned and met her halfway. "Ms. Armstrong, what is it?"

"Do you have a moment, please?" Kazuko panted between words. "I have some new information I want to show you. I need your help."

Clayburn nodded pleasantly. "Let's go inside. It's a little cool out here." He switched on the lights. "What's up?"

"Mr. Clayburn, I've found a picture of the photographer who took my family's pictures." Kazuko handed over her recent purchase.

Clayburn examined the old photograph and looked up. "How do you know that this"—he looked again at the picture—"Leonard Marks is who you're after?"

"Do you see that cane? One of the people who was there that

187

day told me about the photographer. He remembered the cane hanging vertically from the tripod. And, look here, the date," she said, pointing, "just four years after my pictures were taken." Kazuko hesitated before asking, not sure if she wanted to hear the answer. "Does the name Leonard Marks mean anything to you, Mr. Clayburn?"

Clayburn shrugged his shoulders. "I'm afraid not. But I see what you're saying. That's such an odd detail." Suddenly, he squinted and appeared puzzled.

"What is it?"

"The name Marks does ring a bell though."

"A former client, maybe?"

"No, I don't think so. I'm trying to remember."

To disguise her impatience, Kazuko took a sidewise glance at her watch, knowing that time was running out. "Do you have a phone book we could check, please?"

Clayburn returned to the same desk he had used in her earlier visit and pulled out the book beneath his phone. He paged his way to the M's and ran his finger down the columns. "Sorry. There're no Marks listed."

"Darn!" *Why couldn't there still be a relative living here?*

Clayburn blinked.

"What is it? You're remembering something?"

Without answering, Clayburn rotated in his chair toward the monitor sitting on the opposite side of his desk, at the same time reaching down to switch on the computer on the floor. "It's coming back to me. Something happened in this town involving a Marks."

Kazuko stood quietly while Clayburn peered at his computer monitor. Peeking over his shoulder, she could see that he was scanning the archives of the *Herald and News*. Probably the local paper for Klamath Falls, she thought.

Before long, Clayburn focused in on one particular page. Kazuko could read the headlines: "Tragic Accident Kills Two Teenagers." He kept paging through the archive.

Kazuko fidgeted, knowing that she had to get going.

"I remember now!" Clayburn exclaimed finally. "Sylvia Marks. That was her name." He gestured toward the monitor. "This happened back in 1982. I have no idea whether she's related to your Leonard Marks, but it's possible."

"What happened?" Kazuko couldn't help herself, and she looked again. It was 4:45.

Clayburn folded his hands on the desk in front of him. "Sylvia Marks broadsided a car driven by a high school senior; she killed him *and* his date. She had run a stop sign. It was a tragedy for everybody."

"Was she drunk?"

"I don't think so. But there was a trial. She was convicted of vehicular manslaughter, but served only a couple of years in prison. Word at the time was that her attorney's fees ate up most of her money. She did keep the house and, after prison, moved back. I have no idea if she's still even alive."

Sounds promising. "How old was Sylvia back then, do you think?"

"Somewhere in her fifties, I'd say."

"Then it *is* possible she's Leonard Mark's daughter! And if so, there's also a chance she's kept all her father's stuff."

Clayburn couldn't disguise his skepticism. "I guess it's possible."

Kazuko pointed. "If she's not listed in your phone book, where do you think I could look to find her address?"

Clayburn seemed pleased with himself. "I *can* help you there. I don't know the exact address, but I can give you directions. I remember driving by the house when the trial was going on." He gestured toward the window. "The sun doesn't set until after six. There's still enough light that you'll find it easily. It's about five minutes away, and it's unusual enough you'll be able to pick it out." He wrote out directions and handed them over.

With both hands, Kazuko shook Clayburn's hand warmly. "I can't tell you how helpful you've been. Thank you so much."

"I wish you luck, Ms. Armstrong. You certainly seem determined." Clayburn handed Kazuko his card. "I'd be interested to know how this all turns out."

"That's the least I can do to repay you."

As Kazuko turned to go, Clayburn called her back.

"Yes?"

Clayburn closed his eyes. "A lot of this is just coming back to me. Whether or not this woman is related to your Leonard Marks, there is something that you need to know before you go out there. The accident devastated this woman. She had killed two people and knew that she was at fault. After she finished her time in jail, word was . . ." Clayburn acted as if he didn't want to say it, ". . . that she lost her mind. I don't know what that meant. On the other hand, that information is some fifteen years old."

Kazuko thanked Clayburn and left the store. It was going on five o'clock. As she walked up the street toward her car, the debate in her mind raged full force. Unless she headed—right now!—to the airport, she'd miss her 5:45 flight. But, practicality aside, Kazuko knew there was no way that she could keep herself from following through on this new lead.

With her brain searching for a way out of this dilemma, Kazuko realized that there was a solution to her transportation predicament: her rental car. Back in Monterey, she had checked the distance to Klamath Falls. Four hundred and fifty-four miles meant less than eight hours of driving. If she missed the plane, she could still arrive back in Monterey only a few hours later than when her plane would have landed.

With that decision behind her, Kazuko felt energized and jogged to her car, squealing the tires as she exited the parking lot, directions held in place by one thumb on the steering wheel.

Hang in there, Mom! Please don't be mad at me. Before you leave this world, I need to know what it is you are hiding from Patrick and me.

* * *

Clayburn's directions were straightforward, and Kazuko arrived at what was obviously the Marks house. It was a solitary structure, with no neighbors close by and out-of-place for southern Oregon: a two-story structure more suitable to the South during the Civil War. Although the house needed work, the grounds were tidy, indicative that either someone lived there, or there was a caretaker.

Kazuko parked on the street opposite and walked briskly toward the gated driveway. To the side was a walk-in gate with one hinge barely hanging on. Beside that gate was a metal mailbox. Kazuko opened it, not sure why she was doing so. The space was crammed with mail, junk and otherwise. Considering briefly whether it would be proper to deliver the contents to the house, she decided otherwise.

Dreading the thought of an eight-hour drive back to Monterey made Kazuko pick up the pace; planes were occasionally late, and she still might be able to make it. Stepping smartly up the three steps to arrive on the wraparound porch, Kazuko pulled open the dilapidated screen door and knocked. She listened intently. Nothing.

Kazuko tried again. She knocked loudly for some ten seconds straight. About ready for a dash to the car and a speeding-ticket-eligible drive to the airport, she sensed movement from within and looked down to see the doorknob turn.

The door opened, and Kazuko came face to face with a vision of someone who certainly looked the part for Clayburn's story: a woman somewhere in her late sixties or seventies, thin, and dressed in clean, but dated, clothing. She looked out, but said nothing.

Kazuko chose to be direct. "Are you Sylvia Marks?"

No response.

"Please, ma'am. If you are Sylvia Marks, I need to know if you are related to the photographer, Leonard Marks."

With the mention of his name, the woman's expression changed instantly, now warm and welcoming. "Do you know my daddy?"

Interesting! Without the visual reinforcement, one could have been forgiven for thinking there was a child behind that voice.

But with those five words, Sylvia Marks had given Kazuko two critical pieces of information. First, that she was, in fact, the daughter of Leonard Marks. And with that acknowledgment, Kazuko's time pressure vanished. She knew that she was facing a long drive home.

Second, however, Sylvia's reply implied something else. She had not said, *Did you know my daddy?* This meant that either Leonard Marks was still alive—unlikely considering his apparent age in the photograph from 1947—or that Sylvia thought that her father still lived. Kazuko didn't want to think about what that alternative meant.

"No, I don't know your daddy. My name is Kazuko Armstrong, and I've flown here from Monterey, down in California. Your daddy took pictures of my family back during World War II, and I came here hoping to find the negatives of some pictures he took." Kazuko paused, waiting for a reaction. "Can you help me, please?"

"Then you don't know my daddy?" Sylvia was clearly disappointed.

Kazuko replayed Sylvia's voice in her mind. Even her mannerisms mimicked those of a young girl. "No, I do not."

It took only a second before Kazuko regretted her response. Sylvia proceeded to close the door behind her. Surprised at the reaction, Kazuko, desperate and without thinking, stuck her right foot into the gap to stop the door from closing.

"Please, Ms. Marks . . ." It was time for a different approach. "It's true that I do not know your daddy, but my daddy, James Armstrong, does know Leonard." Kazuko decided that using the present tense might provide an advantage, as well as using Mr. Marks's given name.

With Kazuko's plea, the door opened again, and Kazuko witnessed a replay of that hopeful expression on the woman's face. "Do you know if my daddy is coming home today? He told me before he left that he wouldn't be gone long. He had to deliver some pictures."

What Sylvia had just said, coupled with the childish expression on her face, gave credence to Kazuko's earlier suspicions. "Sylvia, when did your daddy go to deliver the pictures?"

"Last weekend. He said he wouldn't be gone long."

Trying to keep her face from revealing what she now knew for a fact, Kazuko had a moral decision to make. Should she play along to get what she needed or leave now to inform community services of a woman in Klamath Falls who desperately needed help? Determined to find the photographic negatives at all costs, she decided she could do both.

"Sylvia, your daddy took some pictures for my daddy, but my daddy lost his pictures. My daddy needs the negatives so that he can make new pictures." Kazuko, eager to know whether Sylvia would be of any help, chose to push the envelope. "Do you know where your daddy keeps his negatives?"

Sylvia put her hands on her hips. "Of course, I know. I help my daddy all the time. He keeps all of his picture things in the basement."

Having already decided to speak at Sylvia's level of comprehension, Kazuko continued. "Because your daddy knows my daddy, do you think he would mind if you let me get the negatives for him? You would make my daddy very happy."

Sylvia pursed her lips, shaking her head rapidly back and forth.

"Daddy told me that he always makes sure he gets paid before he delivers his pictures."

"Your daddy is very smart, Sylvia. That's the way a businessman has to think. Otherwise, there are people out there who would cheat you. I can pay you for the negatives. I bet you've worked with your daddy a long time. Maybe you know how much money he would charge for them."

Sylvia answered confidently. "Yes, I do! For something like this, he would charge at least twelve dollars."

Kazuko opened her purse, removed her wallet, took out a twenty-dollar bill, and handed it across. "Sylvia, here is twenty dollars. If you will let me look through your daddy's negatives, and I can find the ones your daddy took for my daddy, I will give you another twenty dollars. Does that seem fair?"

Sylvia rocked back and forth on her feet, perhaps debating whether Kazuko was trying to cheat her.

Kazuko decided that she needed something else to win her over. She handed across the framed picture she had been carrying. "If you want, I'll give you this picture of your daddy. I'm sure he'd want you to have it."

Sylvia took a quick look and handed it back. "That's not my daddy."

The impact of Sylvia's statement caused Kazuko to back up a step. She closed her eyes. It was all she could do to not yell out, *WHAT DO YOU MEAN, THAT'S NOT YOUR DADDY?* Instead, she composed herself, took a deep breath, and asked in a calm voice, "Isn't your daddy, Leonard Marks?"

"Oh, yes, but my daddy's not that old. That sort of looks like my daddy, but it's not."

Kazuko slowly released her breath. Sylvia's memory of her father was obviously one from childhood—which went hand in hand with her girlish behavior now.

Kazuko tried to get things back on track. "Well, I'm positive that your daddy would want to help my daddy, don't you think?"

"I guess. You *are* paying for them after all."

And with that, Sylvia Marks opened the door and motioned for Kazuko to come inside. There, Kazuko saw what she least expected. "You certainly keep a tidy house, Sylvia."

"Oh, yes. Daddy always insists that I keep things up."

Kazuko didn't want to pry but had to know. "Do you have a mommy, Sylvia?"

"Mommy died when I was born. It's just me and Daddy now. I love my daddy."

Blinking rapidly to control her emotions, Kazuko looked about. Although the house was tidy, the furniture and furnishings were dated, from perhaps the 1940s and '50s. Kazuko followed Sylvia through the living room to the kitchen where there was a door that Sylvia stopped in front of.

"Daddy's studio is in the basement. I know where he keeps his negatives, so I think we can find what you are looking for."

Sylvia switched on the light at the top of the stairs, and Kazuko followed her down. The basement was neat and organized. Sylvia pointed left. "Daddy's darkroom is behind that door. That's where he develops all of his pictures. Over here on the shelves are all of his jobs."

To the right stood shelves reminiscent of a library, and on each shelf were rows of folder boxes, going back some ten to fifteen feet deep into the basement. As Kazuko scanned the labels, she realized that Leonard Marks was nothing if not organized. Each folder was labeled simply with the year. Often, there were multiple boxes for a single year, labeled (a), (b), (c), and so on. Although light was dim between the stacks, Kazuko found the earliest date, 1923. Leonard Marks's professional career had apparently begun two decades before Kazuko's father called on his services back in 1943. As she had walked back through the shelves, Kazuko noticed that not all of them to her right were dated. She scanned the dates and located the last folder there: it read, 1963, no doubt the year Marks retired.

With Marks's filing system understood, Kazuko followed the years until she arrived in the 1940s, a period at least initially when there was only one folder per year, undoubtedly an indication of reduced business during the war. Finally, there it was: one labeled 1943. Kazuko reached down to remove the folder. "I've found it, Sylvia. I think this is it."

"Daddy has a light over here at his desk. You'll be able to see better."

Sitting at the desk, and removing a series of manila envelopes from the folder, Kazuko examined the writing on each, again simply written, this time in the form of a surname, a month and year. After only four other envelopes, Kazuko looked down on her trophy. It read, *Armstrong, April 1943*.

Kazuko gave Sylvia the thumbs-up sign. "Here it is, Sylvia. This is what my daddy's looking for!"

Realizing that her search might soon pay off, Kazuko's pace quickened. She opened the envelope and pulled out the contents. Inside was a written contract, including a signature she recognized as her father's. Also inside was another envelope that contained multiple negatives.

Kazuko reached inside her purse and removed the old worn photograph. She then held each negative to the light for comparison. When she found the one that matched, she handed the old picture to Sylvia. "Sylvia, this picture shows my mommy and daddy. That's me in the blanket. This negative here is a match, which means that your daddy definitely took this picture."

Sylvia then surprised Kazuko with a logical question. "Why do you need the rest of the pictures?"

Kazuko decided to be completely honest with this ten-year-old living within a seventy-year-old body. She deserved the truth. "Sylvia, I think that my mommy's hiding something from me and my daddy, and I'm hoping that the rest of these pictures will tell me what that is. Besides, there are pictures here that I've never seen before. There's one here of my Uncle Masao who died in the war, and pictures of most of my family when they were young."

With that last statement, Sylvia's face turned sad and, considering her obvious condition, said something remarkably astute. "I know what you mean. Sometimes I think that my daddy is hiding something from me too or that something has happened to him. I don't know why he doesn't come back. It seems like I've been waiting for him an awfully long time."

* * *

Kazuko quickly paid Sylvia the second twenty. She was losing it and couldn't hurry fast enough to her car. Inside, she buried her face in her hands and sobbed. As frustrating as her own personal situation was—a dying mother who may be harboring a secret—Kazuko's predicament paled compared to that of Sylvia. Here was a woman living in the past, probably sixty years in the past, waiting for a father she imagined to have left her and would never return. Clayburn had said that Sylvia was never the same after the accident. In her own troubled mind, Sylvia had escaped the pain from the tragic accident by reverting to her childhood, back to a happier time in her life. Within that refuge, she was trapped.

Kazuko wiped her eyes, looked at her watch, and started the engine. Remembering the sign on the door, she knew she had fifteen minutes before the store closed.

* * *

With streets now mostly deserted, Kazuko parked in front of Sherman's Photography and ran inside. He was closing up shop.

"Ms. Armstrong, you're back. Was John any help to you?"

"Yes and no. But, yes, remarkably, I was able to locate the negatives that I was looking for."

"Really? I could have sworn that you had tackled mission impossible."

There was little time, and Kazuko made her pitch. "Mr. Sherman, I need you to print these negatives for me." She took them out of their envelope and handed them over. "Please."

"I can have them ready for you by noon Monday." Sherman reached for his coat on a hook on the wall.

"Mr. Sherman, I need them now. It's very important."

"Ms. Armstrong, I'm headed home for the night. My wife has dinner waiting."

Kazuko reached inside her purse. Briefly, she considered haggling, but realized there was no point; he could have it all. She handed across her wad of emergency cash. "Mr. Sherman, here is five hundred dollars. It's all I have on me, but I can give you more with a credit card. I need you to print these photos now! Please." Kazuko was emotional and shaking visibly.

Sherman stood still for a moment, obviously bewildered by the strange request. After several seconds of thought, he handed back the bills and shook his head. "If this is that important to you, I don't want your money." He pointed to the phone. "Give me a second. I'll call my wife to tell her I'll be late. Tell me, what is it you want?"

"I need a blow-up of each negative, something big, like an 8 x 10."

With that settled, Kazuko took a deep breath, composed herself, and asked for a phone book. In light of the urgency, she realized there was yet another solution to her transportation problem.

* * *

Just south of San Francisco, California
Late Saturday evening, October 28, 2000

Kazuko stared out the window at the city lights as they continued south. The only passenger in the twin-engine Piper Seneca, she shifted from side to side to take in the view and get the most from the three-hundred-dollar per hour it was costing her to charter this aircraft. She checked her watch and saw that they were on schedule to land in Monterey at eleven, just a little more than two hours after they departed Klamath Falls. In fact, she'd arrive ahead of when her commercial flight would have landed.

Worried while in Klamath Falls that her mother might not be able to wait the extra hours it would take her to drive to Monterey, Kazuko had made the expensive choice to charter an aircraft. Mercifully, Mr. Sherman had not taken advantage of the money she had offered. It was going to take more than double that to pay for the plane.

Kazuko resumed looking at the pictures and paged through the nineteen 8 x 10s Sherman had printed. Seeing all the members of her family in good, quality photographs was a moving experience. Having seen Sato just days earlier, she now looked at the face of a much younger man. The same was true of her Uncle Masao and her father, all men just on the north side of their teenage years. Masao would never have a birthday beyond his twenty-third.

It was true what Shizuka had told Kazuko so many times: Keiko and Misaki looked so identical, it was impossible to tell them apart. Images of Grandpa and Grandma Tanaka warmed Kazuko's heart. And there was even a close up of Kazuko lying in the same plaid blanket Kazuko had seen in the small picture.

The pilot looked back and yelled over the engine noise, saying that they would be landing soon. Kazuko's car would be waiting, and she'd rush off to the hospital. With luck, her mother would still be alive, and she'd have time to say her good-byes.

Earlier, not even thirty minutes after takeoff from Klamath Falls, a close examination of the blown-up photographs that her mother had *lost* decades earlier—twice, in fact—gave up the secret. Her aunt's strange reaction at the hospital the day before now made perfect sense. Kazuko recalled Shizuka grabbing the small photograph and holding it close to her eyes—scanning it for the critical clue. But, at that moment, the secret had been safe: the picture was too small. As the new evidence leaped from the 8 x 10s, Keiko's eyesight turned fuzzy, emotion overwhelming her brain.

And now that Kazuko had uncovered the truth, Kazuko wanted—no, needed!—to know why. And the one living person who could provide that detail was her aunt.

One way or another, Aunt Shizuka, before this night's over, you're going to tell me what happened at Tule Lake in the spring of 1943!

32

KEIKO'S LOSS

Tule Lake Relocation Center, California
Friday, July 30, 1943

On the day Misaki died, June 1, it snowed. It was a Tuesday and within weeks of the summer solstice. Those who had been at Tule Lake the previous year remembered that the weather had been a bit crazy then too.

Misaki's death came without warning. Why had this healthy young woman left this earth so early? She had been sick for only a few days prior, having apparently caught the same illness that Shizuka had endured twice. Shizuka had fallen to one bout of the grippe, but then came down with it a second time, a week before Misaki got sick.

One minute Misaki was among the living, and the next she was gone. Her family was in shock. The doctor from the hospital said that her heart had probably given out. Things like that just happened, he said.

"God has decided that Misaki is worth more to him in heaven than here on earth," their minister said. As comforting as he intended his words to be, those sentiments made no sense to the grieving family.

Misaki's family mourned alone—in the sense that both her brother and fiancé had left the camp weeks earlier. The sad news would make its way to Mississippi's Camp Shelby by letter. Akemi grieved not only for her lost daughter, but also for her son and Misaki's new fiancé. They'd be just as devastated and would have only each other with whom to share their sorrow.

Although the Tanaka family was Christian, they chose to adhere to the traditional Japanese custom of cremation. Accordingly, they shipped Misaki's body to a crematorium in Portland. For an additional fee of five dollars, the facility agreed to store Misaki's ashes until the family requested them.

Although Akemi, Isamu, and Shizuka suffered greatly, Keiko knew that they could never understand how much Misaki's passing affected her. It was like losing her mirror image—a picture-perfect reflection she expected always to be there. It came as no surprise to Keiko, then, when her mind turned in on itself, and she fell into a well of depression. Nothing else mattered.

Keiko entered this state of melancholy within days of Misaki's passing, and it became obvious to her family immediately. Contrary to her stated determination to nurse her daughter for well past a year, Keiko quit. Akemi interceded, transitioning Kazuko to a bottle and formula in rapid fashion. Fortunately, Kazuko took the change in stride.

Keiko also refused to leave the apartment, forcing her parents to bring back food from the dining hall. When her boss visited to encourage her to return to work, she refused to see him.

Unexpectedly, during Keiko's descent into despair, a most welcome change came over Shizuka. If the family tragedy had led to anything positive, it was her overnight transformation from a selfish, self-centered teenager into a responsible adult. During her depression, Keiko vaguely recognized that Shizuka's behavior seemed odd. But it was afterward, when Keiko took her mother aside, discreetly asking her what she had done with the sister she had grown up with and Akemi shrugging her shoulders in reply, that Keiko realized that there had been some fundamental change.

It was this sudden onset of maturity that enabled Shizuka to comprehend and address a significant problem that arose during this period. After more than a year's worth of training, James had finally become an active part of the war effort. He had arrived in Pearl Harbor not long after his Tule Lake visit. His ship, the *Santa Fe*, set sail on April 15. Since leaving the continental United States, his letters had become sporadic. But although James was now aboard ship, Shizuka knew that Keiko had written him letters daily. All her writing had come to a halt, however, with Misaki's death. Accordingly, Shizuka had written immediately to tell him what happened. Otherwise, she knew, he would worry. She explained that Misaki's passing had devastated her twin, and that she needed time to adjust. Keiko would write again soon, Shizuka had assured him.

In addition to the letter to James, Shizuka had taken on the added responsibility of writing to Masao, Takeo, and the Armstrongs. Letters to Misaki's brother and fiancé were the most difficult, and she spent considerable time composing the right words. For the Armstrongs, the tragedy at Tule Lake echoed other bad news received from Bellevue the previous week. Barbara had reported that Harrison had had a heart attack. It had been a mild one, the doctor said, but it did mean that Keiko's father-in-law would have to alter his lifestyle and slow down.

The Tanaka family breathed a sigh of relief when Keiko returned to her normal self about a month later. The first thing she did was to reassume her responsibilities as a mother, offering to try her hand at bottle-feeding. Next in line was her obligation to her correspondents.

Naturally, Keiko's first letter went to James. She apologized for the lapse, but explained how much her sister had meant to her. As twins, they had been so close. In some respects, her sister's death had seemed like her own. Seeing firsthand how precious life was, she told him she had decided not to return to work at the hospital, because she wanted to spend more time with Kazuko. She might reconsider later.

* * *

Aside from the heartbreak that overwhelmed the Tanaka household, stresses endured by the internees at Tule Lake and the nine other relocation centers continued. Ill will caused by the loyalty questions festered. Those inclined to protest and make trouble did their best to foment discord among the others, usually those who wanted no part of their thinking or actions.

In response to this worsening situation, the Senate of the United States on July 6, 1943, sent a resolution to President Roosevelt, urging him to segregate disloyal Japanese Americans from the others. Those internees considered disloyal included several categories: those who had asked for repatriation back to Japan; those who had gotten into trouble in some way; those who had voted no/no on the loyalty questions; and, finally, those who had refused to register or answer those questions. Among those in the first group were Sato's parents who remained adamant about their decision to return to Japan. It wasn't long before a decision came down from Washington. Segregation would begin in September.

On July 20, the *Tulean Dispatch* reported that a second edict was on its way, this time from Dillon Myer, Director of the WRA. Tule Lake residents cursed their luck. It was *their* camp that had been chosen to be the site to which the disloyal would be transferred.

"Why did they pick us?" residents of his block asked Isamu. He said that he didn't know, but suspected that the rather high percentage of Tule Lake residents who had either voted no/no or who had failed to register at all probably had something to do with it.

Those Japanese considered loyal, those who had voted yes/yes, learned that they would have some say as to their next destination. Most of those who had moved from the Pacific Northwest figured that the Minidoka camp in Idaho would be their best choice. Not only was it the next closest camp to home, but there were friends and relatives there who had also moved from Washington.

A few within his block told Tanaka that they preferred to stay at Tule Lake. To them, he recommended that they think twice before making that choice. After all, judging by the trouble the no/no people had caused, he couldn't imagine that putting them all together in one place would make it any more peaceful.

At the same time, the pace of the government's reaction to its implied admission that the internment had been a mistake intensified. Specifically, by the end of July, Dillon Myer made another pronouncement that would signal the end of internment for many: 76,000 loyal Japanese would soon return to their former civilian lives. As good as this news first sounded, it did not apply to the Tanaka family or to most of the Japanese from the Pacific Northwest. The government had decided that for reasons of security, the West Coast was still off limits. Except for Shizuka, who still hoped to move to Chicago, the Tanaka family accepted its fate that they would stay in one camp or another until war's end.

To Keiko, home was Bellevue, Washington. She had grown up there, and her in-laws lived there. When she, her parents, and Kazuko returned, she'd wait for her husband, and they would pick up the pieces of their lives. In the meantime, as difficult as it would be, she'd lay Misaki's memory to rest. The one they called Keiko would be the one to carry forth the legacy of the Tanaka twins.

33

MYSTERY SOLVED

Monterey, California
Saturday night, October 28, 2000

Kazuko's chartered plane touched down at the Monterey airport a few minutes after eleven. She rushed off to her car in the long-term parking lot. On the way, she called Patrick. He reported that he and Shizuka were standing vigil at Keiko's side. He told her to hurry.

Twelve minutes later, Kazuko burst into the room. Patrick and Shizuka looked up. Kazuko walked to her mother's bed and took her mother's hands into her own, not knowing what to expect. Somewhat to her surprise, she didn't look any different from when Kazuko had seen her the previous evening. She drew close and gave her a kiss on the cheek. Drawing back a few inches, Kazuko memorized what she saw, marveling over the flawless complexion her family's genes had blessed Keiko with.

Kazuko turned to her brother. "What does the doctor say, Patrick?"

Instead of answering, Patrick stood and motioned toward the door.

Kazuko leaned forward a second time and whispered into her mother's ear. "I love you, Mom."

Outside the room, Patrick pointed down the hallway. "There's a room down here we can use."

The space featured a sofa, one chair, a coffee table, and various other amenities, including a large picture window that looked out into a flower garden accented by spotlights. Shizuka took a seat on the sofa and Kazuko the chair.

Patrick closed the door. "We saw the doctor a half hour ago, and he doesn't think it'll be much longer."

Shizuka looked worried. "I hope that you don't disagree with what we're doing?"

Her aunt's question surprised Kazuko. "Not at all. I know this is what Mom would want."

Shizuka seemed relieved, and she stood. "I think that we should get back. We need to be there for her."

Kazuko remained seated. "Aunt Shizuka, if I could have a few minutes, there's something I want to talk about before Mom dies."

The worried look returned, and Shizuka retook her seat. Patrick sat down beside his aunt.

Kazuko wasn't sure about the best way to broach the topic. As necessary as she knew this to be, she also recognized that what she was about to say would upset her aunt considerably. From her earlier attempts on the subject, Shizuka had been uncooperative. "Aunt Shizuka, I need to tell you where I was today. I flew up to Klamath Falls, Oregon, to get to the bottom of the secret you've been hiding from me and Patrick."

Shizuka stalled. "I have no idea what it is you think you know, but there is no secret." At once, she stood and headed for the door.

Kazuko removed the pictures from the folder she had been carrying and threw them down hard onto the coffee table.

Startled, Shizuka asked, "What's that?"

"Aunt Shizuka, I think you know what they are!" Kazuko pointed. "These are all of the pictures that the photographer took at Tule Lake."

Kazuko next took out the tattered photo she had been carrying all day. Reaching for the top picture on the stack, she held them both up for Shizuka to see. "This is the one I found at Mom's house, and this large one was printed just this evening. You can see that they are identical."

Shizuka's eyes grew wide, but she quickly regained her composure. "So, you finally found the pictures. Congratulations. Where did you find them, by the way? I'm curious."

"That's why I went to Klamath Falls. I found the daughter of the photographer who took the pictures. She sold me the negatives."

"Well, goody for you!" Shizuka's sarcasm was blatant. "We can all reminisce about the good old days later. Right now your mother is a little more important than a bunch of old pictures."

"It's ironic that you put it that way, Aunt Shizuka. I agree that my mother is a little more important than some old pictures."

With Kazuko's eyes lasered onto Shizuka's, her aunt blinked. Even so, she continued toward the door.

Kazuko continued. "You tried to make me believe that Mom lost these pictures. And then, this morning, I knew for certain that you were hiding something when I talked to Uncle Wally in New Jersey. He told me that Daddy had a second set of pictures sent to Grandma and Grandpa Armstrong. When they died, Uncle Wally said he gave them to Mom. I suppose you'd say that she lost those too. Aunt Shizuka, I have an idea of what happened at Tule Lake. But I need to hear it from you."

All the while, Patrick sat quietly. He gestured toward Kazuko, mouthing, "What's going on?"

Shizuka was about to enter the hallway.

Kazuko needed to raise the stakes. "Aunt Shizuka, if you don't tell me what happened, I'm going to show Daddy these pictures. He still has days when he thinks clearly. Since he was there when they were taken, I bet you he'll be able to explain what happened."

Shizuka stopped but did not look back.

Kazuko removed a second picture from her stack and held it up adjacent to the first. "Aunt Shizuka, you might want to take a look at these two. They're the ones I'll show Daddy."

In slow motion, Shizuka rotated and looked. Abruptly, she returned to the room and ran to the window. Seconds later, she turned, her face now crimson, and swore at Kazuko.

Patrick leaped to his feet. "Will someone please tell me what's going on here?"

Kazuko leveled her gaze at her brother and finally revealed the secret that had been kept from them their whole lives. "Patrick! Our mother is not Keiko!" She paused briefly to rephrase because the truth was more complicated. "Or at least yours isn't. The woman we've known most of our lives is, in fact, our Aunt Misaki. Which means that you and I have different mothers."

Patrick fell backward into the sofa, looking up at the ceiling. Just as quickly, he grabbed for the two pictures.

Kazuko felt sorry for her aunt. She walked to the window and placed her hand on Shizuka's shoulder. Shizuka turned, took Kazuko in her arms, and wept openly. Kazuko whispered in her ear. "Aunt Shizuka, you've been carrying this for too long. You know that I'm not going to feel any different toward you *or* Mom. Before Mom dies, I want to know what happened. I think that you owe that to me and Patrick."

Kazuko stared down at Patrick, who by now had solved the mystery revealed by the two photographs. One was the blow-up of the small picture Kazuko had found in her mother's house; the other was a separate shot of their Aunt Misaki and her fiancé, Sato.

Shizuka returned to the sofa, and Patrick handed her the pictures. She stared at them for some time. "I can't believe it's been over half a century since I've seen these."

Kazuko retook her seat and waited. Patrick handed his aunt his handkerchief. "It's funny," Shizuka began. "I had no idea how I would feel if this ever came out. But now that it has, it's like a big weight's been lifted off my shoulders."

Shizuka stood, walked back to the door, and closed it. "I'll tell you what you want to know, but you have to promise me that you'll never tell your father. He's never known this, and he never will. It would break his heart, he loved your mother so much."

"I promise, Aunt Shizuka."

Patrick, eyes glazed, nodded.

Shizuka took a moment to compose herself. She sighed and began. "On the morning of June 1, 1943, your mother, Keiko," Shizuka nodded toward Kazuko, "passed away. She had gotten the grippe—that was what we called it back then—from me.

"We three girls, along with you, shared one room, if you can call it that, of our apartment. It was about four in the morning. Your mother had just nursed you for the second time that night. Misaki and I were both sleeping when we heard some unusual sounds. We knew right away that something was wrong with Keiko. Misaki wanted to take her to the hospital, but Keiko insisted that we wait until morning, that she didn't want to wake our parents."

Kazuko and Patrick sat mesmerized.

"Misaki didn't want to wait. But then it happened so fast. Keiko must have known that something was wrong. Here's what she said to Misaki; I'll never forget her words: 'If something happens to me, I want you to be me. I want my husband to have a wife and Kazuko to have a mother. I love them both so much.' Within a minute, Keiko was gone."

It was Kazuko who now sat disbelieving what she had just heard. She had deduced from her own detective work that it was Keiko— and not Misaki—who had died in the camp. But the reason Misaki had taken over Keiko's role as mother and wife, Kazuko could never have imagined. *On her deathbed, my mother asked her twin sister to take her place!*

Shizuka looked closely at the two pictures. "If only Keiko hadn't tripped on that train down from Washington, this would never have come out."

"Is that how she got the scar?"

"Yes, we were on our way to Pinedale in California. That was the Assembly Center we had to stay in until Tule Lake was ready. She tripped getting into the train and hit her head on one of the benches. It left a noticeable scar."

In contrast to Kazuko, who had had several hours to ponder what she imagined happened, everything said in the room was new to Patrick. "And so, Aunt Misaki became Keiko?" he asked. "Is that what you're saying? But why would she do that? She was engaged to be married."

"You weren't there when we grew up," said Shizuka. "You wouldn't understand. Keiko and Misaki were like this." She crossed her middle and index fingers on her right hand. "I was a selfish brat when I was growing up, but part of the reason, I've always rationalized to myself, is that I was so jealous of what my twin sisters had together. They were special. They lived in each other's worlds. And I could never be part of that. So what I'm saying is that when Keiko asked Misaki to become her, Misaki agreed without hesitation. If that's what Keiko wanted, that would be what Misaki would do."

"I understand what you're saying, that Misaki would do anything for her sister," Patrick continued. "What I'm questioning is *how* she could have pulled off something like this. There's no way she could have fooled her parents." Patrick paused. "And what about your building? From what I've read, there were multiple apartments and sound traveled easily. Others would have heard something going on."

Shizuka smiled and nodded. "You ask good questions. And I have to admit, luck played a huge part in keeping the secret. At the time, a lot of people had been leaving the camp, and it so happened that on that night, we were the only ones in our barracks. After Keiko died, we woke up our parents and told them what happened. There was instantaneous grief, of course, and we all sat around together crying. No one had expected something as tragic as this.

"You can imagine the bewilderment on your grandparents' faces when Misaki told them what Keiko wanted her to do." Shizuka took Patrick's hands. "They had the same look that you had just now. Since I had been a witness to what happened, I confirmed what Keiko had asked of Misaki. Mama and Papa argued with her but, in the end, I guess they felt that they had no right to overrule what their daughter had requested from her deathbed. They couldn't believe that she could pull it off either. But they agreed to try, and they became coconspirators."

Patrick couldn't stop fidgeting. Finally, he stood and began pacing the room. "It's one thing to get your parents to agree to something, but quite another to convince the rest of the world. How could she have fooled everybody?"

Shizuka's face lit up again. "You two have no idea how clever my sisters were. There is one example I'll never forget. In high school in one of their classes, over a three-month period, just for fun, they traded seats *every day* and took on each other's names. *No one* ever noticed."

Patrick remained unconvinced. "It's one thing to fool a teacher you see for a short period every day. But in the camp, with coworkers? And Dad? There's no way Misaki could replace Keiko and he not know it."

"I understand what you're saying, but Misaki had a few things going for her. You look back and, to you, everything happened around the same time. What you have to remember is that nearly three years went by from when your Dad visited Tule Lake"—Shizuka gestured toward the pictures—"and when your mother saw him again after the war. Three years! People change in three years. Besides, she had all that time to become a person she knew intimately. But there is something else you may not know.

"You do know that your father served on a cruiser in the Pacific. Terrible things happened on that ship that he never could erase from his memory. It was horrible, he said.

"The reason I bring this up is that, when your father came home, he wasn't himself for a while. We now call it post-traumatic stress disorder. Back then, we didn't have a name for it, but James definitely had it. It took a couple of years but, thank goodness, he got over it. His mental condition couldn't have helped the memory he had of his wife."

Patrick wouldn't give up. "What about the day-to-day people at Tule Lake? It's one thing to look like another person but quite another to know what's inside their head." Patrick reached for the pictures and pointed. "But, in fact, they *didn't* look like each other. Keiko had a scar, and Misaki didn't. That's how Kazuko figured this out."

Shizuka answered confidently. "Obviously, Misaki knew that. Which is why, for the next four weeks after Keiko died, Misaki did not leave the apartment, except at night when she'd go out for walks, for exercise. We'd bring back food to her from the mess hall, and she took no visitors. Our parents explained to neighbors that Keiko had gone into a deep depression over the death of her twin sister. All she wanted to do was sleep, they told them.

"One of the problems Misaki faced was Keiko's daily letters to James. Misaki knew that she needed to do her homework before resuming those letters. For that reason, I was the first one to write, to explain that Misaki had died and that Keiko was too heartbroken to write. In fact, I wrote *all* of the letters to our relatives, in particular the Armstrongs and Masao. I was the one who wrote to Takeo Sato too, telling him that his fiancée had died. That one was especially hard for me. I was telling a lie. I remember being convinced that I would go to hell for that." Shizuka pursed her lips. "It was during those weeks when Misaki *became* Keiko. You won't believe it, but she even altered her personality. She changed from the reserved, quiet Misaki to the more outgoing Keiko. One advantage she had were all of the letters from James and Barbara. She studied them and studied them so that she knew what it was they knew. To make sure her handwriting could not be distinguished from her sister's, she spent hours practicing. After four weeks, she felt confident enough to write letters on her own."

Images flashed through Kazuko's mind as she imagined the enormous task Misaki had taken on.

"What about the scar, Aunt Shizuka?" Patrick hadn't forgotten. "When she finally came out of the apartment, everyone would see that she didn't have a scar."

Shizuka smiled in satisfaction. "When Misaki made her formal debut, she *had* a scar. I was the one who designed it. I put glue on her forehead and let it dry. I must say, it looked pretty good. To cover any imperfections in my handiwork, Misaki covered it with makeup. The glue was pretty durable, and Misaki sometimes left it on for days at a time before replacing it."

Shizuka dabbed at her eyes. "But, as you're implying, there were a lot of things that could have gone wrong. For one thing, both Keiko and Misaki had regular jobs at the hospital. Misaki understood that there was no way she could fool people with whom Keiko had worked. For that reason, Misaki chose not to go back to work—again under the guise of being heartbroken over her sister's death and wanting to spend more time with her daughter.

"And then, just months later, something else happened that inadvertently solved a lot of Misaki's problems. You remember about the questionnaires and the yes/yes and no/no answers?"

Kazuko answered. "We were talking about those with Mr. Sato just two days ago."

"Well, because of that the government decided to use Tule Lake for all of the troublemakers. Those of us who had voted yes/yes were encouraged to move to another camp. That was why we moved to Minidoka in Idaho. And that was a big break for Misaki; it sort of wiped the slate clean. Except for a few friends who also moved there, everyone was new. From then on, we didn't even bother to fake the scar. If it happened to come up in conversation, Misaki told me that she'd just say that it had finally faded. To my knowledge, no one ever asked. And I think you know that it was from there that I left for Chicago."

"What about Grandma and Grandpa Armstrong? She fooled them too when she got back?"

"As far as I know, yes. After the Armstrongs brought my dog to Tule Lake, they never visited again. Harrison had a heart attack, and the doctor told him that he could not go again on such a long trip. It would have been two or three years before Misaki would have seen them again back in Bellevue. By then Misaki had so become Keiko that I think that she could have handled almost any situation thrown at her. Also, remember that Misaki continued to write not only to James, but also to Barbara. There would have been two years plus of letters that formed memories between her and Misaki. Anything that happened before those letters, Misaki could have attributed to forgetfulness."

Kazuko looked at Patrick and wondered what he was thinking. His perspective was different from her own. Misaki had given birth to him and was the only mother he ever knew. It was different for Kazuko and her father, who had mother and wife replaced by a biological twin. Having spent a lifetime as a stepdaughter, Kazuko had to admit that she had never been treated any differently than had Patrick. Misaki had transitioned perfectly into her role and accepted her niece as her own.

Kazuko wanted to make amends. "Aunt Shizuka, I want to apologize to you for all of this. I know that you've been protecting Mom. And you know what's strange? After knowing what I know now, I don't feel sad or cheated in any way. It brings me to tears when I imagine how close my mom and Aunt Misaki must have been. First of all, for my mom to ask her sister to do what she asked, but then for Misaki to actually do it. It boggles my mind."

By now, Shizuka had pulled herself together. "I've hidden this for so long. But as I said before, we must make sure that what we've talked about here never leaves this room. Your father, especially, must never know. I saw how he loved Keiko before he left for the war, and I saw how much he loved Misaki afterward. To him, there was no difference. And amazingly, I'm sure that Misaki loved him every bit as much as Keiko had. I guess the one person who truly lost in all of this was Takeo."

Patrick held up his hand. "Did you know about Mom inviting him to visit? He was, in fact, her fiancé."

"I did not. When I saw him the other night, I said to myself: *What are you doing, Keiko?* I can't imagine that your mother intended to reestablish any kind of relationship. She was too in love with your father. The only thing I can think is that she was looking for a connection to her past. Think about it. From those she knew from the camp, I'm the only one she has left. Everyone else is gone. And we can't forget that Takeo would have been the last person that she knew who saw Masao before he died."

"Aunt Shizuka, we'd . . ." Patrick gestured toward Kazuko, ". . . I think we need your opinion on something. Kazuko and I talked about whether we should tell Dad about Mom's stroke. She convinced me that there was no point, that if he understood at all what we were saying, it would hurt him too much. I agreed with her at the time. But when Mom goes, I think that we need to tell him. It wouldn't be right not to, I think. What do you think?"

"I think you're right, Patrick. When it happens, he needs to know."

Kazuko thought about it and nodded. *This time I agree with you, Patrick.*

34

WAR'S END

Bellevue, Washington
Sunday morning, January 26, 1947

Keiko was finishing washing dishes from the previous evening and looking out the window of their two-bedroom apartment. James was still in bed on this lazy Sunday morning. His full-time load at the University of Washington—made possible by a new program called the GI Bill—left him little time to catch up on sleep. A week earlier, James and Keiko, for the first time since they married, had moved into their very own place. Living with her in-laws after James's return from the war had been acceptable for a while, but the younger Armstrongs finally informed their landlords that they wanted a place of their own. Barbara agreed, but only on the condition that she could have regular visits with her two grandchildren.

"Mommy! Patrick's waking up." Kazuko had been leaning over the side of his bassinet, patiently waiting for her baby brother to come around. "Can I hold him now?" Only two months old, Patrick was a pleasant child to be around, much like his older sister had been back at Tule Lake, Keiko remembered.

"Let's just leave him be for a little bit. Okay?"

As she turned back to the sink, Keiko took note of the calendar on the wall, surprised to see that exactly one year had passed since James had returned from the war. That meant that it was also four years since Kazuko came into the world at Tule Lake. In some ways, the time spent away from Bellevue seemed like not that long ago, even though their last day at Minidoka had ended nearly two years earlier. Memories formed during those times had been significant and would last a lifetime. In March 1945, they had departed Minidoka after nearly three long years away from home. The Armstrong and Tanaka families would have to wait almost another year before James completed his military obligation to be together again.

* * *

Coincident with the sadness connected with Misaki's passing in June 1943, the lives of everyone at Tule Lake began to change around the same time. When it became obvious that many of the Tule Lake residents would be leaving, replaced by those whom the government considered less than loyal to the United States, the fabric of life built up over the preceding year changed markedly.

By early September, all schools at Tule Lake closed, the buildings converted into residences to house more incoming internees. About the same time, the *Tulean Dispatch*, the camp's daily newspaper, published its farewell issue. Most of the staff were either leaving the camps permanently or being transferred to another. Still barred from areas considered militarily sensitive on the West Coast, the Tanaka and Armstrong families chose to move to Minidoka. They arrived there on October 7, part of a group of five hundred.

Life at Minidoka was both different from and similar to that at Tule Lake. Located in the southern center of Idaho on a desert plateau, the Minidoka camp had a population smaller than that at Tule Lake, about seven thousand. Those who had experienced living at both places reported that summer and winter temperatures were similar, but that there was less wind at Minidoka.

Contractors at Minidoka had done a better job of constructing the barracks, with wood floors and built-in closets, a pleasant upgrade. Mess halls were superior too, but the hospital seemed the same. Compared to the frequent water shortages at Tule Lake, there was plenty of water. Another welcome change was the lack of barbed wire around the camp, with guards posted only at the front entrance. Residents felt as if they had more freedom, with frequent passes allowed for trips to the nearest town, Twin Falls.

Even considering the advantages Minidoka had over Tule Lake, those from the Pacific Northwest still missed their lush surroundings back home. Like Tule Lake, the harsh desert-like environment was something they were looking forward to leaving.

In light of the school closings, Shizuka was fortunate to have graduated from high school the previous spring. True to her word, she didn't stay long at Minidoka. By early November, she left for Chicago, looking forward to a job as a dental assistant. Of the original six-member Tanaka/Armstrong family to arrive at Tule Lake, only three remained. Isamu and Akemi missed their departed children and wrote frequently to Masao and Shizuka. Although the pain of losing Misaki dulled somewhat as months passed, it didn't help that her living twin was a constant reminder of their loss.

All the while that Masao and Takeo remained stateside, letters between Camp Shelby and Tule Lake—and then Minidoka—were frequent and regular. The recruits from the internment camps were not the first of the Japanese Americans to train in Mississippi. That distinction belonged to those who hailed from Hawaii and had volunteered immediately after Pearl Harbor. The 100th Infantry Battalion, a segregated unit, represented the first of the Japanese Americans to face combat. It wasn't long before they distinguished themselves in battle, in Italy in the fall of 1943.

By the spring of 1944, Masao and Takeo, as part of the 442nd Regimental Combat Team, finally arrived in Europe. There, in early June, the 442nd teamed up with the 100th. It wasn't long afterward when Masao's letters informed his family that his unit was finally engaged in combat. Communication was sporadic thereafter, and his parents' hopes and worries awaited the receipt of each letter. But on August 30 their fears came to pass.

Having never before received a telegram, Isamu, who again had been in charge of mail reception for his block, suspected what it was when he saw that it came from the War Department. Not wanting to open the letter alone, he returned to the apartment where Akemi was working outside. When she saw his face, she knew that something was wrong. They opened the telegram together. Keiko, sitting outside with Kazuko, later told Shizuka that until the day she died, she would never forget her mother's scream that echoed through the camp. Masao had died in action on August 20. It would take more than a year for his body to return home.

Losing two of their four children within the space of fifteen months devastated Isamu and Akemi. A few months later, the family received a letter from Takeo. It was the first they had heard from him since his reply to Shizuka's letter concerning the death of his fiancée. In addition to telling them again how much he missed Misaki and how sorry he was that his friend, their son, died in combat, Sato reported that he had been in a different area when it happened. But he did speak to those who had been there, and they reported that he had died instantly—and with valor. From what Masao's comrades told him, Masao had been a hero and would likely receive a medal for his bravery.

When the war in Europe ended, the 442nd/100th became the most highly decorated unit for its size of any combat group in World War II, with eighteen thousand medals. Beginning in 1943 with the initial successes of the 100th, Americans back home read in their newspapers about the unit's bravery and sacrifices. In no small measure, the heroic, patriotic actions of those Japanese-American soldiers countered the suspicions, fears, and racism of those who had lobbied to have Japanese Americans interned.

While the Japanese-American fighting force was making its mark to the east, James and his shipmates were doing the same aboard USS *Santa Fe* in the Pacific. A Cleveland-class light cruiser, the ship's thirteen Battle Stars—citations assigned to a ship and its crew for achievements during a particular campaign—together with its record of seeming invincibility, gave the warship its nickname, *Lucky Lady*.

From the day it set sail from the East Coast on March 1, 1943, until it berthed in Bremerton, Washington, the *Santa Fe* had propelled itself through a lot of water, 277,000 miles of it. When it arrived there on January 25, 1946, James left the ship. He jokingly told his family that the ship's captain, in appreciation for James's wartime service, had agreed to drop him off as close to home as possible.

James talked about the heroics of his ship and its crew. One episode that was particularly noteworthy was a rescue operation involving USS *Franklin*, an American carrier hit in March 1945 by two Japanese bombs; that single incident killed more than eight hundred men. James himself had witnessed the first bomb hit the ship. Under considerable danger maneuvering alongside a severely damaged larger ship, together with exploding ordnance from the onboard aircraft hit by the bombs, the *Santa Fe* carried out its duty in heroic fashion. Over three hours, she rescued more than eight hundred sailors and helped bring fires under control. Because of their actions, the much larger *Franklin* did not sink and was towed back to port. For her efforts, the *Santa Fe* received the Navy Unit Commendation. James would often say that his involvement in that operation was the proudest moment of his Navy career.

In an emotional contrast to this heroism, there was James's postwar duty in Japan. Following VJ Day on August 15, the crew of the *Santa Fe* visited the area surrounding Nagasaki, the second of two cities leveled by atomic bombs. He said that he would never forget the destruction nor the stench of death that hung in the air.

Happier moments for the *Santa Fe* followed afterward when the ship took part in *Magic Carpet* duty. Starting in November, she returned many troops home from the Pacific theater.

The Tanaka family's experience with the nation's ill-conceived plan to segregate them from the rest of the population ended two months before Germany's surrender, and five months before Japan's. In the three years that passed since their train first headed south to Pinedale, California, on May 20, 1942, they had lived in three separate facilities.

On their arrival home at the train station, the senior Armstrongs and their youngest son, Wally, were there to meet them. Benjamin had followed James's lead into the Navy; he would return by the following fall. Attrition from the preceding three years had reduced the returning Tanaka family by three, but Kazuko had made up some of the difference. Shizuka's dog, Princess, was also among the returning party. Hugs and tears were shared by all. Kazuko, who had just turned two, received the most attention. She had been only two months old when Barbara and Harrison saw her last.

Compared to the plights of many of the Japanese who lost homes and possessions, the Tanakas fared well. Harrison had kept his word: the Tanaka house, their leased farmlands, and their possessions were still intact. Isamu recognized immediately that some of his farmland had fallen fallow during his absence, but he also knew that Harrison had done the best he could under the circumstances. The Tanaka share of the profits raised through the sale of their farm products came to a tidy sum that went a long way toward helping them get on their feet again.

Although the senior Tanakas had the good fortune to return to their home and possessions in Bellevue, the Bellevue Japanese-American community that had existed prior to the war essentially disappeared. Most of the others had taken advantage of early releases from Tule Lake to move to states where work was plentiful—and which were located outside the militarily sensitive West Coast. Keiko often realized how different their lives might have been had she not married James.

* * *

"What's going on out here?" In pajamas and bare feet, rubbing sleep from his eyes, James padded into the kitchen. Kazuko stretched her arms upward. He reached down, lifted her high into the air, and blew into her belly, shaking his head back and forth, making shrill sounds. "Is this what you want? Huh? Is this what you want?"

Kazuko giggled and struggled to free herself. "You're tickling me!"

"I am, am I? That must make you happy since you're laughing so hard. I guess that means you don't want me to stop."

About this time, Patrick was making noises, and Keiko lifted him from the bassinet. With Kazuko now sitting on James's arm, the family of four formed a circle.

Over the preceding five years, Keiko had learned how precious life was and how quickly it could all be lost. She held her family tight. All was well in Keiko's world.

35

FINALE

Monterey, California
Sunday Morning, October 29, 2000

Kazuko looked across the seat at her brother and wondered what he was thinking. She was at the wheel, and they were on their way to their father's skilled nursing facility over the hill, near the village of Carmel. It was a little after eight in the morning. As Dr. Siradnamalah had predicted, Keiko's end had come quietly and without drama, three hours earlier. Shizuka, Patrick, and Kazuko had been by her side.

The drama of the preceding night's conversation with Shizuka, followed by the loss of their mother, together with physical exhaustion, had left them numb. After an early morning breakfast with Shizuka at a diner in downtown Monterey, Kazuko and Patrick drove to their homes separately to shower and to prepare for their next step. They had agreed that they should tell their father as soon as possible.

As they crested the hill on Highway 1, Patrick spoke. "Are you okay, Sukie?"

"I'm all right, Patrick. If Mom were here, she'd tell us to get on with it. And she'd say she was glad that all of this lasted only a week."

Patrick gestured. "You were right, you know."

"About what?"

"Recognizing that Aunt Shizuka was hiding something. You

followed your instincts, and you pulled it off. I could never have done what you did this past week."

"Are you upset with me?"

"No. I guess that you could argue that it might be better if none of this had ever come to light. But I don't think so. I think we're better off to know. I still can't believe it though, can you? Mom pulling off what Aunt Shizuka said she did?"

"We've always known that our mother was one resourceful female, and now we know just *how* resourceful."

"And the same for Keiko, *your* mother. How does it make you feel? It's different for me. When you look at that picture and know that your real mother was Mom's twin? It must feel really strange."

"It does, Patrick, but you know what? As I said earlier, it's okay. Even though we had different birth mothers, Misaki is the only Mom I've ever known. To tell you the truth, it makes me feel warm and fuzzy inside. I didn't have just one mother. The first one loved me so much that she couldn't bear the thought of my growing up without a mother—and unselfish enough that she didn't mind if another woman got credit for it. And on the flip side, the woman who took over that responsibility loved her sister—and me, I guess—so much that she actually did it." With one eye on the road, Kazuko tried to gauge Patrick's reaction. "Do you see what I mean?"

Patrick nodded. "Yes." As he said it, they turned left onto Carmel Valley Road. From there, it was only a short drive to Hierman's Valley View Manor Estates.

Kazuko pulled into the parking lot, found a vacant spot, and turned off the engine. "Do we need to discuss how we're going to handle this? I have no idea how Daddy will react."

James's behavior varied considerably from day to day. There was an afternoon about a month earlier when Kazuko swore that her father's Alzheimer's had gone into remission, he had been so cogent. In contrast, most times their conversations led nowhere. Those who knew him likened his condition to a deep depression. And there were days when Kazuko wasn't sure he even recognized her.

Patrick thought about it for a moment. "I think we should just go ahead and tell him. Depending on his condition today, we'll know pretty soon whether he understands what we're saying."

As they walked through the double set of doors at the front of the facility, Kazuko glanced at her watch. It was 8:55 a.m. About this time, James would normally be finishing breakfast in the dining room.

For those there who could appreciate it, Hierman's was a beautiful place to live. As they walked past the business office, the hallway opened into a very large dining/general purpose room, with dramatic gables that gave the space an airy look. Wall-to-wall carpet, walls accented with beautiful paintings, and dramatic gold chandeliers gave the area a luxurious appearance. Expansive floor-to-ceiling windows allowed the residents to look out at the mountains that faced them from the south, across Carmel Valley Road.

The room was so large that not all of it was needed to support those who chose to eat outside of their rooms. A piano, large-screen TV, fireplace, and numerous sofas and stuffed chairs took up the half to the right. In the back right corner was a community jigsaw puzzle that residents took turns working on. Management often brought in musical entertainment, and those events occurred there. At any time, the room was an inviting location for relaxing or entertaining guests.

Most of the residents had finished eating, and attendants were clearing the tables. Kazuko scanned the area to her right, to the table where her father usually sat. As she recognized her father and walked in his direction, she noticed that he was still eating. At the table were his usual partners in crime, George and Bob, two men who had various physical problems, but whose minds were generally intact.

"Hello, Daddy!" Kazuko projected ahead as she approached the table.

James turned to look. Although he didn't answer verbally, his response indicated that he did recognize his daughter. As the Alzheimer's had taken hold over the past few years, his family had witnessed his spirit and personality wither away. In Kazuko's mind, she imagined the disease to be a thick absorbent blanket cocooning his brain, preventing outside stimuli from reaching her father's soul. Occasionally, gaps and tears in that imaginary fabric allowed him to experience the world again in all its glorious detail. But those occurrences were becoming less and less frequent.

Kazuko hugged her father and whispered into his ear. "How's my daddy today?"

To her surprise, James backed off and spoke clearly. "I'm pretty good today. How 'bout you?"

"I'm good, Daddy."

Kazuko stepped back to allow Patrick his turn.

Kazuko had gotten to know George and Bob fairly well over the past year. "And how are you two gentlemen on this beautiful day?"

George was the more talkative of the two. "Can't complain. And your Dad's in pretty good form himself. We've been discussing the state of the world."

"You have, have you? And has my father given you his opinion?"

"I'm afraid that he uses language I can't repeat in mixed company."

As Kazuko laughed at this response, Patrick rolled up two chairs. While no one else would have made anything of George's implication, Kazuko understood differently. Her father's disease had affected his vocabulary. In days past, he would never have uttered any sort of profanity.

Kazuko took her father's fork from his hand and began to feed him. Half of his breakfast was still on the plate. He responded to her encouragement and finished his scrambled eggs and ham. Strawberry yogurt remained, and he finished that as well.

Twenty minutes later, an attendant cleared the table. James's tablemates excused themselves and headed back to their rooms. Like him, they were wheelchair bound, but mobile nonetheless.

Patrick stood and removed the towel-like clothing protector used by many of the residents. By this time, the dining area had emptied out. A few people had moved across the way to watch *Meet the Press* on the large-screen television.

"Daddy, would you like to sit with us in front of the window for a while? It's so beautiful outside today. Do you mind?"

"No, I don't mind." This was only the second time that James had spoken since they arrived.

Kazuko backed her father out from the table and pushed him toward the adjacent windows. Patrick placed two chairs together so that they could sit facing their father. After Kazuko moved the wheelchair into position facing the window, they took their seats.

James pointed toward the window. "The view is *that* way."

Kazuko and Patrick smiled at each other. Their father hadn't yet lost all sense of logic.

As quick as the smile came to Kazuko's face, it left. It was time to tell her father something he definitely would not want to hear. She looked at Patrick.

Leaning forward, hands touching between her legs, she began. "Daddy, we're here to tell you something."

Patrick placed his hand on his father's knee. "We have some bad news."

The disinterested look on their father's face registered a change, a show of concern. *This is going to be so hard!* Today was obviously one of his better days because he understood the word *bad*. Ironically, Kazuko had been hoping for the opposite: that the blanket had no holes in it today.

Kazuko exhaled. "Daddy, this morning at 4:45, Mom died." As she made the statement, she felt wetness forming in her own eyes, tears not for her mother but for the man sitting across from her. "Daddy, she's on her way to heaven now." Kazuko removed a tissue from her pocket, blotted her eyes, and waited for a sign that her father understood.

At first, there was nothing. But before long, it happened, and Kazuko was unprepared. Short shallow breaths preceded an anguished expression on his face that evolved into a look of disbelief.

James's eyes remained locked onto Kazuko's. "Misaki died?"

As if struck by lightning, Kazuko recoiled. *Misaki died?* Her head snapped toward Patrick, whose saucer-sized eyes revealed his shock too.

"Daddy, your wife is Keiko. Aunt Misaki died during the war."

To Kazuko's further bewilderment, her father shook his head in reply. By now, tears were rolling down his cheeks. Seeing this, Kazuko lost all control. She knelt in front of him, took him in her arms, and they sobbed together. Patrick joined the pair. The three held each other for some time.

After a moment of reflection, Kazuko didn't know what to do. She looked at Patrick. *What did Daddy mean? Is his mind playing tricks on him?* Kazuko knew that she had to play this out.

"Daddy, you remember that Aunt Misaki died at the Tule Lake internment camp, don't you?"

James shook his head again. The agony displayed on his face was obvious, and the rest of his body soon joined in a demonstration of his grief. Rocking back and forth in his chair, he began to moan, and his hands rose to cover his face as he wept. From there, they returned to his lap where each washed the other repeatedly.

Her father's agony was tearing Kazuko apart. *But could it be? I have to know! I have to!*

Kazuko covered her father's hands with her own, holding them still. She repeated her earlier question. "Daddy, look at me! You do remember that Aunt Misaki died during the war, don't you?"

For the third time, James shook his head no. Kazuko's mind raced. She prayed that what she had just witnessed meant that her father had accidentally picked the name of his sister-in-law somewhere from out of the recesses of his subconscious. Kazuko decided to ask a second question. If he shook his head for a fourth straight time, she'd know for sure that he had no comprehension of what it was he was saying.

Kazuko spoke slowly and deliberately. "Daddy! You knew?"

Kazuko's pulse thundered inside her head as she waited for his reply. *Daddy, please shake your head no!* She was sure that her heart skipped multiple beats when that didn't happen. Instead, he nodded, his chin coming to rest on his chest, tears flooding his face and dripping from his chin.

Unconsciously squeezing his hands even tighter, Kazuko drew close and asked what she knew she had to ask. "Did you tell Mom that you knew?"

When James shook his head yet again, Kazuko arched her head backward, her face now as awash with liquid as her father's. *Daddy knew all those years, but kept it a secret?*

I have to ask one more question. "Daddy, *how* did you know?"

James deliberately withdrew his hands from his daughter's and leaned forward. Kazuko instinctively closed the gap between them. As she did, he reached out and took her head in his hands. He drew close and whispered in her ear.

* * *

Two hours later, Kazuko and Patrick left the building together. They had arranged for the nurse to give their father a sedative. Before he fell asleep, Kazuko made sure to tell him that she'd return later that day.

Outside, brother and sister wandered through the gardens as they meandered their way to their car. The day was turning out to be warm and cloudless. When a bench beneath an arbor appeared before them, they took a seat.

Patrick turned to Kazuko. "So, are you going to tell me what Dad said?"

Kazuko shook her head. "I was so hoping that he'd say something that would tie everything together, to make sense of his responses. But what he said was pure nonsense."

"So you don't believe him, that he *did* know?"

Kazuko had no idea. "I don't know. It's possible, I guess, but I don't think so. But between you and me, I say that we don't tell anyone about what just happened. Particularly Aunt Shizuka. She thinks that her family executed the perfect cover-up. There'd be nothing to gain by telling her otherwise. Okay?"

"I agree."

A moment passed before Patrick said it again. "I'm still bigger than you, you know. Are you going to tell me what Dad said, or do I have to beat it out of you?"

"As I said, it was nonsense. When I asked him how he knew, he said the following, and I quote: *She could never show me how much she loved me.*"

After a moment, Patrick conceded. "You're right, Sukie. That *is* nonsense. Anyone who has ever been around those two would know that Mom spent practically every waking moment of her life showing Dad how much she loved him."

Kazuko took Patrick's hand. "Let's go home, Patrick. I'm exhausted."

EPILOGUE
UNFINISHED BUSINESS

United Airlines Flight, San Francisco to Klamath Falls
Wednesday Morning, November 29, 2000

Events set in motion by her mother's stroke four and a half weeks earlier had been life changing—and life affirming—for Kazuko. Less than a week following his wife's death, James joined her in the afterlife. It was early Friday morning, November 3, when the nurse responsible for periodic checks on James found him unresponsive. The doctor on duty told Kazuko later that it was probably a stroke or heart attack that had taken him. When she heard the phone ring at four in the morning, Kazuko suspected immediately what had happened; it had come as no surprise.

She was the first to arrive at Hierman's some thirty minutes later. The doctor asked if it was important to know what actually killed him. Kazuko was sure that she spoke for the rest of the family when she told him that it was not. No matter what an autopsy revealed, she knew that her father had died from a broken heart. The Alzheimer's had destroyed much of what made James the man he was. But even that dreadful disease hadn't been potent enough to erase memories of a bond built up over a lifetime.

Later that day, Kazuko remembered her promise to Sato. She phoned to give him the news about Keiko and James. Afterward, she imagined how different life would have been had her birth mother lived. Sato would have been *Uncle Takeo*.

Before making the call, Kazuko had stressed over the pictures. If she sent them all to Sato, he'd be reminded of Keiko's scar. Although it was unlikely he would remember her perfect complexion from the hospital, could Kazuko afford that risk? Another option was to send him only the picture of him and Misaki. Either way, there was a danger. If Sato asked why Keiko had hidden the pictures, Kazuko would have had to lie to keep Sato from knowing what happened after he left the camp for Mississippi. Ultimately, Kazuko decided that the risk was not worth taking and did not mention the pictures. There'd be nothing to gain from his knowing this half-century-old secret.

The wills left by Kazuko's parents stated that, for the first to die, his or her ashes were to be stored until the demise of the other. At that time, their cremains were to be mixed together, flown aloft in an aircraft, and distributed over the Pacific Ocean west of Monterey. Patrick and Kazuko had followed through on that wish the previous week. To make sure that their parents' request was handled properly, they went along on the flight.

Having thought that she was fully prepared, psychologically, for her parents' deaths, Kazuko was surprised at the intensity of her reactions, her emotions, in the days that followed. For that reason, she sought some way to provide closure for herself.

Not long afterward, Kazuko decided what form that closure would take: she would return to the site of the Tule Lake internment camp where she had been born. She wanted to stand close to where that had happened and transport her mind back in time to that January day in 1943. She'd picture her birth mother and the rest of the family as they went about their lives far from home. She'd then move forward in time to early April when her father arrived at the camp to see his wife after so many months of separation. She'd visualize Leonard Marks—along with his daughter—walking slowly with his cane, positioning his subjects for the pictures he would take.

Kazuko would then hold up each of the photographs into the light of the day and imagine that the spirits of both those recently deceased as well as those long gone were standing there beside her. To her way of thinking, doing this would bring her full circle and provide the finality she needed. Patrick offered to go along. Telling him not to be offended, she said that she felt it was important that she do this on her own.

But before driving to the Tule Lake camp, on Thursday, Kazuko had some important business to take care of. Through her statewide contacts in social work, she had spoken to the appropriate authorities in Klamath Falls and was scheduled to meet them this afternoon. Their research had located a living relative of Sylvia Marks, a niece, who was also flying to Klamath Falls today. Importantly, this niece had agreed to intercede for her aunt.

Kazuko had asked the local office of social welfare not to contact Sylvia until she arrived. Recognizing the precarious nature of Sylvia's mental state, Kazuko wanted to be the one who knocked on the door. It wasn't that long ago when she had established a bond with this woman. Kazuko hoped to be a trusted intermediary who might ease Sylvia's transition into the care of her niece and the other social workers concerned with her well-being. To no small extent, Kazuko felt deeply indebted to Sylvia.

Besides Sylvia, there was one other duty that remained in Klamath Falls. Kazuko had promised John Clayburn that she would tell him how this had all worked out. Without both his and Sylvia's help, she would never have solved her puzzle before her mother died.

"We are on the final approach to Klamath Falls. Please place your tables and seatbacks in their full upright positions."

As the plane descended, Kazuko stared out the window but saw nothing, her view blocked by countless mental images competing for dominance in her consciousness. Ultimately, those amorphous representations revolved around her parents' love affair, a romance that had truly withstood the assaults of time and human failings. In her parents' lifetimes, those troubles included a society that had frowned upon a marriage between two people who happened to look a little different from each other, but who had fallen in love with each other's soul; a country that imprisoned some of its most loyal citizens behind barbed wire fences; a world war that separated loved ones and caused untold suffering and casualties; all in addition to the normal lottery of death, sorrow, and misfortune that befall humankind.

With their definitive expressions of love, Keiko's parents—all three of them—had weathered those tribulations and emerged victorious. A grateful daughter could not have asked for a better inheritance.

CAST OF MAJOR CHARACTERS

- AKEMI TANAKA: Matriarch of Tanaka Family, mother to Keiko, Misaki, Masao, and Shizuka; arrived as picture bride to marry Isamu Tanaka in 1919

- BARBARA ARMSTRONG: wife to Harrison and mother to James, Benjamin, and Wally Armstrong; to become mother-in-law to Keiko

- BENJAMIN AND WALLY ARMSTRONG: younger brothers to James

- ISAMU TANAKA: Patriarch to Tanaka family; emigrated to Hawaii from Japan in 1905; married Akemi in 1919

- HARRISON ARMSTRONG: Patriarch to Armstrong family; husband to Barbara and father to James, Benjamin, and Wally

- HIROMI: Takeo Sato's sister

- JAMES ARMSTRONG: oldest son of Harrison and Barbara Armstrong; fiancé and future husband to Keiko Tanaka

- KAZUKO ARMSTRONG: first child and daughter of James and Keiko Armstrong; born at Tule Lake Internment Camp in January of 1943

- KEIKO TANAKA/ARMSTRONG: one of two (identical) twin daughters of Isamu and Akemi Tanaka

- LEONARD MARKS: photographer who took pictures of the Tanaka and Armstrong families at the Tule Lake internment camp

- MASAO TANAKA: oldest and only brother to Keiko, Misaki, and Shizuka Tanaka; volunteered to fight in World War II

- MISAKI TANAKA: twin sister to Keiko

- PATRICK ARMSTRONG: Kazuko's younger and only sibling, born after World War II to James and Keiko Armstrong

- PRINCESS TANAKA: family dog, a collie

- SHIZUKA TANAKA: youngest sibling to Keiko, Misaki, and Masao Tanaka; Aunt to Kazuko and Patrick

- SYLVIA MARKS: daughter of Leonard Marks

- TAKEO SATO: neighbor to Tanaka Family back in Bellevue, Washington, and future fiancé to Misaki Tanaka

GLOSSARY

Assembly Centers: temporary facilities used to house the Japanese before the War Relocation Authority completed the ten permanent Relocation Centers

Executive Order 9066: infamous order, signed by President Roosevelt in February 1942, that uprooted 120,000 Japanese Americans and placed them in internment camps

14th Amendment to Constitution: 1868 update stating that anyone born in the United States was automatically a citizen

442nd Regimental Combat team: Japanese-American unit that garnered great fame because of their heroism and the numbers of combat medals received

IV-C, Enemy Aliens: Selective Service classification given to Japanese Americans during World War II

exclusion zones: During World War II, geographic areas considered militarily sensitive

Gaijin: Japanese word for a foreigner

Gentleman's Agreement of 1907: accord that followed years of anti-Japanese sentiment that crested not long after the great San Francisco earthquake of 1906 when the San Francisco Board of Education attempted to school Japanese-American children together with

Chinese-Americans. In exchange for Japan halting immigration, the Board of Education backed off its decision to integrate the children

hari-kari: a form of Japanese ritual suicide by disembowelment using a sword

Issei: Japanese immigrant to the United States

Immigrations Act of 1790: naturalization act that applied only to "free white persons." Congress updated law in 1870, but only to include Africans

JACL: Japanese American Citizens League; founded in 1929, community-based organizations formed to advocate for the rights of Japanese Americans

Kibei: a Japanese American born in the United States but educated in Japan

Manzanar: one of ten permanent government camps built to house Japanese Americans; this one was located in southern California

Military Area No. 1: World War II exclusion zone that included coastal portions of Washington, Oregon, and California, as well as the southern half of Arizona

Military Area No. 2: World War II exclusion zone that included those parts of the four states not in Military Area No. 1

Minidoka: one of ten permanent government camps built to house Japanese Americans; this one was located in Idaho

Nikkei: Japanese term referring to Japanese Americans

Nisei: second-generation Japanese Americans who were born in the United States, and thus were citizens

Omamori (from *Wikipedia*): Japanese amulets (charms, talismans) commonly sold at religious sites and dedicated to particular Shinto deities as well as Buddhist figures, and may serve to provide various forms of luck or protection

Osechi ryori: traditional Japanese foods eaten on New Year's day

Picture Bride: female bride from Japan chosen by male Japanese living in the United States; marriage agreement legalized before couple even met

Relocation Centers: ten permanent government camps built by the War Relocation Authority to house Japanese Americans; located in Arizona, Arkansas, California, Colorado, Idaho, Utah, and Wyoming

Selective Service Form DDS 304A: divisive form given to male Nisei Japanese Americans that asked them to swear unqualified allegiance to the United States—even though they were being interned, many were US citizens, and the remainder who were not (citizens) had no legal channel by which they could become citizens. A similar form, the War Relocation Authority Application for Leave Clearance, applied to Issei and all female Japanese citizens

Senninbari: otherwise known as the "Thousand Stitch Belt"; originating in modern Imperial Japan (period beginning in 1868), a good-luck charm presented by a woman to a man going off to battle. Made of cloth, the belt required single stitches sown by 1,000 different women

Tri-State High: Tule Lake high school, thus named because most internees had come from Oregon, Washington, and California

Tule Lake: one of ten permanent government camps built to house Japanese Americans; this one was located in northern California

Tulean Dispatch: official newspaper (written by internees) for the Tule Lake Relocation Center located in northern California

Tsukimi: Japanese tradition of celebrating the harvest moon of September, considered the brightest of the full moons

USS Santa Fe: World War II light cruiser, called the *Lucky Lady* because of its success in the Pacific; instrumental in preventing the carrier USS *Franklin* from sinking after it was hit by Japanese bombers

WAAC: the Women's Army Auxiliary Corps; other than nurses, women serving in the WAAC were the first women to serve in the Army

War Relocation Authority: a government agency formed to handle the internment during World War II

DISCUSSION QUESTIONS

Cedar Fort asked me to write a few book club questions for *How Much Do You Love Me?* I thought that was a great idea considering the many moral and ethical challenges presented to the characters in my book.

In the final proof of the book, however, I noted that these questions were going to appear at the end of the book. Because they were so accessible, and because these questions necessarily revealed secrets that would spoil any reading of the book, I suggested that they appear instead on my web site.

Here are instructions for retrieving those questions:
1. Go to www.paulmarktag.com
2. Click on the cover (at the bottom of the home page) for *How Much Do You Love Me?*
3. Next, click on "Book Club Questions."
4. Enter username "BookClub" and password "BookClub"

If you have any difficulty, please contact me through my website.

ABOUT THE AUTHOR

*P*aul Mark Tag graduated with multiple degrees in meteorology from Pennsylvania State University and worked for the Naval Research Laboratory as a research scientist for over thirty years before retiring to write fiction. For years prior to retirement, and the following year exclusively, he honed his skills writing short stories. These have been published in *StoryBytes*, *Potpourri*, *Green's Magazine*, and *The Storyteller*, as well as *The Errant Ricochet: Max Raeburn's Legacy*. In 2005, he self-published his first thriller, *Category 5*, which took advantage of his knowledge of meteorology and weather modification, followed by *Prophecy and White Thaw: The Helheim Conspiracy*. With his historical novel *How Much Do You Love Me?* he has switched genres. He lives with his wife, Becky, in Monterey, California. Please visit Paul at www.paulmarktag.com.